Father, Son
And
Holy Spirit

Father, Son
And
Holy Spirit

James K. Zavez

Get In Line Publishing
New Hampshire, USA

In loving memory of my mother, Elenore Zavez, who edited the first section of this book in 1994. Her love of libraries and words on the pages opened my eyes to endless possibilities. Both real and imagined. I'll always remember us sitting together at the kitchen table on Monroe Street, discussing ideas that somehow became a novel. I miss you.

• • •

In loving memory of my good friend, Mike Lenoce, who passed away at a young age leaving us to wonder why. My memories of Mike remind me that big boys do cry. Quite often. I miss you, too.

Acknowledgements

To my loving wife Marsha, who read my manuscript at least a dozen times prior to editing. We talked through the story, word by word, line by line, chapter by chapter till it all made sense. At least to us. Much of my story is told through her eyes and the love she has for children. Marsha's both a teacher and accomplished artist. While I'm a newcomer to the world of creativity, she lives and thrives in that environment. Thank you for sharing your world with me.

To the human brain. Capable of storing all our experiences from day one, hidden in the grey matter just waiting to be sprung. I beg everyone who reads this to search for it. While it might not make you a good writer, athlete, musician or president, it will help you find peace within yourself. A peace so desperately needed in today's world.

J.K. Zavez

Prologue

TWO MEN IN BLACK SWEATSHIRTS adjusted their backpacks, pulled their hoods tightly around their faces and slipped away from a small crowd of festive people that was headed for the local cemetery. The Dia de los Muertos celebrations had just begun and the city was coming to life even at this early hour. The Dia de los Muertos, a day for family members to spend time with the spirits of their kin, of children and adults who have passed on. The scent of flowers and burning candles began to dissipate as the crowd moved past the two men now crouched in a doorway directly across the street from the American Embassy. As the parade of voices trailed off into the darkness, the cries of a girl could be heard coming from the open embassy windows several floors up, while exploding fireworks echoed throughout the alleyways welcoming the spirits of the dead back into the city.

Waiting for the right moment, one of the hooded men sprinted from the doorway to the twelve-foot fence surrounding the embassy. He quickly threw his backpack over the service entrance gate, climbed the fence and dropped down onto embassy property with physical strength and grace. Once inside, he looked across the street, shot out a quick wave, then ran about fifty feet, disappearing into an underground parking lot and threw himself under an old Chevy Impala. Catching his breath, he suddenly realized he'd left the backpack near the fence. The hooded stranger froze for a moment, hearing the girl screaming again from somewhere in the complex. Forcing himself to focus, his heart raced as he crawled out from under the car and ran back to the gate to retrieve his pack. Making it back to the garage undetected, he opened the pack, checked the contents, and began to put his plan in motion.

• • •

FLASHES OF LIGHT FILTERED through the dusty, olive green curtains that blanketed the large, open windows, casting an eerie glow throughout the musty smelling bedroom. In the center, a massive canopy bed's bright white sheets blew wildly in the breeze, creating the illusion of a landlocked sailing vessel. The décor was early Spanish, with tiled arches and clay-colored walls. The electricity had long been out inside the embassy, as well as most of the city streets in the vicinity; numerous dripping wax candles caused shadows to rise and fall over the walls and white textured ceiling.

There were four people in the room. Three were visitors, two women and a short plump man with a stethoscope hooked around his fat hairy neck. The man clutched a small white towel which he used to wipe the sweat from his balding, extended forehead: Señor Garcia, a local doctor, provided his services along embassy row, lining his pockets with highly valued American dollars, getting rich off the highly respected representatives from many countries around the world. He had an excellent reputation for discretion and a shady reputation for transferring his profits into off-shore bank accounts.

Accompanying Doctor Garcia were two nurses, there to assist should any complications arise. The *doctor en Medicina* firmly believed that guidance and hand-holding were a must, especially in this case.

The fourth person in the room, the center of attention, was lying on the bed, a tortured look on her face. Her long brown hair was matted down with sweat and her light green eyes were tearing in pain. Salt stung the cracks in her lips. She was a small-framed girl of about five-foot-six, weighing slightly over a hundred pounds, currently with an additional thirty pounds in the vicinity of her waist. Her pale legs were trembling and spread wide, positioned to give birth to her first child. Caroline Dustan, no more than a child herself, had celebrated her sixteenth birthday just a week ago.

"Señorita Caroline, please, you must continue to push so this bambino of yours can see the light of day," Doctor Garcia said soothingly, wiping sweat from his forehead. "We practiced these birthing methods for months now. Please work with me: five short breaths and push, five short breaths and *empujar*, push, *empujar*, push. Good, Caroline!"

"I'm trying, I really am!" Caroline screamed in the doctor's ear, "but no one prepared me for so *much* pain." She breathed and pushed – and hugged her one-eyed Raggedy Ann doll, a present she received on her tenth birthday from her recently deceased grandfather whom she missed very much.

• • •

THE LOUD VOICES AND Caroline's distinct cries penetrated the walls of the embassy, winding their way through the ventilation ducts into the large, airy study of Deputy Ambassador Steven Dustan. The sharp, sweet smell of oiled leather furniture and moth balls caused him to leave a window open even during the harshest of weather. The walls were blanketed with ancient hard-cover books, ranging from *The Complete Works of Shakespeare* to *Mein Kampf* by that one-hit wonder, Adolph Hitler. At the far corner of the room near an oval stained-glass window a man stood, leaning over a large teak desk holding his face in his hands.

Six feet tall with a strong, muscular build and dark green eyes that had seen their share of hard times, Steven Dustan looked like he belonged in the fields of a farm in the Midwest United States rather than playing the role of a diplomat in a foreign country. His weathered face with its deep mosaic lines around his eyes, and the streaks of grey that were winning over his black hair, made him appear older than he was. He was forty-one years old, a lawyer who decided early on that he wanted to follow in the footsteps of his father working in foreign countries spreading democracy to those interested.

Several candles flickered in this room as well, revealing the presence of another man standing against a dark, wooden column that looked not unlike an old telephone pole. Virgil Sanchez was not only Steven's second in charge, but had also become a good friend soon after Steven had arrived in Mexico. He was an ugly man, with greased black hair combed straight back, and several scars running north and south along his pock-marked face. Virgil's small eyes were pushed back into his head, giving him the appearance of squinting all the time. In his mid-fifties, he had worked in several other embassies prior to Steven's arrival in Mexico City.

"Señor Dustan, come now, you must not blame yourself," said Virgil. "It's not your fault. You're doing the best you can in a very stressful situation. Some things are beyond our control whether we like to believe it or not. Caroline is a strong young woman like her mother, God rest her soul," Virgil said. His voice trailed off as he closed his eyes, his right hand making the sign of the cross: forehead, chest, shoulder, shoulder, lips.

"I could have done something, spent more time with her, looked for clues in our conversations, especially after her mother died. I was too wrapped up in my own grief to notice that my only daughter had gone from my little girl in pony tails to a woman of sixteen who's now giving birth to a child!" Steven snapped. "If only her mother was still alive. She'd know what to do. I can't go through this alone!" he said, slamming his right hand on the desk, knocking books and papers to the floor.

"Your daughter is young and having a difficult time giving birth," said Virgil. "I wish we could have taken her to the hospital, but the lack of electricity and the Dia de los Muertos celebrations in the streets would have caused great delays."

"Damn you, Virgil, don't you think I have ears! Is it not my daughter who cries out in pain for which her father cannot do a single thing!" shouted Steven. "Look, I'm sorry, Virgil. I just feel so helpless. Since I came here, I've had nothing but problems. Two years in your country. My wife dies in a car accident, I'm charged with spying by your government. And now my little girl – who is just a child herself – is about to be a mother. And she refuses to tell me who the father is, except to say that he's in the Mexican army. Even the local priest knows of this soldier by day and child rapist by night, but is sworn to secrecy by his God. I cannot take much more of this, Virgil! Once Caroline and the new baby are able to travel, I will leave this country and never return. I'll be free of Mexico's authoritative democracy and drug laced corruption. Bitter memories will remain in my heart. I will pray for your country daily."

● ● ●

"DOCTOR, DOCTOR GARCIA, I can see the head!" Maria, the embassy nurse shouted across the room.

"Señorita Caroline, the baby, *lo lamento*, I'm sorry, the birth is almost complete," Doctor Garcia said in a hoarse voice, his English broken. "You must continue to push and breathe. Don't finish, stop now and push! You are doing much good, *muy bueno*, very good. *Gracias*, Señorita Caroline, *muy bueno, gracias*."

"Please, doctor, tell me it's almost over!" cried Caroline. "The pain is unbearable and I feel I'm close to passing out. Get my father! Please call my father!"

"Just a few more minutes, Caroline, I promise," Doctor Garcia gasped, wiping his forehead yet again with his towel. "Please, a few more minutes, one strong *empujar*, push. All right, yes, *si*, that's it! Good girl, Caroline. Señorita, your *el papa* is *el venida*, coming, on his way."

"The baby *es nacido*, born!" Maria screamed while performing the sign of the cross and pointing at the baby. "What a full head of dark hair!"

"Congratulations, Señorita Caroline," said Doctor Garcia. "It's a boy. A fat, *grande* boy at that. Let me remove, snip the cord, so I can give the baby to you."

The lights in the bedroom came on suddenly, highlighting the tears still streaming down Caroline's face. The baby was crying loudly, but Caroline wasn't bothered by that. Her father rushed into the room, bent over his daughter and new grandson and kissed them both on the forehead.

"Daddy," whispered Caroline, "I will name him Joseph, after Grandpa."

"That would be nice," said her father. "Pa would have been very proud, as proud as I am feeling right now. I love you, Caroline."

The other woman in the room suddenly came to life, leaping out of a chair when she heard the doorbell echo throughout the building. "It must be Padre Reyes!" Sister Angela said excitedly. "I hope it's all right that I called him when you went into labor. I asked him to come over and bless the new baby."

Moments later, a thin man dressed in a black cassock entered the room holding a small cross in one hand and a clear glass bottle of holy water in the other. Father Reyes was only in his late forties, his hunched back and severe limp the result of time spent in Mexican jails that had broken him physically, not mentally. He was both a friend to the Dustan family and to the stranger in the Mexican army who came to him one night and confessed to being the father of Caroline's baby. The next morning, the confessor was shipped out on military exercises somewhere in Southern Mexico. That confession had taken place close to six months earlier. Father Reyes had promised both the stranger as well as Caroline that this secret would go with him to his grave. He stood over the bed and began the blessing ritual in near-perfect English. "Oh Lord, with all your holiness and grace, please bless this child," recited Father Reyes, "in the name of the Father, Son and the Holy Spirit."

The lights in the bedroom flickered a few times until they finally went back off again. Candles, snuffed when the lights had come back on, were relit and the haunting glow returned. The voices of celebration continued in the streets as the baby softly cried, tucked in the loving arms of his mother.

Caroline, anxious for sleep, drifted off into dreams that helped alleviate her pain as she prayed for strength. She realized that from now on she would have to be brave for the sake of her son – her Joseph. It did not take long for her breathing to slow to match that of her son, now fast asleep. She never heard the explosion in the embassy's underground parking garage which killed her father instantly as he walked Doctor Garcia to his automobile. The tremor was felt, however, by the one hidden stranger lost in the shadows across the street. He pulled his prized Swiss Army knife out of his pocket, sprinted to a newly formed hole in the embassy fence and disappeared into the nearly demolished parking garage in search of his partner.

An evil man seeketh only rebellion; Therefore a cruel messenger shall be sent against him.

Proverbs 17:11

Chapter One

Monday, January 21, 2013 / 3:20 PM
US Inauguration Day
Washington DC

"**H**EY, MISTER, THE PRESIDENT has been shot!" screams a young boy wearing a Washington Redskins hat as he holds tight to his mother's hand, afraid of being trampled by the quick-moving crowd. He's just one of the many people I see running across Pennsylvania Avenue, away from the presidential inauguration festivities. The sounds of rapid gunfire and small explosions echo throughout the streets of Washington DC, mixing with screams from a fleeing public, sadly reminding me of the 24/7 news footage of the terrorist attacks in New York City on September 11, 2001.

Crouching behind an empty white DC paddy wagon, I can't help but think that this crisp winter afternoon was supposed to be the most important day in the free world. Today, a new president was sworn in to take his place in history to lead our country for the next four years. Now with havoc breaking out all around me, and a temperature of 28 degrees, I am reminded that I forgot my Colt 1911 and my heavy jacket back in Florida. I left my mom's condo early this morning and joined the throngs of people lining the streets to catch a glimpse of America's new commander in chief who promised change and new hope.

Fumbling for my iPhone behind the van, I almost get knocked down by what appears to be a young kid playing dress-up in a police uniform. "Get out of the way," he shouts, sweating profusely even on this cold afternoon. At least his voice sounds old enough to be a cop. "We need to make room for emergency vehicles!" I gotta believe this rookie officer never thought in a million years that his short time on the force would throw him into the middle of such bedlam, especially during such an historic event.

I put on my New York Yankees cap as freezing rain begins to fall throughout the city, coating all its inhabitants in a shell that I fear will not protect us from the days to come.

Sprinting back to my mom's building a few streets over, I hear the loud thumping noise before I actually see the unmarked black Bell Helicopter 430 navigating about 350 feet over my head. With my limited experience in the cockpit, I can't help but think that the pilot must be either crazy or very skilled by the way he – or she – is dodging electric poles and street signs. I lose sight of the Bell as I cross over Virginia Avenue and run towards the Potomac River behind the Watergate Complex. It's amazing that an unmarked helicopter has been able to penetrate Washington airspace without being intercepted by our military, especially on Inauguration Day.

Pacing the sidewalk on Rock Creek and Potomac Parkway, screaming into my iPhone, I've just alerted my office as the Bell 430 reappears. Crossing Theodore Roosevelt Island, it's headed in my direction at a good hundred miles per hour. Fearing it might crash into the building, I race into the quad of the Watergate complex and look up at the seventh floor only to see my mother standing on her balcony looking at the Bell through binoculars.

As my thumb hits Mom's number on speed dial, I momentarily lose sight of the 430 as it disappears around the building, followed by the sound of smashing glass. Chasing it into the recreational area of the complex, I see the helicopter hovering less than five feet above the steaming, heated pool. It sounds like its Rolls Royce engines may have sucked in some debris, causing them to misfire. Looking up at my mom's balcony from this angle, I can see that she's yelling something down to me as I slowly approach the backfiring helicopter.

I'm about ten feet from the sick bird when it tilts hard to the right, forcing me to the ground as the rotor blades almost take my head off. I can see the pilot waving his arms in the cockpit. The rear passenger-side door partially opens and I observe the left side of a man's head at the bottom of the door – vomiting into the pool.

The sick guy turns slowly in my direction and I can see that he's wearing a mask that covers the right side of his face. Then he slams the door, the Bell goes vertical at a high rate of speed, and I get knocked into the pool flat on my back.

The pilot appears to regain control of the helicopter, barely missing my mother's sun deck before it heads southwest on Virginia Avenue. Quickly climbing out of the pool, still thinking about the puking incident, I realize I hear my mom screaming seven floors above.

I look up to her balcony, hear a small explosion and see what looks like a large white propane tank hurtling like a missile in my direction. With very few options at my disposal, I close my mouth and jump back into the heated pool. The last thing I see before hitting the contaminated water are two Sikorsky SH-60 Sea Hawk helicopters flying over the Watergate Complex in pursuit of the mysterious black helicopter.

"Go Navy!"

Chapter 2

SEEING THE BUBBLING hundred-pound propane tank at the bottom of the pool encourages me to leap up the ladder out of the water. Thick black smoke is pouring out of the balcony just a few doors down from Mom's.

Running into the lobby and almost knocking over the doorman on duty, I dash for the elevators. "Sorry, Joe. They're all outta order," Frankie yells. I don't live here, but I might as well, I've clocked so much time helping Mom renovate the place this year.

I throw open the door to the stairs and begin racing up the seven flights. As I take two steps at a time, I ask everyone coming down if they've seen my mom. All shake their heads or say no. On the landing of the sixth floor, I hear one person say Washington is under attack and another "Where are the fallout shelters."

Turning the final corner on the stairwell, I start to smell something burning, but once in the hallway on my mom's floor, the smoke has thinned out and I almost trip over Danny, who's sitting outside his apartment holding a fire extinguisher like a lover. What a strange guy. As I take a left to mom's apartment, a loud voice yells my name. "Where the hell have you been? Don't you know we have an emergency here?" the unmistakable voice of Stella Rinker brays. "Joseph Dustan, please don't tell me you went for a swim. Something is seriously wrong. I can't open the door into your mother's apartment!"

"Stella, Stella, please calm down," I rattle off quickly. "Mom, can you hear me?"

"Yes, Joseph, I can hear you," comes my mother's voice. "Are you all right? I saw you fall into the pool."

"I'm fine, Mom. We need to get you out of here," I say in an alarmed voice.

"Please, Joe, you're freakin' me out. Let me handle this," says Stella calmly.

Knowing I tend to get a little too emotional when it comes to my mother, I move aside and let her friend handle the discussion.

"Caroline, are you okay?" Stella shouts through the locked door. "Can you unlock the door, sweetie? There's a fire in the apartment three doors down from us and we need to evacuate. You know Danny – the weird guy who never leaves the building? He says a propane heater on his balcony was blown over by a strong wind, somehow got itself turned on, broke the window, rolled into his living room and caught his couch on fire – and then rocketed off his balcony. Okay, sweetie, we both know that ugly cream-colored sofa catching on fire is no disaster – but our building burning to the ground is!"

Stella finally loses her cool and rams her right shoulder into the solid wood door, trying to force it open. "I'm gonna report that piece of shit to the condo association at our next meeting. What kind of fool keeps a propane heater on their balcony all winter anyway?" Stella yells loudly, hoping Danny will hear her. "It must be illegal. It can't be allowed in our by-laws! Are you okay in there, darling? Can you hear me? Joe, tell them assholes to turn off those damn alarms!"

"Joseph, Stella, I need you to push my door open!" Mom yells. "I can't see too well and I think I sprained my wrist. The door handle won't move. It must be jammed or something."

"Okay, Mom, move away from the door," I shout. "Stella, move to the side."

Thinking of all the cops shows I've ever seen on TV, I hurl my 150-pound body against the solid wood door. It doesn't budge; I throw myself into it again.

"Stella," I shout over the alarm, "can you find someone who might be able to help? I'm going to get a running start this time. Mom, move away from the door, please!" This time I give myself some distance and plow my left shoulder into the door, only to bounce back into the hallway without an inch of give from the door.

"Joe, Joe, the floor is empty!" screams Stella. "Even that arsonist Danny's gone! Let me give it a try. Come on, Joe, it's my turn."

"Okay, Stella, you try," I say. "But, please, don't hurt yourself. I'm gonna look for something to break it down!" That's all Stella needs to hear as she prepares to ram all of her 203 pounds against mom's door.

"Move away from the door, sweetie!" hollers Stella. "Somebody *please* turn off that damn alarm! Where's the fire department? Please move away from the door, honey!" It takes only two attempts before the door breaks off its hinges. Leaving Stella barely winded.

"Thank you, Stella, thank you," Mom cries as she hurries out into the hall. "I thought I heard explosions out in the street. The next thing I know a helicopter comes screeching not ten feet from my balcony! The blast of air off the helicopter's rotors was so strong it ripped my balcony doors right off their hinges, and blew shards of glass and debris all over the living room. I was thrown against the outside patio wall and my left wrist snapped back, and I dropped your – uh, a glass of water over the edge. And I've got plaster dust in my eyes, and that threw me off balance and I fell onto glass shards scattered all over the floor. The next thing I know, my hands are bleeding and my wrist is throbbing and I'm crawling along the floor and manage to get back into what's left of my kitchen. Stella, where's Joseph?"

"He either went for help – or decided to go for another swim," Stella giggles. Relief's setting in.

Running down the hallway with a fire ax in my hands, I see my mother and Stella sitting on the floor in the hallway hugging each other. "Mom, are you okay. How did you get the door open?"

"Honey, while you were looking for help, Stella just leaned on the door and it opened right up," Mom says with a large grin on her face.

"Well, actually, Joe, it took me two tries to get it open," said Stella with a matching smile.

• • •

AT TIMES LIKE THESE, I am thankful my mom has an ex-roller derby queen as a friend and neighbor. During a recent dinner party I attended at Stella's apartment, I couldn't believe the number of trophies displayed on any available flat surface. In order to simply sit down for dinner, Stella had to move her prized 1980 first-place trophy in the Hell Raisers Roller Derby event held in Baltimore, Maryland.

Having known this wonderful lady for close to nine years now, I've grown to understand the loneliness that comes with being an ex-queen of the hardwood when it's time to hang your skates up for the last time. Stella once told me that she went from signing autographs a hundred times a night to placing her signature on a bank check maybe ten times a month. I'll always remember the story about Stella's husband, who died of a heart attack three years ago during a deep water fishing trip. The captain of the boat said his attack hit during a six-hour cat and mouse game with a thousand-pound marlin. The first mate later confessed to Stella after the funeral that her husband died from having a few too many and falling overboard. The thousand-pound fish story sounded more dramatic, so Stella considered this a perfect ending for her former pro wrestler husband. I agreed. In his profession, white lies and questionable truths weave together to tell a story that's always bigger than life itself.

• • •

I STEP INTO THE apartment and take a look around. Sighing, I walk back out into the hallway in time to hear the super remind us that we need to leave the building until it's determined safe. "You will have to use the stairs," he said apologetically. "The elevator's out." At least we'll be headed down this time.

"Well, Joseph, it looks like we'll need to wear our tool belts again," says Mom. "Oh Stella, by the way, you know those binoculars you loaned me? We'll need to look for those outside when we get to ground level. I might have dropped them off the balcony into the bushes by accident. I'm sorry. Hey, let me ask you both. Have you ever seen the Phantom of the Opera?" Mom asks sheepishly.

"What on earth are you talking about, Caroline?" Stella says as she guides her friend to the stairway. "Did you hit your head or something? Did you say you have dropped my binoculars over the edge? My Nikon Monarch binoculars? I thought you said you dropped a glass of water. And please tell me what the Phantom of the Opera has to do with this? I love you and all, but those binoculars were expensive – and this Phantom talk is crazy!"

I figured I'd shut my mouth at this point. Telling them that *I'd* recently saw a man in half a mask throwing up in the condo association's pool out of a hovering helicopter would make *me* look like the crazy one. "Mom, Stella, I'm gonna get my surf bag and change into some dry clothes. I'll meet you both down in the lobby."

"Joe, please grab the red velour blanket you brought back from Italy. It's on the top shelf in the closet of my spare bedroom," says Mom. "If you find my cell phone, please bring that as well. The city I love has been attacked. Someone may be trying to reach me."

I pull my mother aside and ask in a whisper if she has a weapon in her apartment. Unfortunately, the answer is no, unless you count her collection of exotic cork screws. I'll pass this time.

"Hey, Joe, if you need me to show you how to break down a door, you let me know," says Stella with a wink. "Love you."

"I love you both too. See you in a few minutes."

As those words leave my lips and I watch them turn the corner, the iPhone in my pocket begins to vibrate. I take it out and read a text from my new part-time boss. "Transpo on way to condo for pick up. Be careful. JL Carlone."

I change into some dry clothes, grab the red blanket and put Mom's vibrating cell phone in my pocket. I'm sure that the folks at the *Halls of Justice* have exceeded the capacity of her voice mailbox and need to speak to her right away.

Closing the broken door to my mom's condo, I notice smoke still coming from inside Danny's apartment. I spot Mom leaning on Stella as they move down the second floor landing with a small group of other slow moving people. I'm surprised we aren't greeted by any firemen or policeman as we walk out the emergency doors on the first floor. Stinging, cold air quickly fills my lungs, reminding me that I'm still damp from the pool. I charge over to Stella and Mom, who are both leaning against the outside of the building and quickly wrap them both in the velour blanket.

Huddled alongside Virginia Avenue on Watergate property, it's hard for me not to notice that this major thoroughfare is nearly empty of moving vehicles and that the only noise to penetrate the cold stillness of the air is the fire alarm. We have yet to see the fire department or any other emergency personnel show up, even after several persistent calls.

Just before 5:00 in the afternoon, as a dark haze is beginning to settle over the neighborhood, I see an EMT ambulance pull up with two on board. A man climbs out of the front passenger seat and Stella yells to get his attention. The short, black-haired EMT has what looks like blood all down the front of his white shirt. He doesn't seem to be in a hurry. In fact, he looks like he's way past the end of his shift. Tired, haggard and about to fall asleep, I see him wander over to Mom and Stella.

Joining the group, I notice his name badge says ED, but when I get a closer look, I see that an "FR" on the badge has been partially covered by the same red that's on his shirt. I can tell Fred is very nervous by his disjointed small talk. He lets us know that he's been an EMT in Washington for seven-and-a-half years and really enjoys what he does for a living, most days anyway. He lives with his girlfriend Emma in a small apartment in DC that boasts a White House view if you hang most of your body way out the bathroom window. During parties at his apartment, he says it's normal to have people dangling out that window, hoping to catch a glimpse of something going on at the White House. I guess Fred never heard of C-Span or 24/7 cable news.

"Let me take a look at your arm," Fred says to Mom. "I'll treat your scrapes and bruises back at the ambulance, and get your wrist in an inflatable cast to help prevent further possible damage. Your eyes will need to be examined at the hospital to remove any pieces of debris." As we walk back to the ambulance, Fred's partner, Molly, comes up to him and whispers something in his ear. He looks like he is about to faint, but manages to stay upright as the color drains from his face. When we arrive at the emergency vehicle, Molly tells us that the president was killed near the end of the ceremonial parade walk. There is stunned silence within our small group. Stella holds out the cross she wears around her neck and kisses it. She whispers a quick prayer ending with a murmured, "...of the Father, Son and Holy Spirit." The five of us, our voices cracking, all whisper back, "amen."

• • •

WITHIN MINUTES, TWO DARK blue Chevy Suburbans pull up behind the ambulance. Four men and two women exit the vehicles, three with guns drawn, pointing at the ground. One of the men flips open his wallet to show some type of badge and yells for my mother. "Caroline Dustan. I'm looking for Caroline Dunstan."

I walk up to the guy and let him know I'm her son Joe and that she needs to get to an emergency room. Looking at his badge more closely, I see he's from the Secret Service. He turns and makes a call on his cell phone, then turns back to us and yells out a quick order.

"Joseph and Caroline Dustan, I need you both to come with us right now."

Without a single word, my mother gets up and gives her blanket to Stella. She comes over to me and takes my arm, and we walk together over to the waiting vehicles. Mom looks back one more time at her friend and mouths the words "thank you" and "I'll call you later." It must be standard operating procedure to separate us, as my mom gets in the lead vehicle and I'm ushered into the one behind it. The vehicles are already moving by the time I manage to get the door closed and throw on my seatbelt.

I look out the window of the SUV. The freezing rain seems to have coated everything in the city, including the few human shapes lying over the building's heating grates. I notice that the fire department has finally shown up at the condo complex. I lean back in my seat and start to go over all that's happened during the last few hours.

My reverie is interrupted when I hear rapid popping sounds. The Suburban I'm a passenger in begins to spin out of control, and starts rolling down a small embankment just past the front door of the Watergate Diner.

Chapter 3

THE SMELL OF GASOLINE permeates the air inside our overturned vehicle. Most of the windows have been blown out and the cold rain begins to dampen the inside. My senses awaken me to the fact that I'm still buckled in my seat – and hanging upside down. I see one body lying in the front crumpled on the roof of the Chevy. The driver has somehow become wrapped around the steering wheel.

"Wake up! Hey wake up!" I yell. "Can't you smell the gas? We need to get out of here!" There's no movement up front. As I start to fumble for the button to release my seat belt, I hear voices outside the vehicle and start shouting. "We need help! The men in front are hurt badly and I can't get out of my seat belt. Somebody call the police!"

Just as these words leave my lips, a man's face, large, oval and ghostly white, peers through the broken window opposite me. He has a tattoo of a white tiger on his neck and a small, barely visible Hitler-type blonde mustache. And either he's missing an ear or I'm simply hallucinating from the shock. "We need help, sir," I plead, beginning to feel like I'm about to pass out. "Please."

The one-eared tiger man has other plans, however: he's moved to the front of the vehicle. Reaching in through the broken windshield, he's going through the pockets of the occupants in front, taking their wallets and federally issued firearms. "Hey, what are you doing?" I shout, slurring my words. In the coat of the mangled driver, he finds an old-fashioned silver plated lighter with a MOPAR logo embedded on both sides. This idiot smiles at me while striking the lighter, apparently unaware of the gasoline soaked into the knees of his pants. On the third strike, the lighter illuminates – and flames begin to dance in the front of the SUV.

Black smoke quickly fills the overturned vehicle and I come fully awake, hacking and choking on the fumes. During my coughing fit, a large hunting knife comes through the car window and across my shoulder. I hear a quick zipping noise and fall onto the floor – no, roof of the SUV. Someone grabs my leg and pulls me out through the smashed window, dragging and dumping me behind another car in a parking lot, just as an explosion rains pieces of blue Suburban all over the first two travel lanes of Virginia Avenue. The last thing I see before throwing up is the one-eared tiger man running away in the light freezing drizzle, wearing only his tighty whities.

• • •

"JOSEPH, JOSEPH, ARE YOU okay? I saw what happened," my mother says, out of breath. "It was a shootout, an ambush or something. The FBI's crawling all over this place. Are you all right?"

"I'm fine, Mom, just a little shaken up, that's all," I mumble between coughing fits.

I feel her sit next to me on the ground as she wraps an arm around me and starts to cry softly. Several DC police officers run over and start peppering us with questions. I answer as many as allowed by our positions in the US government.

It takes the sharp eye of an astute Washington police officer to notice that my mother's left shoulder is bleeding through her white sweater. Upon further inspection, he tells me it looks like a bullet might have grazed her shoulder during the shootout.

"Mom, you need to get to an emergency room right away. I'll call your office, let them know you're on your way to the hospital – with non-life-threatening injuries, thank God. I'll get to work and see what the hell's going on. I'll meet you at Washington Medical as soon as I can."

"Okay, Joseph. You be careful, and keep me posted. Sure you're all right?"

"Yeah, I'm fine. Just a little sore. Nothing a few Advils won't fix. I love you, Mom."

After checking in with his boss, the officer in charge is told to take my mother to the hospital with a police escort. Probably some high-ranking administrative type figured out who she is. As I consider the logistics of my journey over to the office, a familiar voice booms out from behind one of the police cars.

"Don't you worry, Caroline, this time I'm not letting you out of my sight," Stella says in a loud, protective tone. "I should have never let you get in that car with those people. Hey, Joey," she screams over the roof of the car to me, "just because some asshole has a badge doesn't mean they know how to drive! Am I right? Shit, look what happened to you!"

"You're right, Stella," I shout back. "Please, take care of my mother, and call me if you need anything. I'll meet you later back at the hospital."

"Take your time, Joey dear. Caroline's in safe hands with the world-renowned five-time roller derby champ from the nineties!" she bawls out the window at me. Her parting thought: "Joey, you need someone to look after *you*."

Their cruiser pulls away and I decide to walk to the office. It's 7:39 PM.

Chapter 4

As THE SUN begins to rise and reflect off its cast iron dome, I see remnants from the day before strewn across the west steps of the Capitol Building. Paper cups, bottles, hats, gloves and abandoned blankets mark a celebration gone badly wrong. The overnight rain washed the puddles of blood away, along with the hope and promise of Inauguration Day.

Pennsylvania Avenue is unusually crowded this early in the morning, with members of all the security agencies – the DCPD, the FBI, DEA, ATF and Secret Service. Even though the attack happened mainly at the end of the parade route near the White House, our job is to cover every inch of ground for clues and record their location, beginning back at the steps of the Capitol.

I'm working with Jim Carlone this morning, a high-ranking Washington DEA agent, scouring the area for evidence, along with other members of our team of eight. It was "all hands on deck" in the DC area, the minute the news hit that there were shootings and explosions going off along the parade route.

As we worked, Jim told me he'd just gotten home to Virginia, for a vacation after completing a temporary assignment in Mexico monitoring the drug trade, when the call came telling him to get his butt to the office right away. Jim and his wife Kim both knew what "temporary" meant in the world of a drug enforcement agent – two months stationed in a highly dangerous part of the world, followed by three months in Washington spending long days in meetings trying to decipher the data and piece together what it all might mean. According to Jim, it goes like clockwork: by the time his nightmares end and he's back into a safe routine with his wife and two daughters, it's time to return to the field. It's obvious the man loves his job and hopes that in some small way he's doing some good for society, and ultimately his wife and children. In my opinion, he's certainly made the world a safer place for all of us.

It's our third time scouring every inch of the 1.2-mile parade route. We work in groups of forensic and law enforcement personnel, crawling along the wet pavement. I've walked this exact route with my mother on many occasions. It usually takes less than twenty minutes. On this particular morning, my Timex Indiglo sports watch lets me know that we just passed the three hour mark.

Our group hasn't found much evidence mixed in with the garbage left behind by the public. At the completion of the third loop, I'm convinced that most of the action took place near the White House seating platforms. "We'll need some help over here recording the location of body parts found under the viewing bleachers," shouts Bob Kelly. "Log, bag, tag and get it all off to the lab for ID."

My friend Bob Kelly's been in the forensic science business for almost forty years. He tells me the last time he saw such carnage was the day the Air Florida flight crashed into the 14th Street Bridge over the Potomac, back in January '82 – ten months before I was born. He said the recovery process was slow, lasting well into the spring. They recovered body parts as small as fingernails, miles from the bridge. Cataloged it all with the hope that something could be identified for loved ones. He enjoys his job – some people say maybe a little too much – but this is his life and all he knows.

I know he's sickened by what happened, but Bob being Bob, he probably sees it as a way to put off his forced retirement at the end of

February. He's sixty-six, with thinning grey hair and a long thick nose covered in scars from several bouts of skin cancer. His eyes are permanently bloodshot, due to a genetic disposition inherited from his mother's side of the family, he'll tell you. When overworked and under pressure, he has a nervous tic in his left eye which causes it to tear excessively. The tic he also blames on family genetics, not the job.

I'm close enough to see that Bob's left eye is in full spasm. Looking away from me, he pulls a wad of tissues from his coat pocket to soak up the tears. He takes Clonidine for it, but he can't stand the dry mouth side effect. That's why whenever I get near him I smell peppermint Lifesavers. I have to assume he's feeling enormous pressure from all sides today. He looks plain tired.

"Skip, I need you over here," yells Bob. "I think I found some shell casings near six, just under the east side of the bleachers."

Skip Sullivan's one of the many FBI agents combing the parade route for evidence. I've heard he joined the Bureau after he failed the Bar exam for the eighth time. He's a short, stocky fellow, built like a fire hydrant without any muscle. No striking physical attributes that would cause him to stand out or be noticed. As a matter of fact, I heard Skip was voted the one most likely not to be remembered by his FBI graduating class. At a recent Washington dinner function, he opened up to me about being a loner. He said he actually didn't mind it, being left alone, and that he gets most of his satisfaction in life from working for the Bureau. He said he was genuinely at ease in his life of anonymity. After our thirty-minute discussion – it seemed much longer – I concluded that he really prefers keeping others from prying into his personal business, which rumor has it, usually ends badly by the end of the typical weekend.

Watching Bob and Skip leaning over body number six less than twenty yards from me, I hear a loud crack, followed by an explosion that knocks me off my feet. Sprawled on the ground still in a state of shock, I reach for the arm lying next me. I recognize the stainless steel Rolex Datejust watch we got Bob Kelly as a semi-retirement gift a few months ago. It's 9:55 AM.

Unfortunately, Bob will no longer need to know the time. Hugging the arm, I realize it's not attached to his body. The last thing I remember before passing out is Jim Carlone's voice telling me to "let go of the arm."

You may have noticed. I'm into watches. I like to know what time it is. It's a military thing.

Chapter 5

T HE LOUD AND RELENTLESS screaming keeps me from getting any rest. I don't know exactly what direction it's coming from, but it feels uncomfortably close. Crying voices reverberate in my ears as I try to stand from my wheelchair, but the ringing in my head forces me to sit back down slowly. My mother is lying on a stretcher in the hospital's hallway directly to my left.

After the explosion on Pennsylvania Avenue that it turned out killed both Bob Kelly and Skip Sullivan, I was driven to Washington Medical to get checked out. The ER doctor found me to be okay, even though I flinched every time I saw the shiny watch on his right hand. I was officially released – in a wheelchair – after two hours, and went in search of my mother and Stella.

I found my mother sleeping, with a splint on her wrist and a small white bandage on her shoulder, holding Stella's hand. I squeezed my wheelchair in next to my mom, carefully, not wanting to wake her, and whispered to Stella to go to her daughter's and get some rest. She agreed, reluctantly, and actually whispered she'd be back soon. I don't think I've ever heard her whisper.

Finally able to stand up without becoming nauseous, I see rows of patient-filled gurneys snaking around a curved corridor that passes the nurse's station and stops at the gift shop, which happens to be closed. Too bad. They probably would have made a bundle today. The strong odor of urine and bleach floating in the air forces me back down into my chair. I can't help but smile when I see the Velcro splint on my mother's wrist already sporting Stella's personal artistic trademark, her name riding on a roller skate. Dozing off for a few hours, I'm actually dreaming something about roller skates when I'm awakened by a loud and familiar voice.

"Can everyone please give me a little air," barks Stella as she walks down the cramped hallway towards us. "I'll be back later to sign more autographs, but first I need to check on my friends. Don't forget to buy my book!"

My mother wakes up and grins when she hears her friend's voice bouncing off the hospital walls. Stella's a local celebrity in the DC area, taking part in many charitable events in which she gives generously of both her money and time. No one thinks – or dares – to tell her to keep her voice down as she high-fives people lying on stretchers and sitting in wheelchairs, wedged into any available space.

"Why, Caroline sweetie, I believe you're starting to look a lot better," says Stella. "It looks like Joseph's been taking good care of you in my absence. Your hair's no longer matted to the sides of your head, and that dirt on your face can now pass as a spray-on tan that's just cracking a little. We cleaned you up a bit when you got here. Believe it or not, those damn nurses thought they were going to keep me away from you. Ha! Oh, please. Don't they know I'm Hell of a Stella on Wheels! Didn't any of them read my #1 best selling book?" Stella takes Mom's hand and gives me a little wink.

"Joe, Stella, tell me what happened," Mom whispers. "The last thing I remember is running along Virginia Avenue, feeling pain in my shoulder and colliding with an albino in his underwear. Wait – Joseph, the car you were in flipped over and caught on fire!" my mother yells hysterically.

"Mom, I'm fine. Please try and calm down."

"Relax, Caroline, don't get yourself all worked up," says Stella. "Like Joe says, calm down and I'll tell you what I know. Is that all right, Joe?"

"Sure, Stella. Thanks."

"There was a terrorist attack along the parade route. The patio doors on your apartment were decimated by some asshole in a helicopter. That shit head Danny from down the hall almost burned down the building. You and Joe got picked up by FBI agents in SUVs. Then some kinda shootout happens across from our building, and the car Joe's riding in flips over and catches on fire. I see you running towards the overturned SUV and you crash into some guy in his underwear." Stella stops momentarily, then barges on.

"Well, guess what. A cop tells me that same bald-headed white dude dragged your son Joseph here out of the burning vehicle before it blew up. I only thank God you fell down when you ran into this guy, since the flipped SUV blew up a few minutes later. I'm sorry, honey, too much information," Stella says, taking in the dazed look on Mom's face. "Don't worry, we can discuss all the details when you get out of here and feel better." But then Stella remembers the last, crowning detail. "Oh, yeah, I almost forgot. And you somehow dropped my million dollar binoculars off your patio after seeing the Phantom of the Opera – or some shit like that." Stella finishes her story out of breath, with a look a relief written all over her face.

"Wait a minute, now I remember" says Mom slowly. "I dropped those binoculars by accident. What's the Phantom of the Opera have to do with this? I do remember that something happened during the inauguration parade. Oh my God, Joe – is the president dead?"

"No, no, Mom, the president's alive," I say, demonstrating my soft hospital voice, trying to set an example for Stella. "Turns out that was only a rumor. That's what the EMTs were saying, the ones that came to your building after the smoke forced you and Stella out into the parking lot. No, the president received some minor injuries from the explosions. He's recuperating at the White House. But his son and his mother-in-law got caught in the crossfire and died. Along with many others."

"Caroline honey, I've heard over five hundred people are wounded and more deaths are expected," Stella says as she looks down at her hands. "No one seems to know who's behind it, but the list of possibles is as long as my arm. The newspapers are saying that the shooters are from the Middle East. Some of the 24/7 news channels say it's homegrown terrorists, like those shit-ass cowards who blew up the Federal Building in Oklahoma City back in the nineties. And they're quoting some people in the government who fear it might be the Mexican drug cartels, pushing the drug wars back on US soil as a sort of revenge for declaring our own secret war against them over two years ago. And tell me, how is that a secret if I know about it? Good Lord, who the hell knows?" says Stella as she gently pushes the tangled brown hair away from Mom's face.

It is at this point that I see my mother pull the hospital sheet over her head and begin to cry softly. Stella, feeling faint, sits down in my wheelchair, holding Mom's hand. She looks up at me and bursts out crying herself. I guess even a once-blond bomber Washington DC Roller Derby Queen is bound to crumble every once in a while. Especially on days like these.

The crying comes to an abrupt halt as two men and two women wearing DEA jackets storm into the emergency room shouting, "Caroline Dustan? Joseph Dustan?" checking gurneys, going in and out of patients' rooms, and interrupting nurses as they cover the floor. Before we can react, the tall, skinny guy in the lead sees an arm rise from under a white hospital sheet. He walks quickly over to us and Mom tells him that she's Caroline Dustan.

Thinking we've met before, I start to introduce myself and ask him what he wants, but before he has a chance to speak, my cell vibrates and I raise a finger, the universal sign for "give me a minute." I move off to the side and read a text message from my iPhone, from Jim Carlone. "DEA picks up Caroline and Joe at Wash Medical. Both attend meeting in DC. Joe on flight from DC to FL tonight. Details to follow. JL Carlone." Before I can give Mom the update, Stella jumps into the conversation with guns blazing.

"Who the hell are you, and what do you want with Caroline and Joe?" blasts Stella. "The last time they got in cars with federal agents, there was a shootout and she and her son almost got killed. She needs her rest. Get away from her! I mean it now, get away from her!"

"It's okay, Stella," says Mom. "I work with many different federal agencies, including the Drug Enforcement Administration. I'll tell you more about it later."

I lean down and whisper the details of Jim's message into my mom's ear.

A short, black-haired female agent, wearing a bullet proof vest under her opened DEA windbreaker, pushes over a wheelchair and helps my mother into it. As they begin to roll her out the door, I'm right behind her. Mom looks over and calls to Stella. "Come with us! Please, I need you to stay with me."

I smile at Stella as she hustles out the emergency room, bumping into what looks like an eighty-year-old security guard blocking the door. She tosses off a quick apology as I see him pull a flyer off the wall, take a pen from his jacket pocket and chase Stella into the parking lot. "You promised me an autograph!" he shouts, his voice quickly winded. Stella rushes back to where the guard is standing, signs his piece of paper, "To My Number One Fan Johnny Z" and kisses him on the cheek. The man slowly sits on the ground, mesmerized by what's just happened, and pulls a silver harmonica out of his front shirt pocket. Watching his roller derby idol on the move with a small entourage of people, he begins playing "Oh My Darling Clementine" like he was six years old all over again.

• • •

TWO DARK CARS IN the lot are waiting for us with the engines running. As we approach the vehicles, the doors swing open. Two agents help Mom into the first car, while the second group, Stella and me included, climbs into the second car. Before Stella can finish saying thank you for the lift, the car takes off down a narrow side street and bursts out onto Connecticut Avenue. The car's flashing lights and shrieking sirens have Stella smiling when she looks over at me. The vehicle takes a hard right and appears to be heading into the side of a building, when it snakes its way into a driveway and begins descending into a parking garage.

By the time I've finally been able to get my seat belt on, both cars come to a screeching halt. The doors fly open and the agents get out of the two vehicles, guns drawn. An unmarked black van with smoked windows has its slider door wide open, waiting to take us on the next leg of this journey. Crossing the lot to get in the van, Stella asks me a simple question.

"Hey, Joe, is your mother really a librarian with the Library of Congress?"

Chapter 6

THE DARK VAN stops at what looks like an abandoned warehouse along the river. As the vehicle passes through the first set of doors, a highly lit area comes into view, with people milling around, and chairs and tables scattered throughout the large room. It's the same type of set up you'd see in a movie, but this time it's all too real. I'm not sure what's going on, since only a few words were spoken on the trip over. A tall red-haired woman wearing a blue FBI hat, black jeans and a tight black turtleneck walks up to the three of us and informs me that my ride to Reagan National will be here in an hour. We find a few empty chairs together in the back of the room and Stella starts talking nervously.

"All right, Caroline, Joe. I'm starting to put the pieces together – you both work for the US government in some capacity. Now Joe, I know you've spent six years in the service, but I thought you got out – over three years ago, wasn't it? And you work for Social Services in – Florida? Okay, forget you for a minute," Stella says without taking a breath as she turns to my mom.

"The more confusing part for me is *your* involvement in the government, Caroline. Listen, I know you're involved in library services and research – I went with you myself to a very boring – sorry – librarian's convention in Las Vegas. All right, we both know what happened, but let's dwell on the positive. You, my best friend Caroline, were stuck in a hot and stuffy hotel room discussing digitalization in the modern age, while I won over ten thousand dollars by the end of the week playing Black Jack," Stella says, shaking her head in disbelief and grinning at the memory.

"Where it all gets a little cloudy is when we celebrated my winnings by going out for dinner with some of my retired friends from my roller skating days. Guess what, Joe? We even brought along a few of your mom's friends from the convention. Old roller derby queens and library nerds out on their last night in Sin City."

Stella moves in closer to Mom and me and whispers the rest. "Joe, Caroline, I gotta be honest with you. To this day, I cannot remember getting on a plane and going home, but I do have scary memories of police, handcuffs, the Hoover Dam, a Celine Dion concert and the Village People telling me to get my ass to the YMCA. I gotta tell ya, I am surely grateful for that 'what happens in Vegas stays in Vegas' thing. Caroline honey, you took great care of me that night. And now, here, all the stealth and secrecy – something tells me you had some kinda outside help that went beyond library nerds and derby ladies," says Stella with an over-dramatized wink for both of us.

"Stella," says Mom, "I know it may seem a little over the top, but it's necessary. Believe it or not I *am* a librarian. A librarian who conducts worldwide research for the US government. At this point, that's all I can tell you, but I'm sure you have a good idea that it's a little bit more complicated than that."

"Caroline, Joe" Stella whispers again. I think she's actually getting the hang of whispering. "Who are these people and what are we doing here? The way the feds came storming through the hospital looking for you two, I would have thought you were either royalty or – responsible for the terrorist attack. It's clear they need you for something very important or we wouldn't be here right now – wherever we are."

As I'm the one with a very low security clearance, I stay out of the conversation as much as possible and let my mother handle the questions.

"Honestly, I'm not exactly sure why I'm here either," say Mom. "I conduct research for the government, file reports and pass them on to the higher-ups. Most of the information I gather is rather basic and can be found by anyone with a good internet connection and investigative instincts." Mom hesitates, then goes on very quietly. "Some of the data is classified. TS/SCI. Top Secret, at the most sensitive level. Things the president might read. Though why I was picked up outside our condo complex and later plucked out of the emergency room and brought here, you got me. Joseph and I are still very much in the dark."

I notice a small door open near a mural-sized painting of the White House. Two men cross the hall to a make-shift podium in the front of the room. An increasing hush spreads like a wave across the floor as those assembled hang up phones, take off headsets and quietly try to find a seat. I offer my seat to an elderly gentleman and stand next to my mother and Stella who, I now notice, are sitting under the map of the world and blocking out most of Australia with their heads. I estimate the room to be at four times its normal audience capacity. I recognize the person taking the podium. My buddy Jim Carlone.

"Jim Carlone. Drug Enforcement Administration," Mom tells Stella. "A good guy – the kind who says little but clearly really cares." Mom knows a different side of Jim than I do. In DC, he may be a man of few words, but in the mountains of Afghanistan, we couldn't get him to shut up.

"Good evening, everyone," says Jim as he taps the microphone to make sure it's working. "As most of you know, I'm Jim Carlone, assistant to the regional director for the DEA office here in Washington. As you all know, there was an assassination attempt on our new president less than 24 hours ago during the inaugural parade. As a result of this cowardly act, the president received minor injuries, but lost both a son and mother-in-law. We have now confirmed 721 injured and 671 dead. No one has claimed responsibility and we have very little to go on. We continue to sift through all the evidence, interview people and most importantly make sure the public does not panic or fall victim to rumors being spread by us or the media. In order to coordinate all our efforts, teams have been set up throughout Washington. We are breaking this event down and assigning one slice to each team to focus on.

"We've been assigned the drug trade angle. We need to determine if one or more of the drug cartels of Mexico, Central and South America had anything to do with this plot. It is our responsibility and obligation to the American people to use all resources available and determine if any of these groups were involved. The public still remembers us going to war in Iraq based on faulty intelligence. We cannot make the same mistake again.

"Each of you will all be assigned to a group with a leader who reports directly to me. All data will go through your team leader and be passed along to a research group headed up by Caroline Dustan." Heads turn our direction as Jim gestures towards us.

"Last but not least, I don't do well with formalities. Most of my friends call me either Jim or JL. I ask all of you to do the same. If we are not friends now, we will be. Remember everyone, time is critical. We'll have to work around the clock to get the answers we need to put this ugly tragedy behind us. Thank you."

Jim walks away from the podium and begins talking to a few people around him. A heavy-set woman up in the front of the room points in our direction and a small contingent of people start toward us. The puzzle is starting to come together in my mind, and I know at this moment our lives are about to change drastically.

Feeling a tap on my shoulder, I turn around as the tall, red-haired FBI agent informs me that my ride is here to take me to the airport. I give my mother and Stella one big, inclusive hug and tell them I'll see them soon. As I start to follow the red head, I hear Stella ask my mom, "Caroline, honey, where can we get our hands on a Bible? I want to lay my right hand on it and get deputized. I wanna help save the world too!"

Chapter 7

Sitting outside on a lawn chair surrounded by who knows how many cats all purring for attention is pretty normal in this old Key West neighborhood. Living several houses down from the famous Hemingway House, I take it all in stride and enjoy their company, especially this morning after a ten-mile run. When I'm here, I often put out milk or scraps of food hoping to see the world-famous felines. The Key West publicity machine boasts that over sixty cats roam the Hemingway property.

The flight in from Washington last night, via a private jet provided by the Navy, tells me that I'm close to leaving the country and getting my passport stamped. Living off Truman Avenue in a studio flat close enough to the ocean to smell and hear the waves crashing along the beach will soon be a distant memory.

Since I don't get to spend much time here, my apartment contains just the basics — a bed, a few chairs and a couch that once belonged to a lovely retired couple. The sofa, an ugly brown, is relatively new and quite comfortable. My neighbor was recently found dead on it, apparently of a heart attack. His widow moved and had no interest in taking the sad memories associated with the sofa with her. She offered it to me

JAMES K. ZAVEZ

at no charge for all the assistance I'd provided them over the last year. I threw an old blue blanket over it to help hide the color and the memory. It barely fit into my one-room apartment, what with all the surfboards, guitars and bicycles that lean against walls or hang off the ceiling.

The truth of the matter is that, spending so much of my life on the road, having to walk sideways through my prized clutter a few months a year to get to the bathroom is just fine by me. I'm the kind of guy who has so many hobbies I've never really been able to get very good at any one of them. I love Key West and consider it my home, but most of the time it's simply a place on a map to store my things and find some peace. And speaking of peace, as my mind goes back to the recent situation in DC, the cell phone in my pocket begins vibrating. The flashing number on the screen indicates it's a call from a business associate in Washington I've been expecting. The conversation lasts less then twenty seconds. My end consists of three yeses, one no and a thank you.

My bag's already packed when I hear a knock at the door and a woman's sexy voice calling my name. Since I don't own a car, my friend Sheila Bennet volunteered to give me a ride over to the Naval Air Station. Sheila's a waitress I met at *Sloppy Joe's* on Duval Street a month ago when I stopped in for a quick beer after getting back from South America. We became quick friends and spent time talking about her family problems, most of which revolve around her younger brother's drug problem and recent disappearance.

Sheila's twenty-five and strikingly beautiful, with long black hair and large olive-green eyes. She's lived in Key West all her life and has a natural tan that one could never get from a bottle or booth. She's mentioned old money in her family, from her great-grandfather's partial ownership in a few big resorts on Miami Beach. While the inheritance was substantial, she said it wasn't enough to keep the members of her generation from having to work regular jobs. The recession and housing bust a few years ago forced most of the Bennet family to

- 30 -

update their resumes and sharpen their interviewing skills. Sheila was proud of the fact that no adjustment was needed for her lifestyle – she'd started working the day she turned sixteen, and has a Master's in business.

But after swimming in the shallow end with corporate brown nosers for a couple of years, Sheila decided that writing romance novels was more her thing. I enjoy our new friendship, but I have no idea what direction it might go. She's not in any hurry for a new relationship, having only recently gotten out of a bad marriage. Even though I'm only thirty, I sometimes get the feeling that she sees me as more of a father figure. Her dad died over ten years ago and with her brother Gary missing, she seems to relish having me as a father/brother-like friend. I never speak about my father, but I'm sure Sheila wants me to shut up when I go on about my mother. She seems to be jealous of the relationship I have with my mother and says she can't wait to meet "this remarkable woman," as she puts it.

Sheila's got the top of her white '93 Mercedes 300 CE convertible down even though the temperature can't be much above sixty. The ride over to the Naval Station takes less than fifteen minutes since it's still early for the tourists, God love 'em. Sheila pulls up to the Boca Chica guardhouse on Saratoga Avenue. When the three men stationed in the guardhouse see this beauty in the driver's seat they fall over each other to see how they can be of assistance. I thank Sheila, give her the keys to my apartment – she uses it to write – and climb out. As she makes a u-turn, I have to work to get the guards' attention to show them my credentials, then stroll down the road to a nearby building complex.

"I have a lot of questions for you, Joseph Dustan, mystery man," Sheila whispers to herself as she turns the heat up, pulls away from the guardhouse and heads for home to meet the new private detective the family's hired to find her brother.

Chapter 8

THE GRUMMAN C-2 Greyhound lifts off the 10,000-foot Boca Chica runway and banks to the southeast over the water before turning northwest toward Panama City, Florida. Its two Allison T-56 turboprop engines are at full throttle, boosting the Greyhound at 2600 feet per minute up to a cruising altitude of 22,000 feet. My watch beeps, telling me its 10:00 AM. Precisely.

Our flight plan includes a stop at the Panama City Naval Station to pick up fuel and supplies; from there our final destination is Andrews Air Force base outside Washington. I calculate our time in the air to be about four hours and our stop in Panama City, to be about two. That will put me at the Washington office at around 6:00 PM.

I hunker down in my jump seat, throw on my iPod and begin to read a letter from my mother that was in my mailbox when I got home last night. It's ironic that I saw Mom yesterday while the letter was written prior to the terrorist attack. It's almost like seeing ripples in a pond before a stone gets thrown in. She talks of her work at the library and all the interesting people she meets, including the ones she doesn't trust. No letter is ever complete without the mention of Stella. After seeing her in action yesterday afternoon, I can certainly understand why. It's obvious in Mom's letter that she thoroughly enjoys going around DC with Stella as she signs copies of her new book, *Hell on Eight Wheels*. What a title.

The last part of her letter revolves around a serious discussion we had a few months ago, having to do with my father, who I've never met. The last time she saw him was two months before I was born; no other contact has ever been made. She has no idea where he might be, or at least that's what she says again in the letter. I have no reason to doubt her, but I sometimes feel there's something more to the story. The only thing I know is that thirty years ago, my father lived in Mexico and that he was in their military. After all these years, my mother assumes he's probably dead. At the end of her letter, she does say that she'll continue to use all her connections and resources to try and find him for my sake.

I put the subject aside for now and fall asleep listening to the passionate sounds of the O'Jays urging me to get on board the "Love Train."

Chapter 9

T HE WHEELS OF THE Grumman Greyhound touch down at Andrews Air Force base at 4:43 PM. My trip back to Washington in less than 24 hours is on schedule and uneventful. I've taken this particular shuttle from Key West to DC on many occasions but have never seen so much security, even after 9/11. The attempted presidential assassination, 48 hours ago now, has certainly put the base on high alert. Military and law enforcement officials are flying in from all over the world, meeting throughout the DC area to piece together what happened and come up with an appropriate response. Assuming that all military vehicles are going to be occupied tonight, I wade through security, throw my surf bag over my shoulder and hit the streets looking for a taxi just as the sun is setting, at 5:21 PM.

Finding a taxi outside Andrews Air Force Base is far more difficult than I'd anticipated. Security is just as high outside as it was inside. Local police are keeping all traffic flowing beyond the perimeters of the base; vehicular stopping is flat out prohibited. Washington lies ten or twelve miles west of Andrews. The best thing I can do is start walking until I can flag down a taxi or possibly grab a ride with a passing military vehicle.

While making my way through the security line at Andrews, I made a few calls to associates in DC to confirm location and meeting time. Another old military buddy, Mike Lenoce, told me he saw my mother earlier this afternoon with her arm in a sling and looking a bit tired. It will be good to see her again in a few hours. Mike confirmed that the DEA pulled a few strings to get her on our team full time.

Mom's well known throughout the federal government for her ability to sift through data, pull out facts and put them in a usable format that even I can understand. She's always told family and friends that she's simply a librarian who works at the Library of Congress, and in fact, much of her time is spent doing just that - working with members of her team digitizing old works to preserve the history of the United States. What she fails to mention is that she has another office, five floors below ground level and that she has direct access to the White House. It's the research she conducts for the government that provides her maximum security clearance and, when needed, 24/7 armed protection. Compared to Mom, I have no security clearance. Basically, they tell me what I need to know, on an hour by hour basis.

"You look like someone who could use a ride," yells a familiar voice. Mike Lenoce is parked by the side of the road, sitting on the hood of his meticulously restored '72 red Ford LTD convertible. "I hope you know that walking these streets at night is dangerous, even for a war veteran who survived several tours in the Middle East."

Walking over to the car, I notice a baby seat in back. It's been a year or more since I last saw Mike. Like I said, we'd served together, reupping together tour after tour, but the day came when he finally decided not to sign up for another two more years. I went to South America in my military-issued business suit and he went to work at his dad's plumbing and heating business in his street clothes. He didn't seem happy about it, but he'd decided he could no longer be away from his wife Joanne for extended periods of time with destinations unknown. Seeing Mike brings back a flood of happy memories – and a tremendously sad one, which chokes me up for a moment. I give my good friend a hug, then hold him at arm's length, surveying him.

"Hey, pal, looks like married life's made you a little soft around the middle. The shape you're in, I'm not sure if you'd be able to save my life again if needed. Seriously, though, my mom told me about what happened to Bobby. I'm really sorry, man. But hey, judging by the baby seat there, I figure there's something you're not telling me. Is Joanne having another baby?"

As the last several words roll off my tongue, Mike's eyes begin to glaze over, and he looks down at his feet. His glasses slip down his nose and his eyes begin to tear.

"I'm sorry I didn't call and tell you what happened," says Mike. "Little Bobby died three days after his first birthday. A rare heart disorder that suddenly dropped his blood pressure so low, he fainted, hit his head on an end table and died instantly. That was over six months ago and we still drive around with his seat in the car." He sagged. "Joanne blames herself for not watching him more closely. It happened in less than sixty seconds as she was making lunch one day. It's still hard to talk about it. I know I should at least put his car seat in the trunk."

I tell Mike I'm sorry again and quickly change the subject. "Well, congratulations on going back to work for the government," I say. "They still need a few good men. Even soft ones." It did the trick, getting us onto safer ground.

"Listen, asshole, give me a month and I'll be in better shape than you. Let me tell ya, working in a family business is tough and you know my father – he'll never change his ways. The promise of me taking over the business after his retirement – turns out that was just a bunch of bullshit to get me close to him so he could tell me 'I told you so' to my face everyday. He's only happy when he knows you're not. Come on, Joe, you know what a miserable son of a bitch he can be. I tried to play the game while setting up his retirement party, which he canceled once he found out that Joanne and I did most of the planning." Mike slides off the hood of the car and opens the driver's side door. I take that as my cue to go around and climb in as well.

"It's Jim Carlone's fault we're working together again, ya know," he went on. "Came into the store looking to buy some parts for his toilet and we started talking about his job at the DEA. I gotta tell ya, Joe, I got so sucked in by our conversation that we took the plumbing parts to his house, repaired the toilet and I ceremoniously flushed the hardware business two hours and a few beers later. I told my dad 'I quit' the next day, and was working for Jim the following Monday. Today, my dad and I barely speak except when he really needs me for something. You know I love my dad. We'll work it out."

He reaches for the key and starts the engine. "Sweet," I say in admiration.

"Yeah," Mike agrees. "The older she gets, the better she sounds." He pulls out into the traffic. "Oh, Joe, I gotta tell ya how Carlone ended his meeting in front of over 45 people. You know he hates formality, right? He makes it a point to let everyone know that he wants to be called either JL or Jim and not James or Mr. Carlone. After the meeting, I personally thanked Mr. James Lawrence Carlone for his honesty and candor," snickers Mike. "He pulled that same shit with those Afghan tribal leaders who couldn't understand an ounce of English. I gotta tell you though, JL Carlone does know how to inspire a crowd."

"Jim must have that "no formality" bullshit written on his arm," I say. "He said exactly the same thing at the meeting I was at yesterday morning. If we're lucky, maybe we'll hear it again."

Mike was never the best driver. He's one of those people who turn their heads to look at their passenger while conversing, and his driving technique has caused me more than a few uncomfortable moments over the years. He probably picked up the habit in the military, where eye contact and face to face discussions are the status quo. Lives can depend on understanding orders, and you always want to make sure that you don't miss anything. I've reminded Mike that even though he now works for the DEA, he's a civilian and really must keep his eyes on the road.

As the Ford's V8 engine hums through the outskirts of DC, I can't help but remember our little clique growing up in the Washington suburb of Arlington. Mike and Joanne were part of the group, and we all knew back in college they'd end up together. I guess some things are meant to be. Then I find myself musing over the mix of good luck and tragedy that Mike and Joanne have had to face. I quickly wake from my thoughts as the car hits a pothole and stops abruptly along Independence Avenue, near the Library of Congress building complex. I release my seat belt and get ready to jump out.

"I'll see you later," says Mike. "I'm going home for a late dinner with Joanne and a quick nap. Carlone wants me back at work at midnight and I want to be on my toes. I may be the new guy, but you know me, Joe, I'm a fast learner. Working in the family business with my father wasn't the life for me. Working with my buddies and trying to make a difference suits me just fine. Joanne agrees and I love her for that. See ya later, Joey D!"

Joey D, a name from back in the day that I truly dislike. I lace my "thank you for the ride" with a heavy dose of sarcasm, get my surf bag out of the back seat and hit the pavement. I forget to ask him why these DEA meetings are being held in the Library of Congress, but I'm sure I'll find out soon enough. I've got a feeling my mother has something to do with it.

Standing on the top step of the Thomas Jefferson Building, I feel like I'm home. My mother's been working here for over twenty years and much of my time as a kid was spent roaming the 530 miles of bookshelves in the world's largest library. It's no wonder I got mostly A's on papers that required research. I made hundreds of friends in this building. Some still have the nerve to call me "little Joey" when I come back to visit.

Tonight, the complex is lit up on all floors and security's roaming both inside and out. I'm not sure what door to go in so I simply walk through the unlocked front doors – causing an immediate lock down of the facility. This is not how I want to make my entrance, but at least my mother will know I'm back in town.

After quite an aggressive pat down by a very large, loud security woman, I'm ushered to an open elevator and escorted down three flights by several security guards. Based on my knowledge of the building's floor plans, I believe this entire subterranean floor consists of high tech meeting rooms. My Timex beeps to let me know its 6:00 PM.

Chapter 10

As THE ELEVATOR doors open, you immediately know you're below ground. Even with an expensive ventilation system, the air feels manufactured and musty. It reminds me of the air you breathe on a commercial airplane.

I'm escorted down a long dark hallway lit only by emergency lighting. The building's generators must be working overtime. We take a left at the rest rooms and an immediate right into a large conference room that's filled to capacity. Jim Carlone's standing at the front addressing his audience in a voice that's flat and tired. Even from the back, I can tell he's drained by his slumped shoulders and the way he keeps shifting his weight from one leg to another. The guy needs a nap. From what Mike's told me, Jim's been running meetings all day. Unfortunately, when things heat up, fighting terror can be a 24/7 occupation.

While Jim continues outlining roles and responsibilities, I quickly spot my mother in a far back corner sharing a bench with Stella. She's of course still sporting the splint on her left arm, but her face is back to being as bright as ever. She's someone who thrives on challenges – her large, green eyes are soaking in Jim's every word, and an occasional nod of her head indicates her agreement with what he's saying.

Looking at her now, I can honestly say she hasn't really changed over the last many years. To me she looks the same today, at forty-six, as she did when I graduated from Georgetown eight years ago. God, she was amazing that day. Bill Cosby was supposed to be the commencement speaker, but got stranded in an airport overseas due to weather. She was asked to step in for him at the last minute – the president of Georgetown's a friend. Though not prepared in any way, she took our class on an hour-long journey through the last hundred years of global history and talked about how each one of us needed to make a positive impact on the next hundred years. She got a standing ovation.

I remember Stella was there too, off to the side of the stage with a huge smile on her face, yelling and clapping for Mom. She was going from there to a tournament right afterward – you could see her roller derby outfit under her coat. Her team, the Washington Roller Coasters had a tournament in less than two hours. My graduation night was spent with my mother, cheering on Stella and the Coasters in a smoke-filled, beer-on-the-floor auditorium in a poor section of DC. After the Coasters swept the visiting Cincinnati Devil Dogs, my mother and I joined the lady Coasters for an all-out celebration. It was amazing to me how beautiful all these women were when they traded in their skating gear for street clothes. It was easy to see how Jim Croce "fell in love with a roller derby queen."

When my mother sees me, she raises her arm with the splint to wave hello and a twist of pain shows on her face. I find it bothers me to see her injured and caught up in this inauguration tragedy. I've missed most of Jim's speech, but recognizing certain people in the room confirms that a plan is being hatched that involves both my mother and me. The two of us have worked together indirectly in the past with positive results and I sense that we will again be donning our team uniforms for a very important cause. As the meeting ends and the crowd begins to move about, I quickly make my way over to Mom and Stella.

"You two ladies look a little too tired to be out this late. Shall we hail a cab and quickly make our escape before Carlone sees us together and decides he wants to talk?"

"Joseph, you have no idea how good it is to see you again so soon," Mom says with a big smile tinged with anxiety. "Unfortunately the news just keeps getting worse."

During a silent moment and quick group hug, I feel a heavy tap on my shoulder. I don't need to open my eyes or turn around to know who it is. The weight that's been lifted temporarily by our little embrace is about to become permanent, for at least the near future.

Chapter 11

SITTING ALONE on a hard wooden bench in the Main Reading Room of the Library staring out into the dark empty streets across to the Capitol Building, I feel myself beginning to relax a bit as I wait for Mom and Stella, who've gone down to the work-out center to shower and change clothes. Spending another night sleeping in Mom's office and wearing the same duds since being forced out of their homes was out of the question. Stella called her daughter Natalie and asked her to go over and get some clean clothes for her and my mom. Target would be Plan B.

Stella's daughter is twenty-three. She came out of rehab a few months ago, Stella had told me, and is learning to live on her own again. She's always struck me as a remarkable young woman. Unfortunately, she got mixed up with the wrong people after her father died. Natalie helped her mother do research for her book, but all the while she was becoming more secluded in her daily life. Stella knew there was a problem, but it was Natalie who checked herself in at a local rehab clinic for 28 days. She ended up staying 93.

Reflecting on what's happened to my mother over the last 24 hours has really put a scare into me. Being raised by a single mother, without any help from a father, we are not only mother and son, but best friends. She's there for every major event in my life, as I am there for hers. When my travels take me to different places around the world, she always makes a point to visit me, unless I'm working undercover. She isn't overbearing, just very interested in my life. I guess being a single parent, she always feels that she needs to be both mother and father.

The subject of my father came up a lot while I was growing up and sometimes ended in anger. The spark of our heated discussions usually revolved around gifts that showed up on my birthday. The packages started arriving when I turned six and were usually left at our house, addressed to me with no return address. In fact, there was never any shipping information on them. They'd be simply dropped off. For all we knew, my father could have been living in the neighborhood watching us shop for our groceries and gas for the car, or maybe he was part of a chain gang we'd see during the hot summer months picking up trash along the highway. (I had a pretty vivid imagination as a kid.) For the first several years, we tried to catch whoever was delivering them in the act, but never got close. If we watched the house, the present would appear in our car while we were in the movies. If we locked the car in the garage, it would be sitting on the front porch.

My mother was sixteen and living with her dad in Mexico City when she had me. She'd known my father for about a year prior to my birth. He disappeared before I was born. Mom doubts she'd recognize him after thirty years if they bumped into each other on the Metro.

The gifts stopped coming after I turned sixteen. We thought he might be sick, or dead, or in prison, or maybe he'd just lost interest. I still have a few of the presents in a closet in Key West. An old baseball mitt. A soccer ball autographed by the great Pelé. The strangest item I received was on my sixteenth birthday: a silver-colored rock about the size of a softball with a familiar looking face carved into it. The attached note said it was from one of the temples of Machu Picchu in Peru. My mother got nervous, took a Polaroid of it and mailed it over to the Smithsonian. When they were somehow able to verify its authenticity, it was sent back to the Peruvian government with an awkward explanation. I stuck a copy of the photo in between pages 48 and 49 of my old high school yearbook. Page 49 contains a picture of my high school sweetheart, Shannon O'Malley, aboard a large white fishing boat named the *Minnow*, along the eastern Maryland shore. We'd been on a biology class trip. We were trolling for aquatic specimens, which were interesting enough, but the real find of the day was a Virginia license plate reminding us that "Virginia is for Lovers." On that beautiful spring day in April, Shannon held a net in her hands while her picture was taken for the yearbook. Three days after our graduation in June, she was killed by a drunk driver.

I am jolted out of my memories by the sound of loud voices that seem to be coming from the main doors of the library. I jump up from the wooden bench and race to the entrance.

Chapter 12

WORKING MY WAY through the small crowd gathered by the doors, I see a woman, about five-foot-eight, with long black curly hair, a dark complexion, a slight build bordering on muscular, and a demeanor that screams she can take care of herself. Attitude or not, she won't be getting by the dozen or so security guards blocking her way into the building. The woman is dressed in faded Levis, brown cowboy boots and a white, buttoned sweater, the top several buttons of which are unfastened, revealing a black lace bra that leaves little to the imagination. As I make my way up to the front of the crowd drawn to the commotion, she spots me and yells for help. Pulling out my ID, I vouch for Stella's daughter, who reaches past the guards separating us to give me a hug that any man would be jealous of.

I haven't seen Natalie Rinker in over six months, but now I really feel like my visit back to DC is complete. Natalie is never shy, and for that, I am ever grateful. Even though we've gone out a few times, she's more like a sister to me than anything else. While on a recent operation in South America, I got almost as much mail from her as from my mother. Once she sent me a photo of herself sunbathing at the beach. Needless to say it went missing hours after I got it.

"Joey honey, I'm *so* glad to see you!" shouts Natalie. "My mother called with very specific instructions and these mall cops don't want to let me through the front door. They say I need special written permission or a damned ID badge. Joey sweetie, help me please?"

"Hey, Nat," I too have to yell over the crowd noise. "Stay right here and I'll get clearance for you."

I make a quick call to Jim's phone, then hand my cell to the person who looks to be in charge and the most pissed. After a few yes sirs and a thank you, he hands the cell back to me, has Natalie put her pocketbook and a big bag from Target on the conveyor belt, and motions to her to pass through the metal detector.

Halfway through, a buzzer goes off and red lights start flashing. The police ask her to empty her pockets onto a plastic white tray, then scan her with a handheld wand from top to toe. The contents of her pockets – keys, lip gloss, condoms – and a switchblade knife. The wand begins beeping consistently as it approaches her left foot. Smiling coyly, she pulls up her pant leg to reveal a small stainless steel Lady Derringer with synthetic ivory grips tucked into her boot.

As Natalie begins to take the gun out, two policemen draw their service weapons; a third one tells her to put the weapon on the floor. As she drops the Derringer, she shakes her head and says something about how a woman has the right to protect herself. I huddle with the cop in charge, who ends up confiscating the knife and the gun with no intention of ever giving them back. Both are illegal in DC. They do give her back her handbag, her keys, lip stuff and the glow-in-the-dark condom, and the bag of clothes from Target.

"Thanks, Joey. I'm sorry," says Natalie. "I shouldn't have brought that stuff into the building. I wasn't thinking. Metal detectors in a library? Who knew? It's just that I've been mugged twice and almost raped once. Each time, I reported it to the cops, names and everything, but guess what – no freaking arrests!" Tears well up in her eyes at the memory.

"Look, Nat, calm down," I say, putting an arm around her. "You know those weapons are dangerous and illegal. After what just happened, we're lucky we weren't hauled down to the station, put in a hot room under a bright light and strapped to chairs while some old fart with bad breath and yellow teeth asks us 'is it safe?'" I get a blank stare. "You know, like Dustin Hoffman in Marathon Man?"

Natalie hugs me and whispers another apology, says she's happy for me, that I'll be safe running a marathon with Austin, whoever he is, and that a little mouthwash might help. I try to explain the "is it safe?" line again, but finally just explain that she won't be getting her gun or switchblade back. Natalie smiles, wipes away her tears and begins to tell me about her recent errands.

"Listen to me, I went over to the Watergate and needless to say they wouldn't let me in. The section where our moms live has some minor water damage from the fire. Their first floor neighbor, Bob Chauvette – you know that older fellow who has MAILGUY for a license plate? The one who always has to tell you a joke? Well, he says everyone should be able to get back into the complex later tomorrow. MAILGUY and his *much* younger wife Ellie told me they'll keep an eye on their condos. He's such a nice man, but he's not very funny. Probably why his wife's always wearing earplugs."

I find a security person to escort Natalie to the employee gym so that Mom and Stella can change. It is now 8:23 PM and I'm starting to feel tired. I'm leaning against a large lost-and-found bulletin board with odd gloves and mittens pinned to it when Jim Carlone comes by to let me know that he needs Mom and me at the DEA building tomorrow morning at eight for a quick meeting. I've been in on enough of Jim's quick meetings to know that any meeting with him is never quick, so I mentally block out the whole morning. He also tells me that he's reserved a block of rooms for us at the Washington Marriott for as long as needed.

As I walk through the law section of the library, I hear a series of six major blasts all within thirty seconds, and feel the ground below me shake. My hope that the explosions are some type of natural occurrence is quickly dashed as air raid sirens go off across Washington.

Chapter 13

THE SIRENS BLARE for five minutes. Word quickly gets around that the blasts came from several fuel storage tanks exploding over at Reagan National Airport. According to one of those so-called reliable sources, CNN is reporting that the air raid sirens were activated by accident and that, at this time, no one knows what caused the tanks to detonate. All I know is that we're all beat and need to get over to the hotel for some sleep.

Natalie has a great sense of humor; it's comical to see both Mom and Stella dressed in identical outfits. Natalie denies that was her motive, claiming that she was just in a hurry and grabbed two of each item in different sizes except for two ugly grey jackets marked "one size fits all." Stella's fits nicely; Mom's falls below her knees with enough room left over for another person.

As we exit the Jefferson Building and head for the area where Natalie told me she'd parked her car, we can hear her start yelling at the top of her lungs. I sprint down to where the screams are coming from only to find Natalie walking in circles in an empty corner of the parking lot.

"Joey!" she yells. "Somebody stole my damn car! I can't believe it! I parked it right here less than an hour ago and now it's gone. Who the hell steals a twenty-year-old Honda Civic? This, Joey, is why I need a gun. What the hell are we gonna do now?"

Putting an arm around Natalie, I turn her to face a sign that clearly reads "No Parking." Vehicles haven't been allowed that close to federal buildings since 9/11.

"Nat, calm down – and *please* stop yelling" I say. "Your car wasn't stolen. It was towed."

"For goodness sakes, Joey, is that suppose to make me feel better?" Nat says sarcastically. "Personally, I'd rather think that someone stole my car because they needed money to feed their family instead of some jerk-off riding the streets in a tow truck looking for innocent prey. Here I am, doing some good deeds and what do I get? Isn't there someone we can call? My mom just told me that your mother knows the president. Maybe he can help?"

"Nat honey, you left your car in a no parking zone and you're right, tow trucks do roam the streets of Washington looking for cars parked in restricted areas. Hey, they've gotta make a living, too. And, by the way, they do help keep us safe."

Stella and Mom come running. From the way they crack up when they hear about the car being towed and Natalie thinking Mom should call the president, it's pretty clear that we're all becoming unglued and definitely in need of rest. Just then, a DC patrol officer pulls over with his window down, asking if we've been partying a little too much, setting off another round of guffaws.

I walk over to the driver's door and explain our situation. Officer Bruce Stenson has a friendly face, and tells me how the last couple of days have been extremely tense for everyone in DC. He apologizes for the car being towed – especially since he was the one who called it in, he admits, winking at Natalie. He's nice enough to offer us a ride over to the Marriott, and promises Natalie that he'll check on the status of the Honda and call her. Smooth operator, getting her phone number that easily. Stella seems to have picked up on the flirting between Natalie and Officer Bruce – she announces that she'll sit in the front seat, leaving the rest of us stuck in the back seat behind the plastic polycarbonate divider like a trio of criminals.

At 10:04 PM, we're greeted like royalty by the front desk staff at the DC Marriott. We've been given three adjoining rooms on the fifteenth floor, with great views of downtown Washington. Mom and I have our own rooms while Nat and Stella share the room between us. We decide to meet for a quick breakfast in the hotel restaurant at seven, after which Mom and I will hurry across town for Jim's meeting. We all share tired good-night hugs, then Mom and I head for our rooms.

As I set up my laptop to check emails and the latest news, my iPhone vibrates – a secure text message from Mike Lenoce letting me know that a car will be at the southeast lobby exit of the hotel at 7:30 AM to pick us up tomorrow. Twenty minutes later, I'm snoring.

• • •

AT 4:14 AM THURSDAY morning, the hotel fire alarm goes off, flashing the lights in my room. I hear people running in the hallway yelling "fire" and pounding on doors. I don't smell any smoke or feel any heat on my door, and when I look through the peep hole into the hall, the immediate area seems clear of both smoke and people. I run over to the adjoining door where I also hear pounding, and open it to find Stella. I run to my mother's door. She quickly opens, just as I see Natalie step out from the middle door into the hallway. But that's not all I see.

Grabbing Stella by the arm, I forcibly shove her into my mom's room and slam the door behind her, then rush over to Natalie, push her back into the middle room and into the bathroom, then throw us both down onto the floor. Glancing back out, I see two baseball-sized objects come rolling into the bedroom like a pair of candlepin bowling balls. Both come to a halt under the bed.

Before I can slam the bathroom door, an explosion rips through the room, blowing the king-size bed out the fifteenth floor window. The ceiling suddenly bursts into flames, telling me that some type of flammable substance has been tossed into the room. The automatic sprinklers quickly kick in, creating an eerie haze as the water mixes with the smoke. I jump up and out of the bathroom, closing the door behind me, leaving Natalie safely huddled around the base of the toilet.

As the fire begins to die down, the smoke starts to clear. I can't see anyone else in the room. The fire alarm continues blasting as I now see people running by our door dressed in all manner of sleep attire. Hotel management arrives in the form of a tall man with short black hair, glasses and a graying goatee. At the same time, Stella and my mother come bursting out of the adjoining room, screaming to see if we are all right.

I'm carrying Natalie out of the bathroom and out into the hallway when firemen and paramedics come running from the stairway door. Over the fire alarm, I yell that Nat's taken in too much smoke. They signal to me to lay her down on the hallway carpet, check her vitals and put an oxygen mask over her face. After a few breaths, she begins to cough and ask questions at the same time. We continue to scream at each other at the top of our lungs, making sure that we're all okay, even after the fire alarm suddenly stops shrieking.

After a quick call to Mike, three DC police officers come panting through the stairway door, working hard to catch their breath after climbing the fifteen flights. As the paramedics are lifting Natalie onto a stretcher, I notice a tattoo of a white tiger just below her hairline on the back of her neck. I'm not sure if she's always had that tattoo, that her long hair simply covered it up, or if it's something new. It's more than strange that in the past forty hours I've seen two different people with what very possibly might be the same tat.

"Joseph," Mom says, "Stella's going in the ambulance with Natalie. To be honest, I'm more than a bit concerned as to what's next. I have to wonder if this incident is related to the events of the last few days. We need to find out quickly before someone gets hurt."

"Mom, I don't know. Let's get down to the main floor and find Mike. I called him right after the alarms went off. He may know something that'll help us somehow piece these events together. It's hard to believe this is all random."

We get cleaned up and dressed, and are escorted by two DC police officers to the lobby. The city's on high alert due to several occurrences overnight in various parts of Washington, they tell us. The mayor may even enact a curfew tonight beginning at nine, allowing only authorized emergency personnel to be out on the streets.

Coming out of the elevators into the lobby I can see the sun rising through the front doors of the hotel. It's hard to believe that it's only 6:20 AM and here we are on the move again. With maybe six hours of sleep, it's clearly evident that my mom is dragging. We say goodbye to Stella as Natalie's loaded into the back of the ambulance. Just before the doors are about to close, Natalie sits up on the gurney and removes the oxygen mask from her face. "Thanks, Joey," she says with a smile. "Now maybe somebody will help me get my gun back. Now do you believe me? A lady really does have to protect herself."

As the ambulance pulls away from the curb, a black Ford Crown Vic pulls up, stops, and the driver-side door flies open. Mike leaps out of the vehicle, runs over and hugs my mother.

"Hello, sweet Caroline", says Mike, then hums a line of the old Neil Diamond song. "We need to get the two of you out of here. Problems are breaking out all over the city keeping us crazy busy and way on edge. We'll find out more at Jim's meeting at eight."

"Thanks for picking us up, Mike," says Mom. "How is Joanne doing? I know she's been going through some difficult times."

"It was tough during the holidays," Mike says almost in a whisper, "but she's back in school teaching chemistry, which has helped relieve some of her grief. We've joined a group of parents like us who've lost a child. It helps, knowing we're not alone, that there are people who truly understand our loss."

"Please let us know if there's anything we can do," Mom says sincerely.

"I appreciate that, Caroline," says Mike. "Getting back to work has certainly helped me get through it, especially that I'm now working for the government. Working in the family business only reminded me of the tragedy. My mother couldn't stop talking about it, and just about every customer who came into the store would want to know how it happened. They all meant well. Just too damn many reminders."

We get into the car and begin heading over to the DEA office. Stella calls to let us know that Natalie's fine and should be able to go home later today. She also tells us that she got a call from MAILGUY letting us know we should be able to get back in their apartments after five this afternoon. Stella's going to stay with Natalie through most of the day, then head home later before dinner time. She promises to update us and tells my mother to be careful. I can hear Stella drop the F-Bomb a few times during the phone call. Her voice carries. The woman has no concept of "private" conversations.

Chapter 14

THE RIDE OVER to DEA's offices is eerie. It's 7:10 on a Thursday morning and the sidewalks are near empty. Everyone seems to be moving in slow motion as they walk the streets of DC, suffering from the shock of the last several days. We stop at a Dunkin' Donuts on the way to grab some coffee and can't help but notice the somber mood of the customers in line. This is Washington's second 9/11 and the continuing nature of this violence throughout the city is keeping its inhabitants nervous, their doors locked and their blinds shut.

We arrive at a satellite DEA office close to 8:00 AM. It's one of those obscure DC buildings that if you didn't know the exact address, you'd never find it, just a regular office complex with no signage out front. This location accommodates about fifty field agents and support personnel. I have both good and bad memories of working with the folks in this office, from receiving commendations to being suspended. It's good to know that even though I haven't reported to anyone in this building for close to a year, I still have many friends here in the DEA. On the way to Carlone's office, Mom takes a few moments to visit a good friend of hers. I grab a chair next to Mike Lenoce's desk as he hangs up the phone.

"So, tell me, Mike, what's your opinion on what's really going on here?" I say. "We have an assassination attempt on the president and bombs going off along the parade route after his family goes by. Is it just bad timing or were the bombs meant to cause public chaos? Mom and I get picked up by the FBI and our rides get caught in a shootout.

My vehicle flips, trapping me inside, only to be saved by a near-naked stranger with a white tiger tattoo. Excuse me, Mike, but this is really bizarre!"

"I know Joe, I know. Try to relax," says Mike as the workers in the immediate area become quiet. "Remember, I got involved in this at the last minute too, but you need to keep something in mind. According to Jim and the other agents, crazy shit like this has been happening all over the city during the last 48 hours. Some events seem to make sense, but others don't. For starters, it looks to me like law enforcement people are targets of some sorta terrorist plot. But then we have incidents that follow pretty much the same pattern, but involving people with no ties to the government. I'm still waiting for the FBI to give me an update on what happened at the Marriott."

I realize I'm not fully aware of all the incidents Mike's talking about, only what I've had time to read in the *Post* and on the *New York Times* web site, or have experienced first-hand. It's obvious, to me anyway, that Washington is under attack, and that the attacks appear to be well coordinated. We certainly have enemies around the world, not to mention home-grown terrorists within our own borders. In my previous life working in intelligence, I dealt with a number of organizations that were out to harm America in one way or another.

The part-time work I conduct for the government today is usually focused on the financial aspect of terrorist groups as they constantly try to bring down our fiscal institutions, hoping to push our economy back into another deep recession or better yet, a full-blown depression. Since 9/11, we've become smarter about how to handle our finances and manage the economy. Don't get me wrong – I'm not some type of banking expert or financial genius, just someone who knows enough about the global economy and doesn't mind being in foreign countries at high level meetings with people who are planning to do bad things. As an undercover intelligence officer, it was my job to get deeply involved in terrorist groups, passing myself off as a sympathizer with money. Learning to make bombs at radical training camps takes financial resources. I made the dollars available, got into their inner circle, found out the place and time, then called in the drones and beat it out of town.

The shelf life for someone in my position is only about two years; terrorist groups share resources and information that help them connect the dots and determine if there's a traitor among them. I've been fortunate enough to get out before I was ever found out. In my two-and-a-half years in the field, I only had to fire my Colt twice. Once in a small village outside Caracchi, Venezuela, during a raid on a counterfeit operation, and once in a taxicab in downtown Kabul, Afghanistan, when a bunch of street kids tried to rob us on a dead-end road.

These days, I spend most of my time working for various non-profit organizations around the world, providing relief to those who need it. Since I'm still in the Reserve, however, I do get called up from time to time to work small undercover jobs, usually in the Americas. Jim Carlone, who was recently promoted DEA Deputy Director, probably has my number on speed dial.

Chapter 15

OUR 8:00 AM MEETING with Carlone actually begins around 9:30, behind closed doors in his office with only four people in attendance. Mom, Mike, Jim and I are crammed into a small office with furnishings that look like they haven't been updated since the cold war. The previous commander was a chain smoker who volunteered his office as the designated smoking area for a few close friends. A fresh coat of paint isn't enough to break the illusion that we're sitting in a giant ashtray.

Behind his desk, Jim's looking stressed. Tiny beads of sweat roll down his forehead from his thinning black hair. Mom and I are sitting in hard metal chairs with thin plastic cushioning opposite Jim. Mike's standing – there isn't room for another chair unless it went on top of Jim's desk. My mother appears to be fighting a losing battle to keep her eyes open as we begin the meeting. The session will have to move fast if Jim hopes to keep his participants actively involved.

"By now, I'm sure you've heard most of what's taken place over the last 48 hours," Jim says. "What I'd like to discuss now are possible reasons for the attack, since no one's yet claimed responsibility. Our people around the world have picked up a lot of chatter but, as yet, can't pin it on any one group. Much of the babble indicates that every single terrorist organization we know about couldn't be happier about what's happened to us but, again, no one even hints of participating."

"How can anything like this take place in downtown Washington without any tips or prior warnings?" asks Mike. "The intelligence community had clues that something big was gonna take place in New

York City during summer of 2001. They just couldn't piece it together quick enough."

"The entire intelligence community worldwide and local police are hunting down leads as we speak," Jim says, wiping the sweat from his forehead with his shirtsleeve. "The bottom line – this puzzle is way too large for any one agency to work on without any coordination. As I said yesterday, the different agencies have split up the pie. Our piece is the drug angle. A few years ago, we declared war on the drug cartels in Mexico, Central and South America. We took the fight into their countries and they vowed they'd bring the war back onto our streets. This might be their revenge."

"Your theory is certainly plausible," I say, shifting my butt around on the hard plastic seat. "But tell me, what does this have to do with my mother and me? I've worked south of the border, but it was mainly about tracking drug money and freezing bank accounts."

"Joe, let me try and explain," says my mother, her eyes for the moment open wide. "Over the last six months, my team and I have been conducting high level research on a very strong drug cartel in Mexico. All the intelligence agencies were sending us everything they knew about this operation. We turned the data inside out and still came up with little to go on.

"Then an ex-Israeli intelligence agent with high security clearance sent me some disturbing information concerning this cartel. He thought that what he was seeing looked like another 9/11-type attack in the making. Two months ago, this same agent was found by a farmer in Arizona – wrapped in a blue tarp. In pieces. It took a couple of weeks to identify the body through DNA. Before he'd been ID'd, though, a DVD came through the mail to the head of the DEA. The disc was over an hour long, showing the man's torture and dismemberment. I never saw it – reading the report on it was hard enough, but I can't help but feel there's a connection here."

"An interesting point to mention is that the man conducting the torture appeared to have the same tattoo on his neck as the man who cut Joseph out of the burning SUV – a white tiger with black stripes and black feet. I remember reading an article in *Newsweek* about a similar tattoo, which I believe it said it was tied into a specific drug rehab program located both in the US and Mexico. And we have agents who swear they've seen that white tiger insignia on trucks – large trucks – on Mexican highways. I'll have one of my staff find the article and write up a quick executive summary and see if it leads us anywhere," says Mom. Going quiet, she tries to stifle a yawn, but it gets the better of her. She apologizes with a polite "excuse me."

"Mom," I say, "when Nat was being lifted onto the ambulance stretcher, I saw what looked like a tattoo of a white tiger with black stripes on the back of her neck, just below her hairline. I'm not sure if it's the same tattoo or just a coincidence, but I think I'll visit her in the hospital to see how she's doing."

"We have more details to discuss," says Jim, "but it looks like this group's too tired to listen right now. I'll just mention one more thing, then you all can go. That unmarked helicopter that flew through the streets and blew in the doors at Caroline's apartment landed for approximately four minutes on the grounds of the Washington Monument. Eye witnesses saw two white panel vans pull up next to it and drop off several people dressed in green uniforms. According to one witness, the people in green got in and took off before the two vans left the scene. A police helicopter and a news chopper tried to tail the Bell, but lost it over Virginia. We had jet fighters in the air along the entire east coast and the helicopter still managed to get away.

"However, we did get a report of a black helicopter with no markings on the ground at a small airport outside Birmingham, Alabama," Carlone continues. "The airport manager was found dead with a bullet to the back of the head under one of the fuel storage tanks last night. The local police and FBI are at the scene now. And, three hours ago, we had an unconfirmed sighting of a black helicopter crossing into Mexico by a pistachio farmer outside of Douglas, Arizona, flying so low it almost crashed into his forty-foot wind tower. The National Security

Administration is reviewing all satellite images from that area over the last 48 hours," Jim says. "I'll have more reports throughout the day. Thanks again, and I apologize for the tight quarters – and the aroma."

The room goes quiet as we gather up our things and begin pondering what we've just learned. My head's pounding from the stale office air and, even though it wasn't mentioned, I know that I'm bound for Mexico to investigate this possible connection. I was south of the border just nine months ago, working with a team from a humanitarian organization that works closely with *Oxfam*. We were there to clean up a polluted water source for a small village outside of Los Reyes, in central Chihuahua. The project was more difficult and took longer than anticipated, but when we were done, the people were able to get clean water from several different locations throughout the town and no longer had to worry about getting sick from drinking it. It's great when you're part of something than can make such a difference in people's lives. I made a lot of good friends in Los Reyes.

"Jim, one more thing before you head to your next meeting," says Mike. "I've assigned two agents to Caroline, to provide security as well as transportation wherever she needs to go."

"Good. Thanks, Mike," says Jim as he ushers us all out of his office. "We're back here tomorrow at eight for an update and to discuss our trip into Mexico."

Is the band getting back together? Will the three Musketeers ride again? Guess I better throw out the abacus and shine up the Colt.

Mom receives a text from Stella saying that it's okay to go back home and that Natalie's now staying overnight at the hospital for observation. Mike's driving my mother home and I'm off to the hospital via a yellow hybrid taxicab driven by a man who looks and talks like George Harrison. On the way over to the hospital I can't help but sing to myself one of his songs about peace and hope, important words written by a good man who passed too early. If we only took the time to understand the lyrics, maybe I'd be going to Mexico on vacation and not a mission.

Chapter 16

EVEN THOUGH THE streets are remarkably empty for 12:30 in the afternoon, the ride to Washington Medical takes longer than expected. Numerous streets are shut down and most stores and small shops are closed. The busiest part of the city appears to be right outside the hospital, where many people are milling around, heads down and hands in pockets, trying to ward off the cold.

The latest information: 805 dead and another 922 injured, and the death toll continues to rise. All the area hospitals are filled to capacity with gurneys in the hallways trying to accommodate the over-flow. I find out from a kindly old woman at the information desk that Natalie doesn't have a room yet and may be still down in emergency. After talking to six different ER nurses, I finally find her in a room designed for four that now holds seven. Her bed is wedged into the corner near a rusting grey radiator. As I approach her, she seems agitated by something, but her mood lifts when she sees me.

"Hey, Nat," I say, cheerfully grabbing hold of her hand. "How're you feeling? You look well, maybe just a little tired."

"Look at me, Joey, and stop bullshitting me!" Natalie says in a voice that attracts the attention of everyone in the room. Needless to say, she takes after her mother in this regard. "I look terrible and you damn well know it! One of my eyebrows is completely burned off, my hair still has fire chemical shit in it, and I smell like I fell down a freakin' chimney. And, by the way, I'm dying for a freakin' cigarette. I can't get any rest because of all the freakin' noise, and when I do manage to fall asleep, a nurse wakes me for my thirty-freakin'-minute oxygen treatment. The good news is that the EMT who drove us to the hospital came back to check on me a few hours ago," Natalie adds, her voice softening markedly. "I was in the middle of my treatment, so we couldn't talk much. Hell, I couldn't talk at all. He said he'd be back to check on me again later. Isn't that sweet, Joey D?"

"Very sweet, and Nat, honestly," I say, using my hushed hospital voice, "for all you've been through, you look good. How many people get caught in a chemical fire and only have to stay in the hospital overnight for observation?"

I mean what I say, but I'm concerned about her mental state. She was almost killed this morning. Eight hours later, I sense she's bothered by something entirely unrelated, in part because of the way she's squeezing the blood out of my hand, she's holding it so tight.

We talk about what happened at the hotel and I let her know that an investigation is in process, and that the police will probably come by to ask her a few questions, if not here in the hospital, then at her home. She tells me her sponsor's coming to see her in an hour so he can "talk her off the ledge." This is meant as a joke, but this type of humor is something I don't respond to. I jump to change the subject.

"Hey, Nat, before I leave to let you get some rest, I have one quick question. All this time I've known you and those times we went out last year, I never noticed you had a tattoo. This morning as the EMTs lifted you onto the stretcher, I noticed a little tattoo of a white tiger on the back of your neck." Natalie does a double-take.

"Come on, Joey. I love that you remember we went out, but what the hell are you talking about? I *hate* tattoos. The only tattoo I ever had was a yellow rose above my left ankle, and I had that removed three years ago. You must have me mixed up with someone else you went out with. Take a look for yourself, Joseph Dustan." She pulls up her hair and twists her neck for me to see. "No tattoo on me!" she says harshly. "By the way, Joey, if I remember correctly you never got close enough to notice such details."

"Okay, okay, Nat, my mistake. I must have inhaled too much smoke this morning. Maybe I'm the one who needs an oxygen treatment. I'll talk to you tomorrow. Get some rest, okay?"

I kiss her on the forehead, then make my way through the rest of her roommates and out into the open area of the ER. It's still crowded, but at least now I have enough distance from people so I don't have to know what they had for lunch. I'm leaning up against the wall outside Natalie's room, trying to force the blood back into my hand, when a young girl with long brown hair in a flowered dress walks over to me and looks up at me, directly in the eyes.

"Excuse me, mister. Excuse me," she says in a sweet voice that has a touch of a southern twang. "I want you to know that I saw the same tattoo you did, on your friend – the white tiger. It had black stripes and black feet. My older sister had a bird tattoo on her back. That's how they identified her when they found her in the garbage dump at the end of the summer. I heard one of the detectives call the picture a tramp stamp."

"What's your name, sweetie?"

"Annabelle."

"Wow, Annabelle, what a pretty name. My name is Joe. Can you do me a favor and keep the tattoo thing between us? My friend's been through quite a lot and I don't want to upset her. Can you do that for me?"

"Sure, mister. My parents tell me that I used to upset my sister and now she's dead."

"Thanks, darlin. You know something, Annabelle, what happened to your sister is not your fault. Bad things happen to people for no reason and those left behind search for answers and sometimes look for someone to blame even though they don't mean to. Being sad is powerful stuff. It can control our lives if we let it."

"Bye, Joe," says Annabelle, wiping a tear from the corner of her eye. "I have to get back in and visit with my Uncle Jim. He fell off a ladder and broke his hip."

"Bye, Annabelle," I say as I wipe more than a few tears from my own eyes. "Take care, and thanks for keeping the white tiger a secret. I hope your uncle's better soon."

As I finally make it back outside, I'm starting to get the feeling back in my hand. In my mind, I go over the conversation I just had with Natalie and quickly determine that she really believes she doesn't have a tattoo on the back of her neck. Based on her traumatic state of mind, however, I don't think now's the time to let her know she does. My thoughts turn to Annabelle and how cruel parents can be sometimes without even knowing it.

I call Mike on his cell and ask him to pick me up. It seems we have some more things to discuss.

Chapter 17

My MOTHER WHISPERS "home, sweet home" as we walk through the door into her torn-up apartment. "Boy, there's a lot more damage than I remembered," she says quietly.

The patio doors have been replaced, but there's broken glass and splintered wood scattered all over the place still. Feeling a little paranoid thinking her place might have been ransacked on top of it all, I tell her to stay by the door while I take a quick look through all the rooms. When I'm certain nobody's hiding under the bed, I return to the living room. Mom turns the knob on the dead bolt, then does her own quick inventory.

"Nothing seems to be missing. Since it's already 7:30, I'll get in touch with the super in the morning and let him know what I found. And I'll call the police and see if I need to file a report," she says with a tired sigh.

Glancing at her answering machine, I notice that the message light's blinking. "Looks like you've got four messages," I say as I hand her a bottle of water from the fridge. Sweeping debris from the cushions, we both sit down to listen to the messages. The first one's the bank, letting her know that someone attempted to log onto her online checking account and was shut out. The second message is a reminder that she has a dentist appointment on Friday at 5:15 PM. The third's a hang up. The last message, left by a man with a heavy Spanish accent, confirms that a package was delivered this afternoon. He leaves no company name or number and hangs up in mid-sentence. "What package?" Mom says. "I haven't seen any package."

We both check all the rooms, but find no package. Mom calls a few neighbors to see if anybody signed for a delivery. All say no, so we decide to pass it off as a wrong number.

Mom takes out a frozen pizza, puts it in the oven and sets the timer. I grab a broom from the closet and begin sweeping the floor. Mom turns on the small TV in the kitchen since, not surprisingly, her 52-inch LCD didn't survive. "We've got twenty minutes to shower and get cleaned up before dinner's ready," she says, coming back out of the kitchen.

"I'll make the salads," I offer and she heads for her bedroom. I hear the overhead fan go on in the bathroom, then I hear her yelling my name.

Running to the room, I find my mother standing with her back against the sink, staring through the opaque shower curtain at the outline of something in the tub. Quickly pulling back the curtain, I find a package in the middle of the tub, a large box wrapped in brown paper. Red twine holds the paper in place. Ten years of experience tells us that the package will have no return address or shipping information stamped anywhere on it. When I flip the box over we read a water-smudged name in big black letters: Joseph Dustan. My mother, feeling faint, sits on the toilet seat. I'm feeling a little light-headed myself, realizing that this is the first time I've received one of these mysterious packages when it's not my birthday.

Chapter 18

IT'S BEEN FOURTEEN years since I've seen such a package, my name written like that in big, black letters on the top. Fourteen years plus. Even though my birthday was over two months ago, it's a reminder that my father may be near and still alive. We both stare at the box, neither of us reaching to touch it or take it out of the tub.

"Mom, I can't believe it," I say nervously. "All these years we thought he was dead – and now this shows up? I'm not sure what it all means, but one message is clear: he knows where you live, and more than likely, he knows that I'm in town."

Expecting some sort of response from my mother, I turn to see that she's left the room. I pick up the box, carry it into the dining area and set it on the table. I hear her in the kitchen rummaging through cabinets and drawers, slamming doors as she goes. I turn when I hear her rapid breathing behind me, and see she's got a pair of scissors in her hand.

"Joseph, there's no point in putting it off," Mom says, sounding harried. "See what your father sent you for your birthday. Maybe there'll be a note inside, explaining why it's late." I turn to look, thinking she's joking. She isn't.

Cutting away the twine and knifing through several layers of clear tape, the brown paper falls away, exposing a nondescript white box that's also taped closed. I look at my mother, who lifts her eyes and shrugs her shoulders giving me the sign to continue. Cutting away several more layers of tape, I finally lift the top flaps to find a layer of crumpled, yellowed newspaper covered in Spanish. I pull out the newspaper and carefully hand it to Mom, then proceed to dig deep into the box.

My sweaty hands catch hold of a metal object under a thin layer of newspapers. I lift a heavy metal cross out of the box and set it on a few pieces of the newspaper. Encrusted with multi-colored stones, it must weigh five pounds.

I lift the box, but judging by the weight of it, it appears that it isn't empty yet. Digging further, I find a piece of ceramic that looks like a black foot emerging from a blue dress. Thinking it might be a part of a broken statue, I look through the box for other pieces, with no luck. My mother seems to be deep in thought, reading something on the back of the cross.

"What is it?"

"I don't know what to make of it, Joseph. The presents from your father – or whomever – always seemed quite normal, except for that stolen art piece that showed up on your sixteenth birthday. While the cross may look old, it's not. On the back, it reads "Misión del Espíritu Santo." Holy Spirit Mission. And a date – November 1, 1982. I guess we both know why that date's important – it's the day you were born." She holds it out for me to see. "I'll take it to work and have my team see if they can find out anything. I want to make sure it's not stolen. Same with the foot. I'll have some experts look at it to try and determine how old it is and where it was made."

"Mom, this seems like more than just a gift. It feels more like it's meant to be a clue, or maybe a message?"

"I really don't know, honey. What I find even more interesting is that the newspaper's only two weeks old, from Mexico City. I'll take that to work too and see what I can come up with."

We eat half the pizza – neither of us have much of an appetite now – and talk for about an hour. My mother's still a bit upset, so I decide to stay over in the guestroom. We say goodnight around 9:15.

There's certainly a lot going on in our lives right now, and the package in the bathtub makes it difficult for me to fall asleep. It's about 10:30 when I hear her turn the radio off in her room. After watching the hands of the clock move for a couple hours, I drift off to sleep around 11:45 PM.

• • •

WE'RE AWAKENED QUITE dramatically – at 6:07 – by the noise of someone pounding on the door of my mother's apartment. As I pull my jeans and an old Navy t-shirt on, I hear my mother open the door and Stella's voice comes booming in the hallway.

I come into the living room to see Stella hugging my mom and sobbing profusely. My mother turns to me with words that come close to knocking me off my feet. "Joe, Natalie is missing!" she cries. "She was taken forcibly, by two men, right out of her bed at Washington Medical!"

Chapter 19

THE THREE OF US dress quickly and are down in the lobby of the condo complex. I've already spoken to Mike, who's pulling together all the information that's available and will meet us at the hospital. In the lobby are two FBI rookies who've been assigned to my mother for safety and transportation. Safety isn't really an issue on this trip, but fast transport is.

We jump into a white Lincoln Navigator, the driver hits the lights and siren, and before we know it, we're traveling down Massachusetts Avenue at over seventy miles an hour. I ask the driver, a woman, to slow down, that we don't want to be checking into Washington Medical when we get there. She apologizes without turning her head and drops the Lincoln's speed down to more like fifty.

My mother barely says two words on the way to the hospital. Stella looks like she's ready for a fight, now that the crying jags have ended. Pulling up in front of the hospital building, I notice Mike's red Ford LTD parked sideways across two handicapped spots. We unload out of the Lincoln and head for the front entrance doors. Through the glass, I see him in conversation with several DC police men and women. As soon as he sees us come through the doors, he breaks away from the group to join us and gives a quick run-down of what they know, then introduces us to Detective Jim Hallene, who's leading the investigation. Mike grabs my arm and pulls me aside.

"Joe, something's not right about what happened to Natalie," he whispers. "We have conflicting statements from several eye witnesses, including a ten-year-old girl. Three say that Natalie was taken by force and carried away. Two say she walked out of the building with two men, of her own free will. The ten-year-old told me that two men woke her up, scared her briefly and that Natalie left with them. Nobody says that she screamed for help or anything. The two are described as white males, late twenties, one carrying flowers, the other a small, gift-wrapped box. We've got a couple of police artists working with the witnesses. Oh, and the ten-year-old, a cute kid named Annabelle, tells me one of the guys was bald with a tiny moustache – and a white tiger tattoo on the side of his neck."

At this point, nothing makes any sense. I can't properly tie any of the events together, but they all have something or other in common. I know my mother will quickly reach the same conclusion. Natalie was acting strange when I saw her last night. Her denial of the tattoo still boggles my mind.

As Mike walks away to take a phone call, Stella and my mother come over to me, pain and fear written all over their faces. "Stella, I need your help on a few things," I say softly. "In speaking with Mike, and based on eyewitness accounts, he says Nat might have left the hospital with two men, of her own free will."

"Joe, I heard the same bullshit from the police and I'm trying hard not to believe it!" shouts Stella. "I was with her most of the day. She never mentioned anything about expecting visitors or seeing anyone. The only person she talked about seeing was the EMT who drove her here. She told me he came back to check on her, and she seemed quite happy about it. Of course, I told her to get well first before she even started thinking about any damn romance. We laughed and that was the end of that," says Stella, her voice trailing off. "Oh, wait a minute – she did mention a possible visit from her sponsor, whoever that is."

"Stella," I ask, "are you aware of a tattoo Natalie has on the back of her neck, just below the hairline? A white tiger with black stripes and feet? I saw it when they lifted her onto the stretcher back at the hotel."

"She never told me about any tattoo. As a matter of fact, she hates tattoos. She had one removed from her ankle, several years ago. The way she wears her hair long, I wouldn't have noticed anyway unless she showed me," says Stella.

"The strange thing is that when I asked her about it yesterday afternoon, she denied it," I say. "She said I must have her confused with someone else. She literally lifted her hair and turned her neck to prove it to me. I saw the white tiger tattoo, clear as day all right, but I didn't want to upset her so I agreed she was right and that I was mistaken. She seemed a little agitated. I didn't want to add to her stress. Bottom line, she truly believes that she doesn't have a tattoo on her neck. A ten-year-old eye witness, a little girl I happened to talk to yesterday, told the police that one of the men who came for Natalie had the same thing on *his* neck." My mother's stares at me when I mention the white tiger markings, knowing that the man who pulled me out of the overturned SUV had the same tiger in the same location.

I ask Stella to sit down with the police and tell them everything she knows about Natalie, including friends, hangouts and work details. Worrying that Stella may be too close to her daughter to be able to keep an open mind concerning her exit from the hospital, I urge my mom to help Stella as best she can. A few moments later, I see them sitting shoulder to shoulder with Detective Hallene. As soon as they're finished, I say goodbye to both Stella and Mom, and Mike and I start to make our way back out through the crowded hospital entrance.

"Joe! Joseph!" Stella screams. "Wait a minute! Now I remember. I met Natalie's sponsor once, at one of my book signings. Oh shit! He was very pale. He was bald, with a tiny blond mustache. And he had a white tiger tattoo on his neck!"

This is crazy, but "oh shit" is right as we notice we're already late for our meeting with JL Carlone. I wave back to her, indicating she should be telling the cops that, but that I have to go. Walking quickly out of the building we find Mike's car missing from the handicap parking section. I guess the official DEA cardboard sign inside the front

JAMES K. ZAVEZ

window wasn't enough to convince anyone not to tow the vehicle. Seeing both FBI newbies mulling around looking for something to do, I walk up behind them, tap the shoulder of the female driver and ask her to give us a ride to the DEA office. Mike speaks to the other intern about staying here and keeping an eye on my mother.

In less than a minute, we're strapped into the Lincoln Navigator and rolling back down Massachusetts Avenue – within the city speed limit. Apparently this one's a quick learner. During our ten-minute ride over to the office, Mike and I are on our cell phones following up on a number of different things.

Mike's on the phone to Joanne explaining how the car got towed from in front of Washington Medical. I hear him doing a lot of back-pedaling, with many apologies thrown in for good measure. Our driver overhears what Mike's discussing and lets him know that her partner back at the hospital already found his car in a back storage lot behind the hospital fitness center. Mike, relieved, tells Joanne he'll have the car back by noon.

I receive a text message from Sheila back in Key West, letting me know that a package was left for me on the kitchen table. She ends the text by letting me know she misses me. Hmm...

I call Jim Carlone to let him know that I need to make a quick detour to Key West prior to getting back into my charro suit and relearning the Mexican hat dance.

Chapter 20

T HE TRIP BACK to Florida seems to take a lot longer even though I'm on a non-stop commercial flight from Reagan Washington to Miami. United Flight 437 is packed. I'm in coach and lucky enough to have an aisle seat for the two-and-a-half-hour flight. Everyone I speak with is either fascinated, terrified or both about the attacks in DC. A short, pudgy woman on the other side of the aisle tells me how relieved she is to leave Washington and go home to her six cats, two dogs and a bird that only knows swear words. She blames the bird's limited vocabulary on her ex-husband who disappeared one day coming back from the track. She told me he owed too much money to some very shady people. "He was a bum and a drunk, so screw him," she says loud enough for people to turn and look in our direction. I give them all a quick smile as I put on my Bose headset and search for Bob Seger's Greatest Hits on my iPod, feeling a palpable need to go to Ka...Ka...Ka Katmandu.

• • •

WE'RE EXPECTED TO BE at the gate in Miami at 10:05 PM. My ride home is via a Naval Gulfstream aircraft due into Key West before midnight. Between announcements by the flight crew and the occasional baby crying, I manage to slip into a deep sleep that only ends when the wheels of the Boeing 747 hit the runway. It takes the best part of twenty minutes to get to our gate and deplane. A very young naval type is standing in the waiting area, eying all the passengers as they walk by her. I sling my surf bag over my shoulder as she approaches and stops two feet in front of me to offer up a perfect salute.

"Captain Dustan, Ensign Kelly Rogers from the Key West Naval Air Station, here to help you with your gear to an awaiting car parked outside baggage claim. There's a plane waiting to take you back to Key West. We should be in the air in less than thirty minutes."

"Thank you, Ensign Rogers," I say, "but I just have the one bag. I can handle it."

Kelly looks relieved not to be carrying my bag as we approach a state police car, its lights flashing. The window rolls down and an officer behind the wheel tells us to get in and that he'll take us to our aircraft. Before I can get the door closed, the Dodge Charger is on its way, miraculously avoiding pedestrians, until we come down a one-lane ramp with a closed gate at the end. Rolling past the guardhouse, the state trooper has barely enough time to flash his badge before we're driving on a closed-down taxiway at 85 miles an hour. I have a feeling that this isn't the first time the officer's taken this route. Kelly and I look at each other, recheck our seatbelts and grip our door handles.

Up ahead we can see a well-lit hangar that's probably our destination. The Charger comes to a quick stop as a British Airways jet takes the right of way onto an open taxiway bathed in blue lights. Once the airliner is safely past and the trooper has permission to proceed, we're quickly back up to eighty. He doesn't even begin to slow down until we're inside the hangar. We come to an abrupt stop at the bottom of the stairs of the Gulfstream and jump out of the vehicle with a quick thank-you to the trooper. Kelly and I look at each other, share a quick laugh and head up the stairs into the jet.

Before we even have a chance to put on our seatbelts, the plane starts its engines and begins moving out of the hanger and out onto the taxiway. The copilot comes out to say hello and inform us that we have a very short window to get off the ground in Miami; a large thunderstorm is moving in off the Atlantic and we need to be on our way if we're going to beat it. Several minutes later, we move to the front of the line for take off. We must have friends in pretty high places.

I settle into a plush leather seat as our jet takes off into the Florida sky and heads south. It is a quick 32-minute flight. At 11:33 PM, I'm hailing a taxi outside the base.

Chapter 21

As the taxi pulls away into the moonlit Key West night, I stand outside my apartment thinking about the events of the last few days. So many questions. So few answers.

Walking up the wooden stairs to my apartment, I hear my next-door neighbors, Steve and Rebecca, fighting again. They're both nice enough individuals, but he has a temper that flares up when he comes home from a night of drinking with the boys, and he was recently laid off from his landscaping job. Rebecca supports them by working two jobs. She only calls the police when he starts to throw things or threatens her with bodily harm, but she never presses charges. Rebecca's told me she feels sorry for him, that things will change once he finds steady work again. Hearing them argue now tells me that Steve's still unemployed and that the fine officers of the Key West PD may be showing up any time now. Once in my apartment, I drop my bag and slam the door, hoping they'll hear me and stop fighting.

I walk over to the kitchen table and find a small box wrapped in brown paper, with my name on it. No return address or shipping label. Here we go again. Under the package is a note from Sheila.

Welcome home, Joey –

Thanks for letting me use your place while you were in Washington. I heard on the news that we still don't know who bombed DC. Who do <u>you</u> think's responsible?

Your neighbor Steve was around most of the time out back with his buddies, drinking beer and smoking pot. They pissed me off yesterday throwing rocks at the Hemingway cats. I went over and told them to knock it off or I was going to call the cops. One of Steve's buddies, an odd looking guy with a pathetic mustache and a blond rug on his head made some rude comment about my boobs. I told him I'd rip that animal off his head if he didn't shut the hell up. Things quieted down when Steve's wife got home from her first job, but started back up the minute she left for her second. I don't know how she puts up with it, but that's a topic for another day.

I don't know how the package got into the apartment. I know I locked up whenever I left. The best I can figure is that it got delivered between three and five in the afternoon. I went out after three for a sub at Ritchie's and got back here a little before five and there it was sitting on the table when I came in. I figure you must have given a key to someone else because I know I didn't leave the door unlocked. Anyway, I hope it brings you good luck. Come by and see me tomorrow at work and I'll buy you lunch. Thanks again for the use of your place.

Love, Sheila

P.S. Maybe your unemployed neighbor saw the person who dropped off the package?

"Love, Sheila." What does that mean? I shake the small box and feel something moving inside. Cutting away the clear packaging tape and removing the brown paper, I'm not surprised to find a plain white box within. Lifting the top of the box reveals a simple silver cross and chain. As usual, the rest of the box is empty – no note, just shredded pieces of Spanish newspaper. Combing through the pieces, I notice that the paper also came from Mexico City, but a date is nowhere to be found.

Moving my hand over the back of the cross, I feel something. Pulling a magnifying glass out of the kitchen drawer, I am able to read my one and only clue: Puebla. I'm not a very religious person. Still, I decide to wear the cross around my neck, hoping that lightning bolts don't strike me dead.

Just as I tuck the cross into the 2009 Yankee World Champion-ship t-shirt I'm wearing, I hear a gun shot outside that scares the shit out of me. I run out the door and down the steps into a small courtyard only to find Rebecca holding a Smith & Wesson revolver like she's Bonnie Parker. She's pointing it at Steve, who's stumbling into a white Dodge minivan as fast as his inebriated feet can carry him.

"Sorry if I woke you, Joe," says Rebecca in a strong and steady voice, "but that son of a bitch is *not* gonna lay another hand on me. If he does, I'll most probably kill him."

As she stands over by the house, I see a patrol car pull into the driveway. I walk over to the open driver's side window and give Rebecca's sister, Officer Helen Donaher, a quick update on what I think might have happened as she gets out. I feel a sense of relief as she locks up the patrol car and walks into the arms of her sister.

• • •

HEADING BACK INTO my apartment, I pull the vibrating iPhone out of my pants pocket and read a four-word text message from Jim Carlone – "don't unpack your bag."

Three hours later, Ensign Kelly Rogers knocks on my door. I open up, she grabs my surf bag lying on the floor and tells me she'll meet me in the car.

It's 3:39 AM as I climb into the front passenger side of a red Jeep Grand Cherokee. Ensign Rogers is at the wheel, talking to someone on her cell phone. As I fasten my seatbelt, I notice that Officer Donaher's police car is still parked in the driveway and all the lights are out in Rebecca's house.

Kelly drops the Jeep into drive and we pull away from the curb in front of my apartment. I make a mental note to call Sheila later this morning to let her know I'm back on the road and that she's free to use my place again. As we take a left onto Whitehead Street and my apartment is no longer in sight, I get a sinking feeling I may never come back here. Thinking about all that's happened over the last 72 hours, I finger the outline of the cross beneath my t-shirt. Who did it come from? Why was it sent to me? Is my mother tied into all of this?

Ensign Rogers looks over, sees that something is bothering me and says a few words to break the silence. "Do you mind if we hit the drive-through at the 24/7 Dunkin' Donuts on the way back to the base? Your chopper ride up to Miami International isn't for another 45 minutes."

Chapter 22

THE AMERICAN AIRLINE flight from Miami to Benito Juarez International Airport in Mexico City takes a little more than two hours. Most of the plane's empty and I have the row to myself, which allows me to spread out my work and get caught up on my new assignment. 9:36 AM finds me standing in a very long Customs line hoping my name isn't flagged in the Mexican computer system. During my last visit to Mexico, I was forcibly escorted by men in uniform to the Rio Grande and told to swim back to America – wearing just my boxer shorts.

Mexico is one of the few Spanish speaking countries that's tolerant of someone who trashes the language but is too embarrassed to carry a Spanish-English dictionary. Overall, the people of Mexico have treated me well and gone out of their way to help me. Maybe they sense my Mexican ancestry, or maybe they're so used to Americans that they just wanted to give this gringo a break. Either way, it's a beautiful country that gets a bad rap from the media and our politicians.

I spend about 45 minutes in line, and grab a warm Diet Coke on the way to the exit. The weather at this time of the year in Mexico City is pretty much the same as Key West. The temps during the day average seventy degrees. Nights can get down in the low fifties. As I wait for my ride outside the baggage claim area, I'm thankful that the city isn't under a smog alert and that vehicular traffic is relatively light today. I find myself sharing a wooden bench with a rather heavy American who tells me she's waiting for her "no good husband" to pick her up in the rental car. She rants and raves about how their flight was late from California, how they didn't serve any food and how it was her husband's crazy idea to come to Mexico to look for a place to retire. He's convinced, she said, that the cost of living is too high in the States. In order to keep up their present lifestyle, they'd have to move.

I can't help but think that moving to Mexico probably means less fast food and more manual labor, but before I can say a word, an old blue Chevy van pulls up and the woman's husband screams "get in" through the open passenger window. He looks even bigger than his wife – he barely seems to fit in the driver's seat. As she climbs into the van, the plus-sized woman turns to look at me like she's about to say something, but stops abruptly, probably because she knows what I'm thinking. When the husband finally finds the right gear, she scowls and sticks her tongue out at me. This gesture strikes me as odd, coming from a stranger who's at least twice my age and twice my size.

Now that I have the bench to myself, I pick through my surf bag and pull out a few files to review. It's been five days since the tragedy in DC took place. No one's claimed responsibility and, based on my limited knowledge, we're no closer to finding the perpetrators. The job of the group I'm a part of is to follow whatever leads we can develop and decide if we are going in the right direction or coming to a dead end. The DEA's job is to either prove or disprove that the acts of terrorism in Washington were executed by one or more of the drug cartels.

There are more than twenty such organizations scattered across Mexico, Central and South America that we're aware of, and who knows how many more we aren't. The DEA knows that the black Bell helicopter flew into Mexican airspace and then was lost somewhere near Mexico City. Our fuel calculations and global satellites give us a

JAMES K. ZAVEZ

good idea where it had to stop along the way in the US before crossing the border and heading into Mexico City. What we don't know is if it simply refueled and headed on to another location, or if it remains hidden somewhere around Mexico City.

There are several large cartels in this area. Our team has been tasked with using all resources available to try and infiltrate these organizations. With my background, I have no problem establishing a cover as a volunteer working in the area helping villages clean up and improve their water supply. Somewhere along the way, Mike will join me. Our major line of support will come from ten intelligence analysts under the direction of my mother back in Washington. While our present team consists of less than fifteen people, I'm supposed to make contact with others inside Mexico who can also provide support. Who they are and what type of support, I haven't a clue.

My job in the field is to gather information, send it back to Washington to be deciphered and await my next orders. Our group is not to take any action on our own. The government has stationed quick response teams throughout the world that can be on the ground in any hot location in less than four hours. Jim Carlone informed me that most of our support will come from a Naval carrier group stationed in the Gulf of Mexico, a few miles from the coastal city of Coatzacoalcos. I'm grateful for the strong backup – since I forgot my Colt, which is locked up in my safe back in Key West, dammit. I'm not sure who or what's picking me up at the airport, but I do know they're already an hour late.

• • •

WHEN I HEAR THE gunshots, I'm not sure if I'm awake or dreaming. Looking around me outside the baggage pickup area, no one appears to be alarmed. Odd. Then I hear the shooting again and finally figure out the source: an old, multicolored school bus with white birds painted on the side and an engine that's backfiring.

As the bus pulls up closer, I can read the black, hand-painted lettering on its side in bold English: Holy Spirit Mission. Mike told me earlier this morning over the phone that I'd recognize my ride when I saw it, and I do believe it has arrived. Letting go of any hope for a last minute limo or SUV pulling up with a chauffeur holding up a sign with my name, I walk slowly over to the bus. With one final, resounding boom, its engine decides it's time for a rest.

Reading the name again off the side of the bus, I make a mental note to see if they're missing a heavy, stone-encrusted cross. If so, I'm pretty damned sure I know where it is – sitting in a box at my mom's office in Washington.

Chapter 23

THE BUS'S RETRACTABLE DOOR slowly squeaks open and I'm fully prepared to see Keith Partridge standing at the top of the stairs. Instead of the groovy '70s teen idol, a young woman descends the steps, wearing a Boston Red Sox cap with a long dirty blonde braid that bounces as she hits the ground in a fast jog, a red screwdriver in hand.

The woman's wearing faded jeans, New Balance running shoes, and a t-shirt that says "Joe's Garage" on the front. At first I'm not sure if the shirt is a reference to the Frank Zappa tune. Maybe there is such a garage. When she climbs onto the bumper, opens the hood of the multicolored bus and begins tinkering with something, it grabs the attention of onlookers, amazed that a woman can actually fix something without the help of a man.

I manage to break through the crowd, which now includes several policemen, and ask her if I can do anything to help. She tells me not yet – at least she didn't blow me off – and thanks me for my offer. Having been around cars most of my life and knowing a little, I can see she's trying to hold open the butterfly on the carburetor to allow fuel to evaporate. "Carburetor running rich?" I say. She glances up at me and hands me the screwdriver.

"Hold the butterfly open," she says, then jumps down. "And keep your face away, in case flames shoot out of the carb," she adds as she runs around and hops back up into the driver's seat, checks the emergency brake, then puts the transmission into neutral. Then this beauty runs back down the steps and hands me a yellow #2 pencil with bite marks all over it. "Keep the valve open with this,' she says. "I need the screwdriver to start the bus." Within seconds she's back in the squeaky driver's seat starting the engine.

The motor catches after a few cranks of the starter as black smoke pours out of the exhaust. The crowd cheers and the young woman in the Sox cap appears at the door and takes a quick bow. I expect I'll have a lot to learn from this remarkable young woman over the next several days. Completing her bow, she hushes the crowd, then yells out my name. I walk around the side of the bus to the open door where she's standing. I've still got the #2 pencil in my mouth, adding a few more bite marks of my own. She looks at me and grins.

"Hello, Joseph Dustan," she says and reaches to give me a firm and professional handshake. "Sorry I'm late. I had to make a few stops here in Mexico City before coming out to the airport. So you're our new water boy. You come highly recommended. As a matter of fact, I spoke to your boss a few hours ago. John Carbone? John Carlone? No, Jim Carlone – yeah, that's it." I nod. "Anyway, I'm Clare Atwater, and this is your ride to Holy Spirit Mission. I can guarantee you that it's hot, dirty and very uncomfortable, but you'll find that out for yourself over the next three hundred miles."

"Thanks, Clare," I say, returning her grin as I drop myself in the first seat on the opposite side of the bus. "I appreciate you going out of your way to pick me up."

"No problem, Joe," she yells over the sound of the engine. "Can I call you Joe?" She doesn't wait for an answer. "If my driving appears to be a little erratic, please know that I don't normally drive this thing. Most of my experience ends once I open the hood and get it started. Our regular driver, Anna, went missing a few weeks back. I drew the short straw to pick you up. Sit back, relax and enjoy the beautiful Mexican countryside. We have to make a few stops along the way."

"Would you like me to drive back to the mission?"

"No thanks, water boy. I should get used to handling this beast in case Anna doesn't come back any time soon. I sure hope she's okay," she adds as she stares briefly through some spider-web cracks in the driver's side window.

"Yes, you can call me Joe," I answer belatedly.

"Okay, water boy," she yells. "Joe it is."

Looking through the dirty bus windows over at baggage claim, I can't help but feel that we're being watched by two young men sitting on the bench I'd just vacated. They're fully dressed in black leather motorcycle garb, with matching helmets on their laps. As the bus pulls away from the curb, I see them get up from the bench, walk over to a pair of matching yellow Ducatis parked at the curb, climb on, hit the kick-starts and pull out into traffic. They're several car lengths behind us and change lanes as we do.

It looks like we'll have company on our way to Holy Spirit Mission. Forgetting my Colt back in Key West was pure stupidity on my part.

Chapter 24

T HE NOISE INSIDE the bus makes it impossible to carry on normal conversation. I'm sitting on a broken bench seat with no cushion, on the right side of the bus three rows down from Clare. I can see Clare's face in the inside rearview mirror. She's got light blue eyes and full lips that turn slightly upward at the edges, the kind that give you the impression that she's always smiling. She must have caught me looking at her, because she reaches into her handbag on the floor and takes out a pair of sunglasses. I follow suit, opening my surf bag and pulling out my Yankees 2009 World Champions hat and a cheap pair of sunglasses I picked up at the Miami airport. Clare glances at me and, without a word, turns her cap around on her head so that I can be reminded of the Boston Red Sox's 2007 World Championship. Game on.

Once we leave the city limits of Mexico City behind us, the streets quickly become quite deserted and very bumpy. I don't see any sign of the two men in black on the Ducatis. The only car behind us is a rusted-out '64 Lincoln Continental convertible with suicide doors, huffing blue smoke out the back while pieces of the convertible top flap in the wind.

Clare tells me we're heading southeast into the Mexican state of Puebla on our way to a small village outside Tepeaca, some thirty miles southeast of the state capital of Puebla and close to a hundred miles from the airport. From what I'm reading off my iPhone, Tepeaca has a population of about forty thousand. The biggest employer is the local cement plant.

I now know, thanks to Clare and a text message from Jim that Holy Spirit Mission will be my temporary home. I'll be working covertly, going out into the countryside visiting villages, presumably to help solve their water issues. My job as a water boy, as Clare would put it, is to only report my findings and make recommendations to the Mexican authorities. I'm strictly forbidden to take any action per an organization that monitors water safety in Central America.

With my reputation of working with international relief agencies and non-profits, getting into Mexico was relatively easy and not heavily scrutinized. So here I am, traveling down a deserted Mexican highway in a multicolored bus, with birds painted all over it, like I'm an honorary member of the Partridge Family. "Traveling along there's a song that we're singing, come on get happy. We'll make you happy. We'll make you happy. We'll make you happy..." I can't get the damned thing out of my head.

• • •

WE'RE ABOUT AN HOUR into our trip, traveling down highway 150, when the two Ducati motorcycles appear out of nowhere and come screaming by the bus to take up positions in front of us. The road is relatively deserted; a few cars and trucks are coming the other way. It looks like we're going to have to fend for ourselves.

"Clare," I shout over the noise of the bus, "those two guys in front of us? They followed us from the airport. I think they're trying to pull us over."

"Yeah," yells Clare, "I saw them in a dry creek bed we passed about ten miles back. They must've been waiting for the traffic to thin out before they made their move. They're probably after drugs and money. They wait for people at the airport who they think make likely targets and follow them. You're basically looking at a modern day hold-up."

Clare slows the bus, enough so the noise lessens and we can talk without screaming. The farther we go, the more deserted the road becomes. We're on our own, and we definitely need some sort of plan.

I've already thought up and rejected half a dozen masterful plans when Clare abruptly pulls the bus over to the side and comes to a screeching halt, sending me sprawling over the seat, landing me in the aisle by her legs. She apologizes, grabs me by the arm and helps me back on my feet. Looking out, I can barely see the yellow bikes on the road up ahead.

"You think we should be stopping here? This is one pretty lonely stretch of highway," I question. "The boys'll figure out pretty quickly that we've pulled over."

"Listen, Joe, we need to take the offensive with these two. Because if we don't, we may meet up with their buddies further up the road. Even though we don't have anything they want, I don't care to be kidnapped, murdered or, at the very least, have our tires shot out. There's no cell phone reception for the next twenty miles. We need to make our stand now."

She throws me a set of keys. "Go to the back of the bus and unlock the storage box. Inside's a pistol and a shotgun. Load them and I'll meet you in back."

I do as I am told and she joins me at the rear emergency door in less than a minute. On her nod, we both push open the door and jump out onto the dirt. I take a quick peek around the edge of the bus. Two pairs of headlights are coming our direction, all right. At a high rate of speed. Clare pumps the double barrel sawed off shotgun, loading the chamber, and walks out into the middle of the road waiting for our friends to arrive. I pull my Yankee cap down over my head and run back up the front of the bus with an old Smith and Wesson revolver in my right hand. I think I've figured out her plan and it's time to execute it.

I hide behind the front passenger-side tire as the bikes apply their brakes, smoking rubber and fishtailing to a stop halfway down the bus, about fifteen feet from Clare. I come around the front of the bus to see Clare pointing the shotgun at the bikers and yelling something at them. I come up behind them with my gun drawn and make a noise to get their attention. They need to see that they're surrounded by armed people.

As I get closer to them, I hear one of them apologize in Spanish as he climbs back on his bike. The other follows suit. As they kick their bikes to start, they both turn to look at me again as Clare slowly moves out of the road and back behind the bus. The two bikers smoothly shift through the gears and head back to in the direction of Mexico City.

Jamming the pistol in the back of my waistband, I walk to the back of the bus to join Clare. As I turn the corner, I see her hunched over releasing the contents of her stomach on the side of highway. She pulls up the hem of her Joe's Garage t-shirt to wipe her mouth and eyes, exposing a firm set of abs. Catching me staring, she says, "Why don't you take a picture. It'll last longer." Her tone is sarcastic and the look she gives me, disgusted. We walk in silence back to the front of the bus.

"Are you okay, Clare?" I ask her. "I apologize for staring. Whatever you said to those two guys sure worked."

"Apology accepted. I just told them the truth, that we have no drugs and little money and live at Holy Spirit Mission, assisting the local community. That's a line right out of our most recent brochure and it seemed to work. They mumbled a little, saw you behind them, then nodded to each other. I got out of their way, they took off. End of story."

"Maybe they thought they were outgunned and didn't want to take the chance of getting hurt," I suggest. "What might have looked low-risk for them at the beginning turned out to be high-risk. It may have just come down to human nature and the path of least resistance, what with you standing there in the middle of a deserted highway pointing a shotgun at them."

"Oh, that reminds me. Do you know how to clear a shotgun chamber? I think it got jammed when I pumped it. Thank God I didn't need to use it." This woman's something else.

"Why don't you let me drive for while, Clare," I say. "You can relax in the back – and enjoy the road noise. I'll check the gun later."

Clare gives in graciously, smiles and climbs up the stairs, grabs her bag and takes a seat in the second row. Something certainly stirs within me as I take my seat behind the wheel of the multicolored bus. I'm not sure what it is. Maybe it's just my nerves calming down after the motorcycle showdown, or maybe it's something more complicated. I look down at the ignition, stand back up, walk over to where Clare is sitting and hold out my hand. Rummaging through her Nike bag, she pulls out the object we need to get this party started. She places the red Stanley flat head screwdriver in my hand with a wink.

I jump back into the driver's seat, start up the bus and manage to keep it running on the first try. As I get it in gear, I look in the inside rearview mirror and can't take my eyes off my passenger in the second row, who's changing into another Red Sox t-shirt. Wonder if she's ever actually been to Fenway Park.

Our multicolored bus is up to sixty. Next stop: Tepeaca, outside the capital city of Puebla, to visit and pick up supplies. I have no idea what that entails, but something tells me it'll be interesting. "Come on, get happy!"

Chapter 25

2:02 PM. THE HOLY SPIRIT MISSION bus rolls into a small town on the outskirts of Tepeaca without incident after our showdown with the men on the motorcycles. Clare's slept most of the way, stretched out in the aisle on top of several blankets to help cushion her from the bumpy ride. She wakes up when she hears screaming as I slam on the brakes to avoid a small crowd of children that have come running out of nowhere in front of the bus. My understanding of Spanish is embarrassingly weak; however one name I do know seems to make up most of the din, and that I easily recognize.

Clare opens the door to the bus, jumps down onto the dusty road and gathers up all the children into the biggest group hug I think I've ever seen. They obviously know her and adore her, and continue to climb all over her as she sits down on a patch of brown grass in front of a dilapidated stone and wooden building. I hear her say something to the kids about lunch, people named TG and Sandy, and pizza. Pizza must be the magic word; at the sound of it, the children relinquish Clare and vanish into the alleys. Clare climbs back into the bus with a big smile on her face, looking energized.

"Wow, Clare, you certainly worked some kind of magic with those kids. For a minute there I could imagine those sweet, angelic children becoming an angry mob and turning over the bus," I say with a laugh.

"Don't be silly," she says, but she's serious. "The reality is that many of these children have little or no food to eat. They live on the streets begging and stealing to survive. Many get kidnapped by strangers, never to be seen again. The lucky ones make it to Mexico City and become hookers and drug dealers. I'm afraid it's not so different than what happens in cities in the US. Some of these kids' parents have thrown them out because they can't afford to feed them. But these kids have amazing spirits and an astonishing will to survive. Many come to the mission begging for work, asking for food, or just for a corner in the building to get out of the cold and rain."

Clare gets back behind the wheel and drives on less than a mile to an unadorned concrete block building with two large picture windows, "Amalfi Pizzeria" neatly painted in the center of each. She parks the bus in a grassy lot opposite the restaurant.

Walking across the street, now we hear children's screams and laughter approaching from behind us. As we turn towards the noise, a small black-haired girl with beautiful dark skin jumps into Clare's arms. I recognize many of the children who only a few minutes ago were climbing all over her a few streets back. The Spanish is flying and I'm desperately trying to keep up, pretty sure I hear words like pizza, party, soda, ice cream and – baseball? Clare gives two of the older boys instructions in Spanish. They run over to the bus, climb inside and start throwing items out the windows and doors.

I follow Clare into the pizzeria where she gets a wordless hug from a big burly man who lifts her clear off the ground, all the while smiling at me warmly. He must be able to tell that I'm linguistically challenged. When he begins speaking, it is in slow, broken English. I can tell already I'm gonna really like this guy.

"Sister Clare, how happy I am to see you!" he says with an all-encompassing grin. "*Los niños*, the children here every day, ask me if you and the colorful bus will come for pizza. I'm sorry – I mean that *you* have pizza, not the bus. My English, it is still not so good. Any day, any how – I mean, anyway, I tell the children I no see you today, but you come soon."

"TG, your English has improved much better than my Spanish has, I'm sorry to say. How can you tell white lies to these beautiful children?" Clare says as she grabs hold of TG's large hairy hand. "You know I've been very busy back at the mission, helping the migrant farmers get through the flu epidemic. Where's Sandy?"

"My lovely Sandy goes to her mother in Carolina, United States. I'm sorry, Sister, for lies – excuse me, my lies, but these children hope something – need something to hope for, and that is you, my sweet friend. We still have parents arriving – no, I mean going to the cities and US, *abandono*, abandoning some of their children. I had a young boy, *un niño pequeño*, in here not yet seven years old who tells me his *madre* is missing and must have found herself lost. He comes home from *escula*, school and finds the doors chained shut with *nadie a casa*, not nobody home. A neighbor finds him crying in the street asking for someone to help him find his lost *madre*. She brings him here for pizza and Coke. While eating at the counter sitting in a stool on top of a wooden box, he thinks he sees his *padre* walking in – excuse me, across the road. He *corrio*, I mean runs into the road and is *golpear*, run over by a cement truck. It kill him *de immediate*, right away, instantly."

Clare must have heard that kind of story way too many times to make her sad anymore. Instead it has the opposite effect – it makes her angry and she goes off in a Spanish tirade that lasts a few minutes. Then she remembers why she's here and orders ten large pizzas, four large bottles of soda and six gallon tubs of ice cream. As he takes off his bright white apron, TG goes behind the counter, yells the order to someone in the kitchen, then bends down below the cash resister and retrieves a green box with the name Spalding on the cover. He opens it up. Inside: a brand new softball. Tossing it to me, he grabs his glove hanging on a nail over the cash register. It is obvious to me it's game on.

During a scattered conversation with TG, I discover that Clare is pretty well known in this area for the things she does for the children. The local street kids know that the mission bus means pizza, ice cream and baseball. Clare, TG says, just wants to remind everyone that they're still just kids.

We carry out a few tables to set the pizza on. The game is in full swing. The only adult allowed to play is Clare. My job is to serve up the pizza and soda, watch and cheer.

Seeing Clare up at home plate, preparing to hit, I'm stunned by her simple beauty. It's in the way she carries herself, and laughs when she swings the bat and misses the ball completely. The children all laugh along with her when she strikes out and then pretend to be furious at the pitcher, dancing around in a circle and booing him loudly.

Clare joins them, and as she spins around in her mad dance, I can't help but notice a silver cross on a chain around her neck, which takes me back momentarily to the one I received in Key West yesterday. Tucking the cross back into the neck of her Red Sox shirt, Clare screams out, "*quien esta listo para el helado,*" which I'm surprised to realize I know means "who's ready for ice cream?"

Chapter 26

IT FEELS STRANGE pulling out of the parking lot across from Amalfi Pizza, waving good bye to TG and all the children. Many of the children are crying; several of the older ones are running after the bus. I'm back in the driver's seat grinding the bus's gears, using all my strength to push the shift into second and then into third. Clare presses her right hand up against the window in a permanent wave as her left hand wipes the tears from her own face. It's easy to understand her sadness, knowing that most of these children will be sleeping out in the streets tonight with no one to tuck them in or read them a story. TG and his wife Sandy do what they can for them by providing shelter, food and blankets whenever possible. What I learned today: when people search for work in the cities many things get left behind, including their own flesh and blood.

We head for Analco Iglesia del Angel Custodio, an old church in the heart of Puebla, to meet someone. Now that I know Clare is a Sister, a nun, going to a church makes sense. I would have never suspected Clare to be a Sister Clare. Aren't nuns supposed to have that thing on their head, like Sister Bertrille in "The Flying Nun" on TV? The only religious thing Clare wears is the cross around her neck. My frustration begins to rise, knowing that not only is she a Red Sox fan, she's married to the Almighty to boot. How's a Yankee fan supposed to compete with *that*?

We manage to park the bus on a street named Calle Diez Sur. After I put the screwdriver in my pocket and lock the door, we walk down a stone path that ends at the stairs of a beautiful church, a simple building of white stucco, with red trim and two tall towers in the front. Clare stops at one of the green benches along the way and sits down. She grabs my hand and pulls me down next to her.

"Joe, I have to go inside by myself. I'll only be a minute. Can you wait outside for me?"

Is she joking? I'd wait anywhere for this woman. However, what I tell her is, "Sure, Clare, even though I was hoping to get a look inside. I'll be right here."

Moving quickly down to the end of the walkway, she disappears into the church. While I wait, I pull out my iPhone, turn it on and am happy to see I have service. I call into DC using a secure line and quickly reach my mother.

"Hello, Mom. I'm in Mexico," I tell her. "I wanted to see if there've been any new developments."

"Joseph, it's so good to hear your voice," she says as only a mother can. "With all that's been going on over the last several days, I've been worried about what you're getting yourself into. I trust you'll be careful. Don't forget to call in the cavalry if needed."

"I know, Mom. Life's a little different down here, but believe it or not, I feel relatively safe. I'm on my way to Holy Spirit Mission and –"

"Holy Spirit Mission?" Mom asks. I can just imagine her face. This is a woman who likes people to think she's unflappable. Even though I can't hear it in her voice, I know she must be bug-eyed at this piece of information.

"That's right, Mom. I have no idea if it's the same Holy Spirit Mission, but if it is – well, I'll let you know if they're missing a cross. What's the latest?"

"The latest. Ah, yes, the latest. Okay, none of the agencies have made much progress thus far," says Mom, climbing back into her official persona. "We still have no one claiming responsibility, which as you know makes it very difficult to get a full-blown investigation started. Based on all the information my group's gathered, I think we're headed in the right direction. If we didn't know about the helicopter flying over the border into Mexico, we'd probably still be stuck at the starting gate with all the other agencies. Our people on the ground in Mexico were able to confirm that the black helicopter flying through the streets of Washington Monday is the same one that recently landed at Holy Spirit Mission. It stayed on the ground for twenty minutes, then flew on to a large farm, Faltan Acres Granja Familiar – Missing Acres Family Farm. Joseph, I feel strongly that Holy Spirit Mission and Missing Acres are somehow tied into what happened in DC. As a matter of fact, the helicopter stopped at the mission at about the same time you were being picked up at the airport in Mexico City."

"Ha...small world. Mom, keep me posted on Holy Spirit. Is there any word on Nat? How's Stella?"

"Natalie's still missing, I'm afraid, Joseph. It's tearing Stella apart, especially since it does look like she walked out of the emergency room with those two men of her own free will. It's an unusual missing persons case, and you know how hard it can be to get the police to take them seriously if there's no evidence of violence, but I'm staying on top of it and local law enforcement's working hard to find her, thank God."

"Oh, Mom," I add, "did you happen to find out anything on that broken piece of statuary?"

"Not yet. The leg's in the lab. The technician's come back with very little so far. The best we know right now is that the blue paint's less than fifty years old. Our best guess is that the leg's covered by some sort of robe. One member of the team thinks it's part of a religious statue. She's been scouring the internet looking at thousands of pictures trying to find a match. The good news is that it has very little value if any, so chances are it wasn't stolen."

"Thanks, Mom. My ride to the mission's walking towards me. I'll call tomorrow. Love you."

Clare, moving at a good clip, walks right past me, then returns and sits on the bench as I snap my phone shut. Turning to me, she recommends we get moving, that it's getting late. It's only 4:42 in the afternoon, but I get up quickly, responding to the look of urgency in her eyes. I'm not sure what went on in there, but something's caused her – meaning us – to break into a run.

When we get to the bus and unchain the door, we quickly climb in, then catch our breath. Which is when I hear a familiar sound racing up the street and getting louder. I look out the back and see our two friends on the yellow Ducatis heading in our direction. They now having matching passengers on the backs of their bikes – who look to be holding shotguns.

I still have the old revolver tucked into the back of my pants, but haven't had a chance to un-jam the shotgun. Just as they're about to pull up alongside the bus, a dark maroon Cadillac SUV with tinted windows comes barreling up from the opposite direction, looking like it's ready for a showdown. Both Ducatis veer to the left to avoid a collision and hit the foot-high curb, which sends one set of cyclists somersaulting off their bike, hitting the dirt like rag dolls, bouncing several times. The other motorcycle manages to stay upright; the driver of that one navigates smartly down a hill into what looks like a park and is quickly out of sight. The downed riders are lying on the ground, motionless.

Next thing, we hear a hard rap at the door of the bus. Standing outside is a very large, dark man who looks to me like an ex-boxer. In his arms: a young Mexican woman with scratches on her face, her hair flattened with something that looks a lot like dried blood. I open the door and come down the steps. The boxer says nothing, just places the girl in my arms. I turn carefully, carry her up into the bus and set her down on one of the seats. Clare thanks the man in Spanish and then closes the door.

As the maroon SUV pulls away, we hear sirens off in the distance. We decide not to wait around to file a police report. It's time for the multicolored bus to go home. Leaving the girl with Clare, I return to the driver's seat and put the red screwdriver into the ignition switch like I've been doing this all my life. It starts on the second try.

As I pull away from the curb and onto the roadway, I can hear Clare and the woman talking behind me. The noise of the bus increases as it picks up speed, but I can make out enough of their conversation through the crying and broken English to know that we have Anna, the mission's regular bus driver who went missing a few weeks ago.

Not seeing any lights behind us, I thank God and pray for justice. The eye-for-an-eye, tooth-for-a-tooth type stuff.

Chapter 27

THE FOUR-HOUR RIDE to the mission outside the town of Acayucan is uneventful, except for some sporadic crying that echoes off the metal walls of the bus. Anna speaks good English. Much of the conversation behind me is in soft whispers, but from time to time I catch snippets of her reliving her story of the last two weeks. She thanks Clare for putting her own self in danger by meeting those men inside the church.

It's obvious that Anna's been beaten up and treated very badly. I can see her in the rearview mirror. She looks a lot older than someone in her early twenties. She talks about going into a small grocery in Puebla, only to be dragged out the back door and thrown into a waiting van. Three masked men drove into the dessert and interrogated her for over an hour. Anna kept telling them they were making a mistake, that she wasn't the woman they thought she was. The men meant to kidnap the daughter of some prominent local industrialist and hold her for ransom. When they found out their mistake, they beat and raped her and left her for dead in an old, abandoned cement warehouse on the outskirts of the city.

Then they came up with another idea, and tried to sell her off as a sex slave to those who traffic in human cargo. They made a connection through the underground community and a meeting was set up at the abandoned warehouse, but the men's plan went to hell when two trucks showed up with eight heavily armed men. There was a short gun battle, and the three kidnappers were dead in less than five minutes. Anna was taken to a local clinic, cleaned up, placed in one of the confessionals at the church and in less than two hours, found herself back on the bus, on her way back to Holy Spirit.

Clare explains to me that TG at the pizzeria gave her the message about Anna being at the church. She also tells me that the dark-skinned man who handed Anna over to us outside the church works for a well know Mexican family, the family that operates Missing Acres.

My mother's initial research loosely tying Holy Spirit and Missing Acres to local drug cartels seems to be on target. It's not out of the question for a legitimate organization to be tied in one way or another to an illegal operation. There can be mutual benefits for both parties, but the question is always how much the legitimate group knows about the dealings of the illegal operation. Getting Anna back into Clare's hands certainly didn't happen by itself. Clare must have had help from some powerful organization, one that wasn't afraid of repercussions or revenge.

While I'm driving and thinking in my own little world, Clare shouts from behind me that I've missed the turn to the mission. I yell out a quick apology and manage to turn the multicolored monster around without getting stuck in a ditch. There are no signs, houses or other landmarks of any sort that I can see as I wrestle the cracked steering wheel into a hard right turn.

• • •

9:13 PM. PULLING UP in front of the Holy Sprit Mission, I stay in my seat as Clare helps Anna down the steps of the bus. A large white man comes over to greet us. He's in great shape and, based on his size, could easily pass for an ex-football player. He has short salt-and-pepper hair, and a nose that's been in a fight or two. He gives Clare and Anna both a strong, lingering hug, then walks over to me.

Before I can say two words, a black helicopter comes screaming over our heads, about three hundred feet off the ground, moving at well over a hundred miles an hour. It's obvious that I'm the only one surprised by the noise and its abrupt appearance. The large white man, who's wearing black Dockers and a white button-down cotton shirt, gets right in my face and gives my hand a strong shake. "Welcome, my son, to Holy Spirit Mission! I'm Father Ed."

Chapter 28

AFTER A QUICK CONVERSATION with Father Ed, I sit outside the mission on an old cement bench, pieces of which are flaking off the surface, turning my pants grey. According to him, the mission was built on an infamous battle site where Spanish conquistadors, led by Hernán Cortés, slaughtered numerous Aztecs around 1520. Under the direction of the Catholic Church, the beautiful stone mission was built soon after. It took over ten years to complete. It was abandoned in the early nineteenth century, after a TB outbreak killed most of the local population. Those who survived thought the epidemic was a punishment from God for building the church on sacred ground. At the same time, they were afraid to destroy the mission, so it fell into disrepair, abandoned for over sixty years, until a wealthy Mexican-American bought it from the government and began to restore it to its original beauty. During the restoration, an earthquake caused several walls to give way, killing over twenty laborers and the new owner as well. His widow donated it back to the Mexican government in 1958. The non-profit Holy Spirit Mission Group bought it for a dollar in 1967.

I can hear the hum of a generator from behind the building, powering the lights, including one that's shining above the outside main entrance door. Holy Spirit Mission, naturally sand-colored, consists of two main floors and four large arches perpendicular to the main entrance. With its large façade you get the impression of a much larger building. Rising above the mission is an old bell tower that's missing the majority of its roof and, most importantly, a bell. Father Ed points out scaffolding and tells me about the three brothers who've been charged with rebuilding the bell tower. He refers to them as the "three *amigos*," doing God's work through physical labor.

One can easily imagine an old, hunched-back monk in a dark robe pulling on a rope, ringing the missing bell to let the locals know that mass was about to start. Closing my eyes and letting my imagination run, I feel someone touch my shoulder.

"Oh, I'm sorry I woke you," Clare says quietly. "May I join you?"

"Please, sit down, and by the way, I wasn't sleeping," I tell her. "I was just thinking about all the bizarre events today that finally brought me to this beautiful place. How's Anna?"

"As I'm sure you can tell, she's in rough shape, both physically and mentally," says Clare. "A local doctor will be coming by tomorrow to check on her and provide any medication needed. We also have many good friends at Doctors Without Borders who'll be coming through the area next week. They always stop here on their way back to Mexico City and give the local people free medical assistance. They have a wonderful woman doctor on staff, Mary Ann, who'll examine Anna. I've already texted her with the specifics, and gotten a quick response letting me know that she'll be with them. You have to understand – the Mexican people are very hardy and resilient. They understand pain all too well, it's so much a part of their daily lives. By the way, Joe, thanks for your help today," Clare says, her manner downright sexy.

What the hell am I talking about, sexy? She's a nun, for God's sake! I make a quick apology to God, smile at Clare, then close my eyes for a minute, feeling the warm air brush across my face. Hearing the low hum of the generator in the background with no other noise except for the breeze filling my ears, I begin to feel sleepy. Clare places her hand next to mine on the bench as our breathing falls into the same slow pattern. I open one eye very slowly to see that her eyes are wide open, her head tilted to the sky. Feeling cocky, I decide I might as well pop the big question.

"So tell me, Clare, how long have you been a sister?" I ask in my most serious tone.

Her response is a soft noise, a cross between a burp and suppressed laughter. She's just turned to answer me when we both hear a scream from inside the mission.

Jumping up from the cement bench, we run inside where a very old woman is standing near an adjacent doorway, a broom in one hand, making the sign of the cross with the other. Clare rushes to the vestibule as I manage to catch the old woman as she faints.

I'm placing the woman on a blanket-covered wooden bench, when I realize that Clare has burst into tears. I look up to see her standing frozen in place, looking in horror into the next room. Hurrying over to her, my eyes follow hers to see Anna, lying on her back on the floor, a large knife protruding from her chest. Her eyes are open wide, staring at the ceiling.

Running quickly over to Anna, I bend down to check her pulse, then close her eyelids. The thought of suicide enters my mind – perhaps, after the hell of two weeks of rape and torture, she now wanted to go to heaven.

Father Ed rushes through the door and sees Anna lying on the floor. Kneeling beside her, he put his head in his hands and begins to pray softly. A strong wind comes through the room's open window and blows out the flame of a large red candle in the corner. The one candle still flickering in the hallway illuminates Anna's face, giving the eerie impression that her features are moving – that she's still alive. But that candle also loses its battle with the breeze, casting the room into deep shadows.

Nobody says a word as the old woman, now back on her feet, comes into the room with a white sheet and hands it to Father Ed.

Kneeling; I pull the six-inch kitchen knife from Anna's chest and lay it on the cool stone floor. Father Ed unrolls the sheet and together we place her body in the center. We wrap her very carefully, then I help him carry her to a small, detached wooden building with a rusted metal door where we lay her on a large, grey stone surface. As I walk back towards the entrance, I turn to see Father Ed on his knees, a simple black rosary in his hands, praying over Anna's body.

Feeling a little dizzy, I go outside, lean against a wall and take a few deep breaths. After listening to Father Ed recite several Hail Mary's, I gather myself together and walk back to the mission, planning to stop at the bus to look for my surf bag. The generator's shut down for the night, and I can see candles being lit in a few of the rooms. Hoping to catch a glimpse of Clare or even hear her voice, I walk over to the bus to grab my things and look for a place to sleep.

Chapter 29

4:48 AM. I'M WOKEN up outside in the courtyard by a tan dog with a white nose who's licking my face.

After I left Father Ed last night, I went back to the mission, grabbed an old green army blanket hanging off a chair and headed out into the courtyard. It was pitch black, except for a few stars blinking through the clouds. I got a flashlight from my bag and shone it along the ground till I found a soft spot with no rocks. Bed.

Waking up to a dog – fortunately only a medium-sized dog – with terrible breath standing on your chest is certainly a surprise. I remember a strange dream that included Sister Clare dressed in full nun regalia whacking my knuckles with a thick wooden ruler.

Hearing men's voices, including Father Ed's, on the other side of the courtyard wall, I push my new friend off me, stand up, brush several layers of dirt off my clothes and head for the opening in the wall. The skies are starting to brighten a bit. I can see a fat, black and white horse hooked up to a wooden wagon. Coming closer, I see Father Ed and an old man with a long grey beard lift Anna's wrapped body from a bench and place it gently into a pine box on the ground next to the wagon. The two then lift the coffin into the wagon, which startles the horse briefly, causing the old man to curse at it in Spanish.

Father Ed nods when he notices me as they tie the box down to the wagon. Once secured, the bearded man shakes hands with Father Ed, climbs up into the seat with much difficulty and snaps the reins to get the horse moving. The dog with the sour breath bolts away, chases the wagon, then leaps up into the front seat right next to the driver. The dog looks back at me, jumps off and runs back towards the mission, not slowing its stride to leap the stone wall into the courtyard. I'm thinking it knows it's time to eat.

"Thanks for your help last night, Joe," Father Ed says as he walks over to me. "Señor Mendoza will take Anna's body back into town so her family can oversee a proper burial. I went over to see her parents last night and tried to explain what happened to her. They are definitely saddened by what I told them, but for some reason not too surprised. They're good, hard-working people who do not deserve such tragedy, especially when suicide is involved. I assured them that God will forgive, though, that Anna will get to heaven."

Father Ed points out a fairly new grey metal building about a hundred yards behind the mission, down a small slope. "It's plumbed," he tells me. "Clean running water, showers. You can get cleaned up. Delores has coffee ready by 5:30."

Thanking him, I head for the building. Halfway there, I see someone sitting against the wall with her head down. Coming closer, I see it's Clare, wrapped in a blue North Face jacket. She seems to be asleep. After finding Anna last night, she probably just walked around until she collapsed right here. I walk past her as quietly as possible. The cross she wears is dangling in full sight by one of her hands. I am now convinced that our crosses *are* identical.

To my surprise, the outbuilding is quite modern, with separate men's and women's facilities that smell of bleach and orange peels. The men's area has six modern showers and ten enclosed toilet stalls with Kohler fixtures. In fact, these bathrooms are a lot plusher than what I have at home back in Key West.

I grab the only towel out of my bag, along with a small bar of soap I saved from my recent trip to Washington. The shower's a bit tricky, but once you understand the process, it works just fine. You start by pumping a large wooden handle that's tied into some sort of gearing under the floor. As you pump the handle, you can hear water being drawn through piping below your feet, up the wall in front of you and into an unseen storage tank overhead. Once you think you have enough water, you stop pumping, then turn a large brass knob on the shower-head to start the water flowing. Gravity fed, you control the flow with the brass knob as it comes through the shower head. There are no separate hot or cold fixtures, but the water's warm, which feels excep-tionally good this morning. As I'm getting into the rhythm of my shower, I hear the door to the men's room squeak open and closed, followed by silence, which again reminds me that my Colt is in Key West.

"Joe, it's me" says Clare. "I thought I heard someone in here so I figured I'd investigate. I saw your bag and knew it was you. Good morning."

"Morning, Clare. I was woken up by a brown dog with bad breath licking my face. I really needed this shower," I laugh.

"Ah, sounds like you met Fina. She's a stray who came to us several months ago and has never left. She and a dozen cats keep down the rodent population around here. Be careful, Joe," Clare warns me, "if she likes you, she'll follow you everywhere."

"I'll keep that in mind – thank you. Do you always come into the men's room when you want to talk or is this just a one-time thing?"

"Don't worry, Joe. It's only my second – or maybe third – time," giggles Clare. "I just felt like talking to someone and you were the closest."

"I'm really sorry about what happened to Anna," I say. "I think she wanted peace and from everything I've heard, she probably thought taking her own life was the best way – maybe even the only way – to find it. I'm sorry, Clare."

"You're probably right. I just get sick and tired of all the tragedy and sadness that happens around here. I came here to help, but it always seems like one step forward, two steps back. You can get so wrapped up in the misery you find yourself getting depressed from time to time."

"Clare, I don't know you very well, but I do know that those children in Puebla couldn't wait to see you," I say through a partially opened door. "You're a hero to them who comes to save the day when no one else will or wants to. It's okay to feel miserable once in while, as long as you feel hopeful and believe things will eventually get better. Everyone would be miserable on some level without the possibility of hope. You provide that possibility."

"Thanks. I appreciate your kind words," she responds, then changes her tone. "Hey, I need to get back to the mission and help cook breakfast, but first I need to clarify something. Father Ed may be a real priest, but I'm no nun. Since I work at a Catholic mission, people just assume that I'm a nun. Sorry for any confusion."

Before I have a chance to say anything the door to the outbuilding squeaks open, then closes. Two thoughts pass through my brain, one right on the heels of the other. Clare isn't a nun? So much for my Flying Nun/Sister Bertrille fantasy. Father Ed *may* be a priest? I need to get a weapon.

Chapter 30

It FELT GOOD walking up the slight incline from the shower facilities to the mission in clean Levis and a sweatshirt. It's close to 6:00 now. The sun's just rising over the east side of the courtyard.

I can't stop thinking about what Clare said but I'm trying not to overanalyze what she meant or didn't mean. After breakfast, we'll be heading off to a small village near the town of El Paraiso, about forty-five miles south of here. The environmental arm of the Mexican government has already spent two years working with the village to clean up the site of a contaminated water well and dig a new one. My job is to make recommendations to the government and the locals on how best to move the clean water where it can be readily accessible for all. Having it piped less than a mile to the town center looks good on paper. Now we need to physically verify the plan and make sure the old, polluted well is capped properly.

As I approach the courtyard, I can both see and hear the bus rolling up the dirt road, hitting every pothole on the way. When it rolls to a stop in front of the mission, a loud cheer goes up inside the bus. I guess I wasn't the only one who felt like cheering when I knew I was getting off that dirty, smelly vehicle. Father Ed steps out the open door. Some twenty people follow him down the steps and into the mission.

Turning into the courtyard, I see six long tables and chairs, the tables all set with plates and utensils. The people I saw getting off the bus behind Father Ed a few minutes ago are now pouring into the courtyard taking seats around the tables. Father Ed, Clare and a few others I don't recognize follow the group into the yard, each carrying large aluminum pans filled with steaming hot food. The sight and smell of breakfast begins to make my mouth water. I count twenty-three people of all ages. Some seem to know each other, while others are definitely alone.

I quickly go past the tables and into the kitchen, looking for some much-needed coffee. Finding Clare serving food, wearing her Red Sox t-shirt and my New York Yankees hat almost stops me dead in my tracks. Nothing better than a sexy, true-blue Yankee-Red Sox fan, especially this far from either the Bronx or Beantown. She has got to be the most beautiful woman I have ever seen. With a mug of hot, strong coffee in one hand and an empty plate in the other, I sidle up behind her.

"Excuse me, Sister Clare," I say plaintively. "Can I please have a little breakfast?"

"Sorry, sir, this breakfast is only for mission members," says Clare in an authoritative tone. "You are welcome to take the bus fifteen miles into town for your breakfast. Don't forget to leave two dollars for the coffee." Turning to give me a little smirk, she continues serving the members.

As I sip my coffee, Father Ed tells me that he drives into town every morning to pick up a small group, feeds them and then conducts a quick mass. He says the bus will usually make two more trips back into town, one mid-morning and the other late in the afternoon. The one in the morning is for those who have some place they need to be. The trip in the afternoon is for those who have no place to go and enjoy working around the mission. "That's our membership," says Father Ed proudly. "We're blessed to be able to help those in need."

Clare returns with a full plate of food and hands it to me. "Thank you, Sister Clare – I mean Clare, or shall I call you Miss Atwater? By the way, that Yankee cap looks really good on you."

I find a seat next to an elderly man who speaks English just about as well as I speak Spanish. We hit it off since we're both talkative, though neither of us exactly knows what we're saying to each other. I talk sports, politics and American history. He spends most of his time talking about a woman he met in California back in 1955 on a family vacation. I don't need to understand Spanish or his broken English to know what he's saying – his hands and facial expressions tell most of the story. Finally, as our conversation slows down to basic head-nodding, I realize that a tall, middle-aged woman across the table a few seats down keeps staring at me. It feels a bit uncomfortable until she finally asks me a question in her broken English.

"Excuse me, sir, are you – no, *do* you know a man by the name of Diego Hugo?" she asks me, sizing me up with one eye closed. "He familiar – *perdón*, he looks like you."

"No, I don't know anyone by the name of Diego Hugo," I tell her. "I arrived in Mexico City yesterday from the United States. Clare gave me a ride from the airport here to Holy Spirit Mission."

She continues to look at me with great suspicion as I finish my conversation with my elderly neighbor. Feeling a little uneasy, I finally excuse myself and head to the kitchen for a refill on the coffee.

"I think she likes you," Clare says in a flirtatious voice. "It sounds to me like a pick-up line I've heard in bars. Listen, Joe, you don't have the time right now to date the local women – or their daughters. I need you focused, water boy."

"Clare, that woman's dead serious thinking I'm someone else. She studied my every move while I was talking to the gentleman next to me. It was kind of creepy."

"Oh, please. Do you know how many times I've gotten that line in the past?" says Clare. "Hey, you look like someone I know. Did we go to high school together? Did you use to hang around with my sister?"

"That's because you're beautiful and guys will say anything to try and meet you. I'm sure they're crushed once they find out that Sister Clare has to be back at the convent by nine o'clock."

Clare takes off my Yankee hat and throws it at me, grinning. I wonder what would have happened if she was wearing my Yankee t-shirt.

"I'll pick you up out front at nine," says Clare. "Don't be late – or you'll be forced to wear my Red Sox hat for the entire day. And Joe, we won't have room for your new girlfriend."

She walks away, then stops, turns in my direction and stares at me for a few seconds before speaking. "You know something? Maybe she wasn't trying to pick you up after all. I think she may be on to something. You *do* look a little like Diego. See you at nine, water boy."

Watching Clare leave the kitchen, I notice a large nail hammered into the whitewashed stucco above the cast iron stove. You can clearly see that something was hanging on that nail not all that long ago; the soot coming off the stove has yet to darken the white paint where the object once hung. And from the shape of the whiter patch, there is no doubt in my mind that the object that once hung on that nail was delivered to my mother's apartment in DC several days ago. I can now tell Mom where the stone-encrusted cross came from.

With Clare gone, I'm left with several Spanish-speaking women cleaning up. Worried that I might be recruited to help, I go back out into the courtyard, where breakfast is over and Father Ed is cleaning off the tables and collecting the trash. Looking in my direction, he tosses me several green garbage bags, and I join him in the cleanup process, starting at the opposite end of the yard. Two little barefooted girls are chasing Fina as she scampers through the yard doing her part in cleaning up, looking for any scraps of food that might have hit the ground during breakfast.

Chapter 31

Aꜰᴛᴇʀ ʙʀᴇᴀᴋꜰᴀꜱᴛ, Father Ed shows me a room in the back of the mission, which the day before was probably a storage closet. The room has no windows, but there's a closed vent in the ceiling about eight feet off the ground. Standing on a chair I borrow from the hallway, I'm able to reach the vent, but can't open it. It's rusted shut – not even enough airflow to blow out a match. I figure this is *my* storage closet for now – I'll sleep outside in the courtyard at night. I unload the nonessentials out of my bag and onto a three-legged cot that's seen better days; the fourth leg is propping the door open. I keep the important stuff in the bag to take on the trip, in case we run into any trouble.

I make it out front with five minutes to spare and hear choral singing coming from inside the mission. Most likely, mass has begun as my watch beeps 9:00.

Standing there, I see an old blue Jeep CJ5 without its top barreling towards me, kicking up clouds of road dust, with an old David Bowie song blasting, reminding me "we can be heroes."

As the Jeep gets closer, it begins to slow and the Bowie tune fades out. Clare's behind the wheel, shifting down through the gears, and comes to a stop two feet from me. She's wearing jeans, a New England Patriots football t-shirt and, of course, her Boston Red Sox ball cap. I say good morning, buckle into my seat, unroll the map and pull my Yankees hat down tight my head. She leans over to my side and points to our first stop on the map, just as my phone begins to vibrate in my left front pants pocket. Clare smells like strawberries and I'm having trouble pulling my iPhone from my pocket.

Before I can look at it, Clare makes a quick u-turn, telling me she's forgotten something very important. The Jeep stops abruptly in front of the mission. She jumps out and goes through the main door, leaving it wide open, allowing me to hear some beautiful singing as I finally take the call.

"Hello, Mom!" I say, looking around at the Mexican landscape, thinking how different everything is here compared to DC where she's calling from. "How's everything back in the States?" The call from Mom is quick, with little news, governmental or personal. Natalie is still missing. Stella continues to search for her night and day through some of the poorest sections of Washington.

Clare's walking back to the Jeep with two steaming coffees in her hand as I finish up. "Yes, Mom, that's singing in the background. Okay, I'll call you later today. Love you. Please give my love to Stella. Bye." She hands one mug to me and we both strap ourselves into the high bucket seats of the CJ5.

As the Jeep begins to move out of the main drive, Clare lets out a powerful whistle that catches me off guard. Spilling half my coffee on the floor of the slow-moving vehicle, I feel like a fool. She gives me a little smirk, then turns to look behind us. I see the real reason why we went back to the mission. Running flat out, kicking up dust, comes Fina the wonder dog, closing in on us. At the last minute, Clare slows the Jeep just enough to allow her to jump into the back. I have the distinct feeling that this maneuver's been done many times in the past.

Fina quickly makes it up to the front and slobbers all over Clare's face. After about a minute of Clare laughing hysterically, the dog jumps into the back, sits up straight and tilts her head to the side. As the Jeep picks up speed, I look back to see Fina's ears flapping in the wind, and what appears to be a smile on her face.

"If you don't mind me asking, who was that on the phone?" asks Clare.

"My mother, calling from the US. She lives in Washington. She was just checking to make sure I made it down here okay. We also have a family friend who's been missing for a few days, and we're all quite concerned."

"Wow. I'm so sorry to hear that. I don't mean to pry, but what happened? Do you think they'll find her soon? Or him? I'm sorry, Joe," Clare back peddled. "You said missing and I immediately thought of poor Anna."

"That's okay. It's a strange situation. I'm hoping she'll turn up on her own, but I fear the authorities will find her in a bad way. I hope I'm wrong, but there's history of drug abuse that's affected her life greatly. Right now, her poor mother's knocking on the doors of crack houses all over DC searching for her daughter. Stella's my mother's best friend – and an ex-roller derby queen who don't take shit from nobody."

"It's so sad, what drugs can do to a person. An entire community, really," says Clare. "I was raised in central Connecticut, and I've seen many of my friends ruin their lives just to get buzzed. They abandoned their families, quit their jobs, in some cases did some truly unspeakable things to stay high. I had a good friend there who got so addicted to meth she just disappeared one day. She was found three months later by a private detective, living in a crack house, working as a prostitute. When they found her, most of her teeth had rotted out of her mouth, she was practically bald, and pregnant. And then, when the police arrived with her parents to take her home and try to get her some help, she jumped off the fifth-floor balcony of the house onto the pavement. As she lay dying, she asked the people around her if anyone had a joint or a little crack to share. Somehow a picture of that, her dying on the sidewalk, made it into the local newspaper. When I saw it, I couldn't recognize any of her features, even though she sat in front of me for three years in homeroom."

Our conversation dries up after that sober image. We ride in silence for the next ten miles or so, the only noise being the wind and Fina panting behind us. On this stretch of dirt-packed road, we don't see another human, animal or dwelling of any sort. The Jeep's traveling at just under fifty, more than fast enough for the road conditions. When Clare does decide to speak again, she tells me a little bit about who she is and where she came from.

"Clare Atwater," she says by way of preamble. "Born and raised in New Britain, Connecticut. Two brothers, one sister. About ten miles south of Hartford. It used to be to be known as the Hardware City of the World, we had so many factories making tools, hinges and ball bearings, but all that was long gone before I was born in New Britain General Hospital on February 25, 1984."

She attended the local high school and was accepted into the nursing program at UConn. Her first job out of school was working at an inner-city hospital in Boston. "It introduced me to a world of sadness I'd never experienced," she told me. During her second summer at Boston Medical Center, she saw a posting on the cafeteria's bulletin board looking for volunteers to spend part of their summer in Mexico working with the poor. She thought it'd be good experience, so she talked her doctor boyfriend into joining her for the two-week program. They flew down to Mexico City as part of a group of 38.

When they got there, they broke up into six small groups destined for different locations. She and her boyfriend went to different villages, based on needs of the community. Sitting outside baggage claim, Clare and five others were waiting to be picked up for their ride out into the countryside, just like I had, when they all heard the popping and banging, then saw the big multicolored bus pull up to the curb. A big hulk of a guy jumped out of the vehicle, onto the sidewalk and saw the six of them reading the big black words painted on the side of the bus, Holy Spirit Mission. He walked over to them and said in perfect English, "Welcome to Mexico, my friends. I am Father Ed."

Clare goes on about the work they did while she was there, and how rewarding it was. She quickly fell in love with the people of Mexico and found their spirit contagious and inspiring. When the working vacation came to end, Clare decided to stay on at Holy Spirit till the end of the year, basically as a volunteer. That was close to two years ago and she never looked back. She does admit that her only real concern is living in an area with increasing drug violence, especially since the mission is located near several large Mexican families supposedly involved in drug trafficking.

With a shrug, she leaves it at that and we move on to something else.

Chapter 32

W E'RE ON OUR way to a small village outside the town of El Paraiso. It must be very small or newly established since I can't locate it on the map. Clare tells me that villages are often established after a company or industry moves into the area. Sometimes wealthy land-owners will even start up a community and name it after a saint or a relative, a son or daughter. Not all of them thrive.

The village we're heading to, Clare tells me, was started by a small Chinese aggregate company that went from boom to bust in less than six months. Several hundred people moved from San Pedro for the promise of work and health benefits. The company employed close to a hundred at the beginning, but closed down quickly after a well-known family in the area put pressure on them to pay their workers a fair wage. There were threats, kidnappings. Two foreigners turned up dead in a roadside ditch across from the plant. When the company closed, most people left the village to find work elsewhere. About 35 families stayed in the area to farm or work for the local family.

"Clare, when you say local family, I have to ask – do you mean a local drug cartel? I know there are cartels in the area, and quite frankly when you talk about a large, family-run operation, that's one of the first things that comes to mind."

"Many of these families that I'm talking about are large landown-ers and farmers," Clare says, her tone protective. "They employ many of the locals and pay them a fair wage to work in the fields. There might be some illegal activity going on, but we have few problems with our neighbors."

Fina the wonder dog, who's been asleep on the back seat, wakes up as we noisily cross a rusting bridge over a shallow river about two hundred feet below us. Looking down, I see what looks like the carcass of an animal – or something – lying in the mud of the river bank near a cement culvert.

Clare makes an abrupt left turn off the main drag onto a long cement driveway that ends at an iron gate about twelve feet high. A sign on the gate says "Faltan Acres Granja Familiar." Beneath that, "Absolutamente Prohibido el Paso." My Spanish is good enough to know that we are prohibited from going any further. What really makes my heart skip a few beats is the image in the center of the sign. A white tiger with black stripes and black feet.

"Welcome to Missing Acres," says Clare, those beautiful blue eyes of hers staring in my direction. "I want to make a quick stop to let Señor Delgado, the owner, know what happened to Anna. You met one of the guys who work for Señor Delgado yesterday. The gentleman who met us in Puebla holding Anna in his arms. She lived and worked here at Missing Acres last year, during the flu outbreak."

"Okay," I say, "but I don't think we'll get past this locked gate, and I doubt there's a hole in the fence we can crawl through."

As she's about to respond, two large Hummers come down the driveway on the other side of the gate, moving at a high rate of speed. Clare doesn't flinch, so I figure we're probably okay and that she's done this before. Fina jumps out the back of the Jeep, chases a rabbit out of the scrub grass, then becomes sidetracked with a need to pee.

The two vehicles quickly turn in opposite directions, only to circle back stopping parallel to the gate. Two dark-skinned men carrying shoulder weapons get out of the back seat of Hummer *número uno*, with no action coming from Hummer *número dos*. The windows of the vehicles are heavily smoked, which makes it impossible to determine how many people are in both Hummers. I only know that we're out-manned and outgunned, since I haven't seen any weapons in the Jeep except for a rusted butter knife I found in the glove box while looking for a treat to please the wonder dog.

One of the men comes over to the gate and says "*hola*" to Clare. After the friendly greeting, my poor Spanish skills quickly come back to haunt me. The two men seem friendly enough towards Clare, but watch me with great suspicion as I climb out of the Jeep. I have a cramp in my left leg and very much need to walk around a bit, but when I start towards the gate, both gentlemen raise their weapons, point them in my direction, and in very loud, very clear English, tell me to turn around and stand in front of the Jeep. Clare protests, telling the men that I'm a friend, her "*amigo.*" Since they have all the firepower and I certainly want nothing to happen to Clare, I back up and lean against the Jeep, bending over to try and rub the cramp out of my leg. I'm glad those bastards didn't force me to grab the rusted butter knife from out of the glove box. God, I must get a real weapon!

"Joe," Clare shouts over to me, "I need to go down to the main house to see Señor Delgado. Can you wait here with the Jeep for a few minutes till I come back?"

"Sure, I'll stay out in the hot sun waiting for your return," I say sarcastically. "Take your time, have lunch, catch up on the local gossip. I'll play with Fina."

Clare says thanks, then sticks her tongue out at me. Whoa! How can it be that, in 48 hours, two different women who barely know me show me their tongues, both in entirely non-sexual contexts?

As the gate begins to open, Fina comes running towards me at full speed. At least the wonder dog will stick by me and keep me company. Wrong. She never slows down, just runs right past me, through the open gate and into Hummer number one. Clare looks back at me and smiles before getting into Hummer number two.

● ● ●

BOTH DRIVERS HIT THE gas and roll down the path towards a maze of white buildings. After losing sight of them, I pull a blanket and a bottle of water out of the back seat of the Jeep and sit on the ground under a nearby tree for shade. Checking through encoded text messages, I see one's from my mother, one's from Jim Carlone and one's from Mike. The message from my mother is coded as urgent. Considering the possibility of eavesdropping equipment here at Missing Acres, I decide to send her a text message of my own.

As I start to type, I notice the signal on my iPhone fluctuating up and down, rendering the device useless. I get up off the blanket and start walking in an effort to get a better signal, but it remains inconsistent. I wonder if my cell could be broken, or if the transmission is being jammed. I know I had a strong signal off the satellites just a mile down the road.

Looking over at the white tiger symbol on the front gate, I spot something in the sky coming towards me from inside Missing Acres; it slows down as it gets closer. As I walk away from the tree and out into the open for a better look, I can now see that the object is a white Hughes 500 helicopter. Two people are seated in front. It stops and hovers about twenty feet off the ground, just inside the gate. Clearly the passenger in the copilot seat is taking my picture, so I decide to continue the tradition and stick my tongue out at him. After they get what they came for, the Hughes 500 swings around 180 degrees and heads back into the compound.

Climbing back into the Jeep, I fire her up and move away from the fence perimeter, thinking that might improve my satellite signal. Parking near an uprooted tree that provides some relief from the sun, I begin reading the three text messages. Mike is in Mexico City and on his way. JL Carlone says we may be getting additional resources since the cartel angle continues to look the best. Mom sadly informs me that Natalie is dead. They found her decomposing body in a trash dumpster in a vacant lot adjacent to a suspected crack house, across the street from a Burger King in Wilmington.

Chapter 33

I WALK AROUND outside the Jeep in a daze after reading the message from my mother. I try to get her on the cell, but the signal is still too unstable and probably not secure. I figure it must be time to drive back over to the gate to pick up Clare and Fina so we can continue our trip. The sky begins to darken and I can see rain falling in the distance, which prompts me to put the top and doors on the CJ. While the portable top will provide cover from impending rain, we'll still get wet, between the gaps in the doors and a small rip in the canvas over our heads.

The two Hummers are inside the fence with their headlights on as I pull in. I park outside the gate, get out of the Jeep as the door on Hummer *número uno* opens and Fina comes bouncing out, followed by Clare. The passenger side door opens on *número duo* and an older man with stooped shoulders and a face hidden by a dark beard and long hair brings a pair of binoculars to his eyes and trains them on me. Even from where I'm standing, I can tell that the beard and hair aren't real. I give him a simple wave, then walk over to meet Clare and her canine companion.

As they walk through the gate, the skies open up and the rain starts falling in sheets. Clare and Fina jump in the passenger side and I run around to the driver's side, throwing myself into the seat as quickly as I can to get out of the rain. Clare's soaked, and Fina thinks this is the perfect time to shake herself off, then settles down for a nap, untroubled by droplets falling on her head. As I watch the two Hummers pull away, it's hard not to notice that Clare isn't wearing a bra, and that her nipples are fully erect against the wet New England Patriots t-shirt. It's enough to make me a Pats fan. However, while the size and shape of her breasts are perfect from my point of view, what I really can't take my eyes off is the outline of the cross beneath her shirt.

Catching me staring at her chest, Clare smiles before putting her hands over her breasts. Turning aside, she reaches into her bag behind her seat and pulls out a new, dry white t-shirt. The sun shower over, she opens her door, climbs out and strips off her wet shirt, wrings it out, and ties the arms of the shirt to the bent radio antenna so it'll dry. Then she turns towards me, with her shirt off and the silver cross hanging down between her breasts, which causes me to stutter, "Clare – Clare, can – can I ask you something? Where did you get that silver cross?"

Looking down at her naked chest, Clare seems mildly shocked by my question and quickly puts on her shirt. She probably thinks I'm gay or in a relationship or something.

"To be absolutely honest, Joe, that wasn't the question I – I was expecting," she responds, almost as flummoxed as I am. "I – I got it at a little family owned jewelry shop in Puebla. It was a gift from the owner, for returning his lost daughter one afternoon several months ago. The little girl got distracted walking back from church and got separated from her family. I found her crying, knocking on the door of the bus. She told me she lost her family and remembered the bus from one of our pizza and baseball days. I knew who she was and was able to walk her back to her family's home, above their small shop. The owner insisted that I take something, anything I want, so I chose this simple cross."

Moving closer, I ask if I can see it. As she looks me in the eyes, she takes it out of her shirt. I take the cross gently in my hands, turn it over and read the word on the back. Of course it says Puebla and is identical to the one I received in a white box several days ago in Key West.

My pulse begins to race as I again smell a hint of strawberries – and again notice her nipples now straining against the fabric of her dry shirt. Forgetting momentarily about the cross, I lean in and give her a brief kiss on the lips. Pulling back into my seat, I fumble through the right pocket of my jeans. Clare's puzzled look turns to one of amazement when I pull out the identical silver cross and show it to her.

"This cross appeared in my apartment in Key West three days ago, in a small box wrapped in plain brown paper – with just my name, nothing else. I saw your cross yesterday when you changed your shirt in the bus on the ride from Mexico City. I didn't say anything because I wasn't sure. It's probably just a coincidence," I say in a less than convincing tone.

"Before you try and kiss me again, I think there's more I need to know about you, Joseph Dustan. It's got to be more than coincidence. There's something you're not telling me."

We sit in silence for a few minutes staring straight ahead, the quiet only broken by Fina's snoring. Clare throws on a grey sweatshirt and brushes her hair into a ponytail. I look at her face and smile, then flinch as the vibration of my phone tells me I've just received a new text message. The tragic reality of Washington comes rushing back. Clare is now involved, and she deserves – no, as she put it herself, she *needs* to know more about me.

Chapter 34

As WE HEAD for El Paraiso, I tell Clare about being raised by a single mother, our lives in Maryland and Washington, my time in college and the military. I purposely hold back anything about my work as an undercover financial agent for the US government, but I do tell her that I'm presently in the Reserves and have an apartment in Key West.

I can tell based on Clare's questions that she is trying to work out a connection between our silver crosses. She repeats herself more than once, insisting it had to be more than just a coincidence that we both have the same cross, from the same small shop from Puebla – from a city the size of Puebla.

"The crosses couldn't have come from the same shop. It's just not possible," I tell her.

"I will prove to you that they came from the same place," Clare says. "We will go back to Puebla in a few days and pay a visit to that jewelry store. I know there's more to the story." I agree, then change the subject.

"So tell me, Clare, what's really going on at Missing Acres? The place is all fenced in with armed guards driving around in military-style vehicles."

"Joe, you have to understand that the owner, Señor Delgado, has been very good to Holy Spirit. For example, the farm manager, Tomás Amos, has a small convoy of trucks that pick up supplies in Mexico City every three weeks or so. On the way back to Missing Acres, one of the trucks stops at the mission to deliver food, clothes, cleaning supplies

- 130 -

and other items to us – at no charge. Since Anna used to work at the farm and was rescued from the kidnappers by the owner's employees, I thought I owed them a personal visit, to let them know what happened and to thank them again for their support."

"Do you find it strange that I was not invited to go in with you?" I ask.

"No, not really. They don't know you."

"Do you find it strange that his employees carry weapons?"

"No! Why? These are dangerous times. They're protecting their land and assets."

"You don't think it's weird that while you were down at the house, a helicopter came to the gate, hovered above me and took my picture?"

Clare thinks for a moment, turns to me and says, "Okay...okay, that *is* weird."

• • •

12:30 PM. A FEW MILES away from town, I notice that my phone now has a strong signal. Now I can call my mother to find out what happened to Natalie. As we arrive at the outskirts of the village, I tell Clare I need to stop and make a call to the States. She directs me to a small house off the beaten path where I park next to a very old and rusted '73 green Ford Grand Torino.

Climbing out of the Jeep to stretch my legs, I notice that all the factory seats inside the Ford are missing. They've been replaced with two short-legged wooden chairs in the front, screwed to the floor, and an old, faded yellow park bench type seat in the back. But the most amazing thing inside the Torino is a vintage Craig 8-track tape player attached to a metal bracket where the glove box once was, with Steve Miller's "Fly Like An Eagle" inserted into the deck. "Dance, Dance, Dance."

I turn around to show Clare my discovery, but she's already at the door, about to knock. She waves at me and I nod my head in return. Leaning against the back of the green Ford with no one in sight, I stop my not-ready-for-karaoke-night singing and make the call. My mother answers on the first ring.

"Hi, Mom," I say. "Mom, what happened to Nat?"

"Joseph, are you okay?" Always her first question when I'm away on assignment.

"Mom, I'm fine. You've gotta tell me what happened to Nat."

"Well, like I said, she was found murdered. In a dumpster, next to a crack house outside Wilmington. With a gunshot to the back of the head, and – and both her arms were broken," she says, then begins to cry. "I'm sorry, Joe, but I can't stop crying. Stella's holding up better than I am."

"Of course you're upset, Mom. It's all – so terrible," I say, trying to wrap my mind around what she's told me.

"It gets worse," Mom chokes. "Someone used a knife to remove a piece of flesh on the back of her neck. And – in the dumpster, next to her, was that bald man who pulled you out of the flipped FBI vehicle last Monday, Joseph, but they didn't know who it was right away. The body was – headless. And handcuffed to Natalie's. Oh, Joseph, I hate to have to tell you all this. And it just gets more terrible. The police recovered the head later, from a homeless person's cart, mixed in with a bunch of bottles and cans. Stella was right – he was Natalie's sponsor."

Completely at a loss for words and sliding down the Torino's trunk onto the ground, I tell my mother I'll have to call her back. Her crying now is pretty much out of control, so she has to hang up. I close my phone and close my eyes at the same time, stunned.

Sitting on the ground behind the Ford, I hear footsteps coming in my direction. Before I can turn to see who it is, Fina jumps into my lap and begins licking my face. Sensing my distress, Clare sits down beside me, gently wraps her fingers in mine and leans her head against my shoulder. I can smell the strawberries in her hair, and the foul odor of Fina's breath.

"Nat's dead, Clare," I say not really believing it. "My mother told me while you were inside Missing Acres. I just got more details about what they found. It's – it's horrible."

Clare doesn't say anything except that she's sorry, and wraps her arms around me as I begin to cry. Fina repositions herself on Clare's lap, probably hoping for someone to rub her ears. With everything that's gone wrong lately – and now the deaths of both Anna and Natalie in less than 24 hours, sitting on the ground with Clare's arms wrapped around me brings me a moment of peace for which I am grateful.

Chapter 35

W E DRIVE IN silence for a few miles into the center of a village that's adorned by a colorful tiled fountain that probably only sees water when it rains. Two old men sit on the edge of the fountain, talking passionately, waving their arms and slapping the old stones as they make their points.

I park the Jeep near a small pink stucco house with a caved-in roof. Clare seems surprised by its condition, and walks over to the men sitting by the fountain. They begin to converse in Spanish. I'm able to make out the words "storm," "fires," "black flying machine" and "missing *amigos*." The two men look over at me, squinting, and pepper Clare with questions. I'm sure they want to know who the gringo is and where he's from. I stop listening and my thoughts return to Natalie.

When I turn to check on Clare, she's on her way back to the Jeep, and I notice the two old men are gone. Fina begins barking as three people come walking down the dirt road towards the fountain. One of the three is a woman who recognizes Clare and Fina immediately, and tosses me a strange look. I walk over with Clare to meet them, pasting on a friendly smile, and pat Fina on the head.

Clare introduces me to the woman, whose name is Abby, and proceeds to tell her what happened to Anna. Abby, I learn, came here from Mexico City to visit her dying father. She has long, straight black hair that hides much of her face, which she constantly pushes from her face, looping the long strands behind her ears.

Abby's very thin, with blue veins visible under the tight skin of her arms and neck. She appears to be a once-beautiful woman who has experienced hard times in her life. Her face is severely weathered, her eyes lifeless, blood-shot and deeply sunken into their sockets. She shakes my hand, almost giving me the impression that she knows me from somewhere by the way she holds onto my arm.

Abby introduces one of the men as Peter, who works for a humanitarian organization located in Mexico City. He tells us that he traveled down with Abby to check on some of his relatives in the area. He looks to be in his late thirties, with an athletic build, a strong face and eye contact that could easily win a stare-down contest. A Los Angeles Dodgers ball cap covers his head of thick, dark curly hair, and he wears a faded black t-shirt that once had either a picture of Mickey or Mighty Mouse on the front.

I know the third man with an officer's issued 1911 pearl-handled Colt 45 visibly tucked into the front of his baggy blue khakis. It's nice that Mike Lenoce finally decided to show up. We try to act like we don't know each other, but don't seem to fool anybody, especially Clare; she gives me a suspicious look. That's probably one of the reasons Mike and I both flunked out of secret agent school many years ago.

Peter tells us that he's also down in the area meeting with several farmers to follow up on a new fertilizer. Mike comes up with some phony story about conducting research on the Redknee tarantula spider for some university in the States none of us ever heard of. Knowing Mike, I think he'd cry like a little girl if he ever actually saw one of these spiders.

After Mike finishes his bullshit spider story, Clare shoots me another look – clearly she doesn't "get" this guy. Mike's untucked Hawaiian shirt and camera swinging around his neck make him look more like a tourist than anything else; the bright orange price tag on the frame of his sunglasses only adds to the weak illusion.

We all agree to meet at 4:00 for an early dinner at a local place called Desperados. It's main claim to fame: it serves cold beer. Before we say our goodbyes, a chorus of screams erupts from the street behind us, a category of screams that sound familiar. As the noise gets closer, Mike's hand moves to the butt of his gun. When the dozen or so yelling children come running around the corner and grab Clare's hands, I swear I smell pizza in the air.

While Clare runs and plays with the children, and Peter and Abby sit on the edge of the fountain deep in their own conversation, I get a chance to speak to Mike alone.

"Hey, buddy," I laugh. "I was wondering when you were going to show up. And please, when you have more time, you really must fill me in on your spider research – and where you buy your undercover attire," I grin, peeling the orange tag off his sunglasses.

"Hey, thanks, Joe," he says. "I'm doing my best to try and fit in." I honestly can't tell if he's serious or not. "I got into Mexico City last night and hitched a ride down here with Peter and Abby this morning. I gotta tell you, Joe," he goes on, and now I do take him seriously, "Mexico's crawling with US security forces. The Mexican government's given us full access and we're taking every advantage of it. Based on your mother's information, we're now quite certain that the attacks on Washington were run by one or more of the drug cartels, either here or in South America – or both. I saw your text about Missing Acres. It's entirely possible that our elusive black helicopter's stationed there. NSA's still reviewing satellite data, trying to piece together the flying history on that bird."

Nodding, I put in my two cents. "Listen, when we got to Holy Spirit Mission last night, what greets *me* but an unmarked black Bell helicopter, at less than three hundred feet. Oh and by the way, I'm like the only person who notices. And you'll really appreciate this – during our visit to Missing Acres this morning, while I was waiting for Clare outside the gate, this small white Hughes 500 flies over to check me out, hovers at twenty feet and I see somebody in the passenger seat taking my picture."

"I hope you weren't wearing something that made you look fat," says Mike, his grin sarcastic. "The camera adds what, ten pounds?"

"I think it's more like twenty. Listen, Clare gave me a brief description of what the place looks like inside the perimeter. Sure sounds like there's enough room to hide an army of helicopters."

"We've been zeroing in on Missing Acres from space since your visit this morning," Mike tells me. "The report I saw less than an hour ago mentioned equipment being moved around the property, but nothing about helicopters, or any flying machines for that matter. The report said that people on the ground were moving vehicles into buildings and covering things with brown tarps. They knew enough to cover their faces so we couldn't ID them. They know we're looking."

"I'm not surprised, especially since they now have a picture of me. If the bad guys keep a good guys database, my picture's probably in it, wouldn't you think? But quick, Mike, tell me how my mom's doing, coping with Natalie's murder – you know, Stella's daughter?"

"I saw your mom yesterday afternoon. She seemed all right, considering. The local police are calling it a drug execution, but the chunk missing from the back of her neck has thrown everyone for a loop. No law agency in the country has ever reported mutilation like that in connection with a drug-related killing. What can I say? They're stumped." Mike scratched his head. "Speaking of stumps, the headless body is another whole story."

"Nice segue," I say grimly.

"Thanks. I thought so. Anyway, this guy pulls you out of a burning SUV. Stella thinks he's Natalie's NA sponsor from the rehab clinic. He's identified via security cameras as one of the men with Natalie as she walks out of the hospital. Less than 24 hours later, a homeless woman's trying to redeem the head at a shopping center bottle collection facility. The FBI and ATF are all over this case. One of the bosses at ATF thinks he remembers a case similar to this one several years ago. They have all available resources working the case. I'll tell you one thing, Joe – whoever murdered Natalie just better hope the cops catch him before Stella does. Her fans are out in droves, passing out flyers and searching for this son of a bitch."

"Mike, Nat had this tattoo of a white tiger on her neck. If you check, I'm sure you'll find the same tat on the guy who pulled me out of the burning SUV – the one handcuffed to Nat."

"You think there's a connection?" says Mike.

"Come on. What are the odds? Oh, and Missing Acres? The sign on the front gate? The name in big black letters – surrounding a picture of a tiger – a white one, with black stripes and black feet. Now, how's that for a coincidence?"

We both stand in silence, listening to Clare and the children play hide and seek around the deteriorating buildings in the square. Abby and Peter join Clare in searching for the kids, breaking out in hysterical laughter every time someone is found. The children start to quiet down when they hear rumbling that only gets louder as the ground begins to shake. Right away, I think earthquake because the sun is shining and there isn't a cloud in the sky.

The noise grows louder and Clare rushes the children towards the center of the square, away from buildings in case the quake should topple any remaining structures. As I feel the ground shake again, I notice Mike looking in my direction, confirming what I already suspected, based on past experience. I run over to Clare who's holding on to several of the smaller children and put an arm around her. She leans against me as we all look up into a cloudless blue sky.

Eight of the Navy's Boeing Super Hornet jets fly in formation at about five hundred feet, screaming over our heads at over four hundred miles an hour. For the few seconds the jets are directly above us, once again I feel my iPhone vibrate in my pocket. Clare looks at me, feeling the vibration and pulls away slightly. The vibrating stops just as the Super Hornets break into groups of two and head in the direction of Missing Acres.

It's nice to know that the tracking device in my phone's working, just in case I do need to call in the big guns. Now that our position's been verified, it's probably only a matter of minutes before one of the satellites positioned above us takes our picture. Mike must be thinking the same thing because he looks up in the sky with a big grin planted on his face. Clare sees me smile at Mike as he prepares to have his Kodak moment, gives me a soft elbow to my side and returns to her chasing after the children.

"Everyone look up in the sky and say cheese!'" Mike yells.

"Cheese," say Peter and Abby, looking up.

I now know who Peter and Abby are working for, and Clare is quickly figuring it out. The cat's emerging from the proverbial bag – and I have no intention of stopping it, unless it puts Clare in any danger.

Note to self: Mike really does need to attend undercover school.

Chapter 36

AFTER THE JETS are long gone and the children are back to their game of hide and seek, I go with Clare to visit people in the village. Peter and Abby head off in a different direction, saying they need to check on Abby's father. Mike disappears to look for the rare Redknee spider, which I have decided is code for finding a secure place to use his phone.

My meeting with the local water officials has been postponed so I decide to tag along with Clare on her medical visits. She provides some basic healthcare – taking temperatures, providing cream for rashes and on three subsequent stops, checking the health of pregnant women. After we complete our thirty-eighth visit, Clare and I find ourselves outside Desperados. 4:05 PM. Not bad.

Mike's already inside as Peter and Abby come walking out of a food storage building across the street. We go inside, grab a seat next to Mike and listen to some more of his bullshit about his quest for his elusive spider. Clare gives me that "how stupid do you think I am" look and breaks into Mike's lame story to ask a question.

"What exactly are the specific mating rituals of the Redknee spider, Mike?" she asks, her face a mask of pretty convincing curiosity. "I hear they're quite fascinating."

"If you could just hold that question for a second, Clare... 'Scuze me but I've gotta find the little boys' room," Mike says. "Be right back." He jumps out of his chair and heads for the bathroom, most probably not to take a leak, but to do a quick Google search on the Redknee tarantula.

Glancing around it would appear that Desperados was at one point somebody's home – it has two garage doors that open overhead when food and drink are available. The place is basically empty except for the five of us and three guys at the bar, a makeshift construction of plywood with red indoor-outdoor carpet screwed down on top. The heavily stained carpet must help to keep down the splinters and hide the spills at clean-up time. Every nook and cranny of this place is filled with religious statuary of the primitive, homegrown variety, from Jesus and Mary to the twelve apostles.

The guy behind the bar has a red bandana on his head and an eye patch over his right eye. He also has a large, handlebar mustache and a long scar running from his right eye down to under his chin. He keeps calling the three at the bar "mates" and "blokes," which I take to be a positive sign, English being my first and second language. He comes over to our table and says a very pleasant hello to Clare. He looks to be about fifty and a little on the soft side. I figure I can take him in a fight if he tries to steal my girl.

His name's Darnell, he tells those of us who don't know him that he came from Australia to live in Mexico over twenty years ago. An ex-army pilot, he forfeited his wings after losing the sight in one eye in a bar fight in New Zealand. The highly physical disagreement happened in a joint called Desperados.

He says that when he was a kid, his father worked for an international oil company, and the whole family lived outside Mexico City for about ten years. He always had fond memories of Mexico and when his wife died in a car accident in Wales, he sold everything and moved here. He tells us that he and his partner have other Desperados locations in Mexico City and Cancun. I imagine those are a bit more upscale, with less of the statuary and plywood.

From the corner of my eye I see a small color TV to the left of the bar, squatting between statues of the three wise men and The Three Stooges. The TV's tuned to CNN and I can barely read the words of the special report when someone at the bar yells "*a su vez lo*" – turn it up. Darnell takes a remote out of his pocket and quickly obliges his customer at the bar, increasing the volume. Filling the screen is the President of the United States, standing behind a podium, looking both pissed and determined.

"Good afternoon. Today I have authorized several military, non-lethal operations around the world. The decision was not an easy one, but I wanted to send a clear message to those who perpetrated the horrendous human tragedy that took place six days ago here in Washington, DC. While no one has yet to claim responsibility, our intelligence agencies are collecting information and it will only be a matter of time until we find those responsible and bring them to justice. I want to make it crystal clear to those countries that may be harboring these terrorists, that the United States will not be deterred by your country's borders and military. We are not looking to pick a fight, but we will not walk away if a fight is required. Thank you, and God bless."

Darnell turns down the TV as the three patrons at the bar begin to argue about what they just read scrolling in Spanish under the president, but it is now crystal clear to three of us sitting at our table the reason for the jet flyovers a couple of hours ago. The arguments at the bar peter out once Darnell changes the channel for their late afternoon viewing of Baywatch, and go to dead silence as an almost naked Pamela Anderson puts sunscreen on her female costar in a red one piece bathing suit.

Noticing that I'm staring at the television, Clare clears her throat to get my attention. I make eye contact with her, give her a quick smile and then return my focus to the TV.

"Never knew you were a Baywatch fan," Mike comments as the show cuts to commercials. "Now, *that's* a fan. His mouth's still hangin' open, even for the tequila ads." Just as he's labeling my behavior as "creepy," I rise from my chair as if in a trance and head for the bar. Clare calls my name and I turn briefly, but my march to the TV doesn't stop. As I approach the screen, the three bar patrons yell at me in both

Spanish and English to get the hell out of the way. The smallest of the three actually starts to get up and come towards me, but turns around and sits back down once he sees the look of determination on my face.

Darnell comes out of a side room to see what all the commotion's about. Still blocking the screen, I reach beyond it for the statue of the three wise men. I take it off the shelf and begin to lose my balance as the reality of what I'm looking at hits me between the eyes. Darnell steadies me as he pulls me from behind the bar, grabs a chair and helps me settle into it.

Staring blindly at the tiled floor, my head between my knees, in a bar outside El Paraiso, I hold a broken statue of the three wise men in my lap. The black wise man is missing a section of the hem of his blue robe. And a leg. And a foot.

Chapter 37

I NEED TO GET some fresh air, so I decide to go for a walk around the village. I get up and go out onto the street, the statue still in my hand. I've only gone a block when Clare comes running out from between two buildings yelling at me to wait up and jumps directly in front of me.

"What's going on, Joe? Tell me what the hell is happening," she cries. "You snatch a statue out of Desperados, and now you're out wandering the streets with it, looking like you lost your best friend. What on earth's the matter?"

"It's nothing, Clare," I shout a little too defensively. "I don't wanna talk about it."

"Okay, fine, just give me back the statue so I can return it. Please. Come back with me and have dinner with us," she pleads. "I won't ask any questions. I promise."

"Here," I say, handing her the statue, but not taking my eyes off it. "Take it back. I'll join you in a few minutes. I need to think. That's all. Let me pull myself together." I finally look up at her and see her concern. "Thanks, Clare."

I watch her walk away with the statue in her two hands, holding it tight to make sure she doesn't drop it. As she rounds the corner, Mike comes out of an alleyway looking equally confused. He walks me over behind the food storage building.

"Joe, what is going on with you?" says Mike. "You give me a hard time about the need to remain undercover. What you just did will be all over town in an hour. Tell me you're okay and I'll catch a ride back to

Mexico City with Abby and Peter. If there's a problem, I'll stay with you, but right now, we need to get out of here."

"Mike, I'm all right, but something really strange is going on and I can't talk about it right now," I whisper. "Look, I didn't think it has anything to do with our job down here, but too many things are starting to add up. Once I get some clarification, I'll let you know and we'll talk about it – I'll explain the whole thing. Right now I can't begin to. Let's just have dinner and get the hell outta here before it gets dark. Oh, but here's another odd thing: those three guys at the bar? They were saying something about the *policia* coming back again tonight, to round up more *gente sospechosa* – suspicious people. Whatever that means."

"I'll tell you what it means," says Mike. "The Mexican authorities are working with reward money provided by the US government, looking for information concerning the cartels. Abby heard that the last few nights people were handcuffed and taken to a farm out in the country for interrogation. Only Peter says it's no farm – he thinks it's an old prison. He also said what they're calling interrogation sounds more like torture. He swears US personnel are not involved."

We go back into Desperados and I apologize deeply to Darnell, Clare, Peter and Abby, making up some half-assed story about an old family heirloom that my great-grandparents brought with them from Europe, how that statue reminded me of them. Glancing over at the television, I see the three wise men are back on the cluttered shelf in their original position.

"Hey, mate," Darnell says congenially, "no major crime. Nothing like a little wacko behavior to break up the day, I always say. Hey, I'll talk to my business partner. It's his. Maybe he'd like you to have it." I smile. I don't trust myself to speak.

Mike, Abby and Peter are anxious to leave and decide to make a last quick stop to see Abby's father on the way out of town. She's been trying to convince him to come back with her to live in Mexico City. Looking at how frail she is, I wonder who'd be taking care of whom – or if the whole story is made up. Clare's hardly said a word or made eye contact with me since I got back to the table.

After we scarf down our meals, Clare goes with me to the bar to pay the bill. She tells Darnell to say hello to Diego for her, and that the food was great. I apologize again and ask him to keep me in mind if they ever do want to get rid of the three wise men statue. He again promises to mention it to his business partner, when he gets back in a few days. I shake Darnell's hand and leave a sizable tip, with more than enough left over to buy the three wise men at the bar their next round.

I'm halfway through the door, when Darnell says, "You know, mate, you kinda remind me of Diego."

I let the words fly over my head, until Clare whispers in my ear, "Diego Hugo. His partner. And that now makes three of us who think you look like him. I only wish he wasn't so ugly." She smiles and grabs my hand as we walk out into the street.

Chapter 38

I CLIMB BACK into the jeep and find Fina sound asleep on the floor, leaning against the red Coleman cooler. She opens one eye briefly, sees it's only me, and goes back to chasing cats in her dreams. Mike appears out of nowhere and hands me a folded newspaper, which I put under the driver's seat. "I'll catch up with you in a day or two," he says. He's reminding me to answer my phone when Abby and Peter pull up in an old green Toyota Land Cruiser. Peter's in the driver's seat. Abby leans out the window to tell me to be safe and get our butts out of town. Mike jumps in back and they all say goodbye.

After a few minutes, Clare appears, glad to see that I intend to drive, and climbs into the passenger seat. Fina, of course, comes instantly wide awake, jumps into Clare's lap and sets to licking her face. She mentions that the villagers are quite nervous about the possibility of another visit tonight by the Mexican police.

6:06 PM. I fire up the jeep, make a half circle around the fountain and start heading north on our way back to Holy Spirit Mission. The sky is clear and full of stars. A dimly lit quarter moon lies low in the eastern sky. Clare, perhaps purposely avoiding the episode at Desperados, takes our conversation in a different direction. "I know we've just met, Joe, but are you planning on telling me what you're really doing here in Mexico?" she asks, looking straight ahead. "You have an excellent reputation working with relief agencies throughout the Americas, but I get the feeling there's more to it than that. If you can't tell me now, that's all right, I guess. I just want to know what I'm getting myself into."

JAMES K. ZAVEZ

"Thanks for understanding. I just need a little more time to sort a few things out. I know that stunt I pulled with the statue seemed a little crazy."

"Ya think?" says Clare, rolling her eyes as she glances over at me.

"Maybe a little. But, for your information, I may have had a very good reason."

"Stealing a broken statue of the three wise men and walking through the streets reminded me of Steve Martin in the movie *The Jerk*," says Clare." Did you see that see movie?"

"Yes."

"Remember the part near the end when he's lost everything and he's walking down the street in a bathrobe with his pants down around his ankles, holding on to a chair?"

"Yeah, I remember."

"That was you today walking through the town with that statue in your hands. At least you kept your pants on. I'm happy about that."

She finally turns her head to look at me and bursts out laughing. It was my turn to look straight ahead and not play her little game. "You know something, Joe? *You* are a jerk." I can only ignore her for about thirty seconds. She puts her hand on my knee and I break out in laughter.

Chapter 39

Driving back to the mission through the quiet Mexican night with Clare and Fina seems oddly normal, like we've done it a hundred times before. My mind continues to race, thinking about statues with missing legs, silver crosses, and white tigers. What bothers me most is that I've put Clare in danger and she doesn't even know it. Worse yet, I don't know how to get us out of it.

Clare and Fina the wonder dog are both asleep when my phone begins to vibrate in my coat pocket. I read the scrambled numbers and know it's my mother. "Hi, Mom," I whisper, trying not to wake my crew. "How are you? How's Stella? Any more details on what happened to Nat?"

"Joseph," she says, still not quite herself, "Stella's trying to stay strong. There's still no update on what happened to Natalie. The police are calling it a random act relating to a neighborhood drug war. Over the last couple of days, Stella's either been at the police station or canvassing the neighborhood where Natalie's body was found. I went with her twice, but nobody seemed to know anything. What you find out quickly is that drug-related murders are quite common and sometimes even go unreported. Everyone we spoke to either knew of someone who'd been killed in a drug-related crime or had a family member who'd been caught in gang crossfire. It's all very sad."

"Mom, what about the flesh from the back of her neck, that white tiger tattoo she didn't even know about? That white tiger's shown up way too many times now to just be a simple coincidence. Don't you

- 149 -

think? Did you have a chance to look at the Missing Acres photos I sent? The tiger symbol's right in the middle of their damned sign."

"My team and a group from the CIA are looking into that," says Mom. "As soon as we know something, I'll certainly let you know. Did you hear about the president being on television today?"

"Yes, we were having lunch at a restaurant that had satellite TV. I saw it. The Navy did a flyover, too – I'm assuming due to my GPS signal."

"Jim told me that they used your GPS to coordinate satellites to get a closer look at Missing Acres. There's no doubt it's a place of interest. It could be a target, depending on what our agents on the ground find out. Please be careful, and please – stick to the plan. You and Mike are there to gather information and act only as back-up if needed. We've got a small army on the ground in Mexico working with local law enforcement to determine with certainty if a link exists between last week and the cartels."

"Mom, all I can say at this point is that my friend Clare speaks highly about the family that runs Missing Acres. They feed and employ the locals as well as give food and medical supplies to Holy Spirit. Then again, they do have a twelve–foot fence. With barbed wire on top. Oh, hey, did you have a chance to find out anything about the broken statue? I'm pretty sure I found out where it came from."

"You did? My friend at the Smithsonian said it's from a statue produced in the last forty-plus years. The paint was made by DuPont sometime after 1965. You think you know where it came from?"

I told her about dinner. "Look at the pictures I sent you, about an hour ago, and let me know what you think."

"Joseph, that's impossible! I'll look at them right away."

Fina's growing restless. I figure she needs a pit stop. I see a break in the road, go down a small dirt hill and park under a large tree.

"Bye, Mom, I'll talk to you later. I love you. Please, look at those photos."

"I love you too, Joseph. Be careful."

• • •

FINA'S A FEW YARDS away from the jeep investigating something in the bushes when Clare starts to wake up. "Are we at the mission already?" she asks sleepily.

"No, Fina was begging to go to the bathroom so I pulled over."

"Was I dreaming or were you talking to someone?"

"I was on the phone with my mother in Washington."

"Is everything okay?"

Hardly. "My mom's terribly upset over Nat's murder, in part because the police are ready to call it a drug-related killing and close the book on the case. Stella's in an uproar, trying to solve the case for them, which apparently is pissing off the police. Nat is – was – like a sister to me. We were pretty close over the last few years. I'll really miss her."

We decide to stretch our legs a bit since we still have a couple of hours to go. We're about ten miles from Missing Acres, and Clare says she'd be happy to ask if we could spend the night there. I figure she's busting my chops a little since I wasn't allowed on the property this morning. Fact: my chances of being invited are slim to none. If I ever get into Missing Acres, it isn't going to be through the front door with a personal invite.

Leaning on the hood of the jeep, I follow the beam of Clare's flashlight out into an open field, chasing Fina. I'm about to join them when I hear vehicles on the road coming our way at what sounds like a high rate of speed. Yelling to Clare to kill the flashlight and stay still, I hustle back to the driver's side and reach under the seat for the newspaper Mike gave me back in town. Inside, I find a fully loaded Glock 30 with an extra ten-round magazine. I put the clip in my jacket pocket and stick the gun in the back of my pants. I don't think the jeep can be seen from the road, but I still want to be careful.

As the noise grows louder, I walk up the small grade and hide in some stunted bushes closer to the road. I count four sets of headlights coming our way and hear the wonder dog bark down by the jeep. The four vehicles blow right by me doing at least seventy and never slow down. Two of the vehicles, I believe, are the Hummers that came out to meet us at the gate at Missing Acres earlier today. The other two are medium-sized refrigeration trucks. All I can say is, they must be very familiar with this stretch of highway. I can barely do fifty on these roads.

I fill Clare in on the details as the three of us get back into the jeep and pull back onto the road. Having forgotten to take the Glock out of my pant's waistband, it's now digging into my back every time we hit a bump.

Clare fills me in on her plans for tomorrow. She says she needs to administer flu shots at three local villages as well as at Missing Acres. While she's pulling out a map to highlight tomorrow's route, I see some red lights flashing about fifty yards off the road. I alert Clare, make a U-turn back towards those lights, pull over and park on the shoulder. Now that the Jeep's not moving, we can see that the flashing red lights are coming from what looks very much like Peter's Toyota Land Cruiser. I kill the engine and we both jump out and run.

The vehicle's lying on its roof. I yell for Mike, Abby and Peter. Getting no response, I peer into the Toyota with a flashlight. It's empty, except for what looks like medical supplies thrown all about the inside and something that might be blood covering the back seat. Clare catches up to me at the overturned vehicle and begins to scream for our three friends as she sets to searching the grounds with her flashlight.

All of a sudden we hear Fina barking, a few hundred feet from us in the dark. I pull the Glock from my waistband and begin walking towards the noise as Clare joins me. She arches an eyebrow when she sees the weapon. As we get closer to the barking, I can now see Fina sitting next to Peter, who is lying on his back on the ground, his face and hair covered in blood. His clothes are ripped and torn, as if he's been in a fight. He's still alive; his eyes are wide open and he's breathing heavily. I lean in close to hear what he's trying to say between gurgles. Clare runs back to the Jeep for her medical kit as Peter's shallow breath forms some distinguishable words.

"Ran off – road. Two – black vehicles," Peter says grasping for air. "Military – style."

"Peter, where are Abby and Mike?" I ask him anxiously.

Peter says "taken," then closes his eyes for good, at 7:08 PM.

Clare runs back, out of breath, but there's nothing she can do except say a prayer. I go over to the Land Cruiser and shine the flashlight inside to see if I can find any clues as to who did this and why. The two Hummers that passed us a while ago must be responsible. I don't want to jump to conclusions – but now I'm positive that those were the same two I saw at Missing Acres yesterday. I quickly scour the area for any signs of Abby and Mike, but find nothing. Having past experience with terrorist-style kidnapping, I think it may very well be time to call in the cavalry.

Clare comes back from the Jeep with a blanket, in which we wrap Peter's body for the trip back to the mission. As we fold the blanket over him, a business card falls out of his shirt pocket. I pick it up and hold it under the flashlight. It's says Desperados on the front, listing all three locations; on the back of the card is Darnell's name and phone number. Listed under his name is Diego Hugo, his business partner, and his phone number. Diego – the one who's into collecting statues. Something's telling me that this Diego Hugo fellow's involved in this somehow. I pocket the card. I figure I'll give him a call in the morning.

Clare and I gently place Peter's wrapped body behind the back seat on the floor, then I run back down to the Toyota with a large garbage bag and collect up all the personal belongings I can find. Using my cell, Clare calls Father Ed at the mission and explains what happened. He tells Clare that he'll get hold of the local authorities about the accident and abduction.

After a heated discussion, we decide not to wait for the police. I'm concerned it might take a few hours for them to get here and think it'd be best for us to avoid questioning by the authorities. Clare takes over the driving as I map out a detour around Missing Acres so we don't meet up with the two Hummers on the road. Turning to check on Peter, all I can see is Fina curled up against his wrapped body on the back floor.

As we speed through the night, I send a text to Carlone and my mother, giving them a brief description of what happened, telling them that Mike and Abby are missing and presumed kidnapped, that Abby's some sort of agent working for the US government, and that I believe Missing Acres is involved, and that we may need to raid that place soon.

Jim immediately texts back that they're trying to activate the emergency beacon in Mike's cell phone. He believes that both Abby and Peter are CIA. He'll get back to me ASAP about Missing Acres. Our top priority, he tells me, is to find Abby and Mike – alive. "But sit tight and don't do anything foolish," he adds. He knows I'm not a patient man, especially when it comes to close friends like Mike.

Our new route back to the mission takes us about thirty miles west of Missing Acres along one-lane back roads covered with natural vegetation that slows us down to under forty miles an hour. Clare, focused on the road, isn't saying much. I'm thinking about my next move.

9:04 PM. We arrive at the mission. Father Ed and another man are standing by the gate to the courtyard. The man he's with, dressed in casual business attire, has a graying moustache and short, dark graying hair that's combed straight back. The two come over to the jeep with flashlights in hand as we begin unloading our gear, deliberately not disturbing Peter's body wrapped in the blanket which now has blood stains soaking through it. Father Ed hugs Clare, thanks God we are safe and informs us that the authorities will be here in the morning. As I turn to say hello to the stranger, Father Ed jumps in with introductions.

"Joe, I'd like you to meet a friend of mine, Diego Hugo."

I figure now's not the time to quiz Diego Hugo about the three wise men. He must have already gotten a call from Darnell telling him about this crazy American trying to steal the statue. Who says I look like him? I don't see any resemblance. I say a quick hello and shake the man's hand.

Chapter 40

CLARE AND I UNPACK the Jeep as Father Ed says prayers over Peter's body. Señor Hugo lifts the deceased out of the back of the Jeep and places him gently on the ground. Once the last Hail Mary is complete and Father Ed sprinkles holy water, they carry him from the vehicle to the locked shed, the same small building where Anna's body rested only the day before.

Clare and I start up the small incline towards the mission's courtyard. Stopping halfway, I remove the Glock from my pants waistband and put it in my surf bag. Seeing the gun, Clare gives me a look that reminds me of any one of a hundred "Here's Lucy" episodes in which Lucy would have "some splaining to do." We certainly have a lot to talk about, especially with Señor Hugo showing up at the mission.

It's close to midnight, and the courtyard's full of people sleeping outside under the stars in several tight-knit groups. Clare had said something about flu shots in the morning. The night air is warm, filled with the sounds of snoring, coughing and a baby's crying as it drifts in through the open doors of Holy Spirit. Clare and I stand in the kitchen waiting for water to boil for some instant decaf coffee. Clare rubs against my arm as she searches for two clean mugs in an open cabinet near the stove. She hands me one with "MSNBC News" and "Morning Joe" imprinted on it. Clare's has a toll free number for missing and exploited children in big bold lettering. I keep checking my phone for any information on Mike and Abby's whereabouts. Nothing yet. We're making small talk when Father Ed and Señor Hugo come through the kitchen door.

"Okay, start from the beginning and tell us what happened," says Father Ed. "Diego has many connections in the area and may be able to help us."

Looking quickly at Clare, then over to Señor Hugo, I begin at the beginning, at least as far as they're concerned. Clare chimes in on details I miss. Father Ed agrees with my hypothesis that Missing Acres is somehow tied to the disappearance of Abby and Mike. He also again reminds us that the authorities will be here in the morning to talk to us about what's happened. I make a mental note to make sure I'm gone before they get here.

Señor Hugo says he will make some calls right away, to find out if any of his contacts have heard anything or have any information. As he stands up to leave the room, my cell phone vibrates.

Excusing myself, I walk outside to answer my phone. It's both Jim Carlone and Mom calling from Andrews Air Force Base, letting me know that they're on their way down to our embassy in Mexico City with a small group of support personnel. Special Forces have already been deployed and are on the ground across Mexico, Jim tells me. He also says there's been increased activity at Missing Acres as well as at other known cartel locations throughout southeastern Mexico.

"Joe, we haven't been able to locate Mike via his GPS," he tells me, clearly frustrated. "Either it was broken in the crash, or someone destroyed it on purpose. We have no indication that Mike's at Missing Acres or anyplace else for that matter. I'm sorry, but I have to take a call from the president. I'll see you soon in Mexico. Stay safe and don't do anything crazy."

"Mom, what's your plan once you arrive in Mexico City?" I ask. "I feel like things are coming to a head – and getting dangerous."

"Joseph, we wanted to be closer to where Mike and Abby might be being held, so I decided to move my team to our Mexican Embassy. They have plenty of room for us, along with excellent technical facilities so we can continue to work the data."

"Have you found out anything more about the statue's leg?"

"No," my mother says with no hesitation.

"Have you ever heard of a man by the name of Diego Hugo, Mom?"

This time my mother does hesitate before answering. "No, Joseph, I –" The signal on my phone drops and the call is lost.

• • •

BACK IN THE KITCHEN Clare's sitting by herself at a small round table, staring into space. I come up behind her and lightly put my hands on her shoulders. At first she starts to pull away, but after a few seconds I feel her relax and push the back of her head gently into my chest. Clare's hands come up to meet mine and she pulls me closer. I reach down to hug her and find she's crying. I grab a chair, pull it up in front of her, take a seat and stroke her arms. Clare looks sad and tired.

"Joe, I'm scared," she whispers. "Something terrible's happening and I'm not sure what to do. I'm used to danger, but this is different. And all this, just since you arrived two days ago. You have to understand, this is my home." I start to say something, but she stops me. "Listen, I'm not stupid. I know evil things go on around here, but I've made a point of staying clear of all that. The Mission's a safe haven for all, but now it feels like a war's brewing with Missing Acres."

"Clare, relax," I say softly. "I know things have been crazy since you picked me up at the airport, and you're not the only one who's worried. Believe me, I have many more questions than answers. It's hard to comprehend that a man I met less than ten hours ago is dead and rolled up in a blanket lying in a storage shed. It's equally incomprehensible that Abby and Mike are missing – and that they might be prisoners at Missing Acres. But, come on, Clare, you saw the same stuff I did."

"Joe, look me in the eyes right now and tell me that today was the first time you've ever met Mike," Clare says, her voice stern. "You both seemed way too chummy to have just met. And please, Joe – don't lie to me."

"I'm sorry. I do know him, Clare. He's a close friend from back home. His wife has probably just gotten the news. God, she must be devastated. That's all I can say for now, Clare, except that I cannot – I *will* not leave Mexico without him."

Clare doesn't blink or say a word. I'm not sure if she's just too tired to ask more questions or if she just hates me and all my secrets. She pushes her chair across the floor and stands up looking in my direction. I'm pretending to stare into my empty coffee cup when she comes over and kisses me lightly on my unshaven cheek and leaves the room.

• • •

AFTER SITTING AND thinking for a good half hour, I get up, go over and open my surf bag and reach in for the Glock. I place it under my shirt, again in the small of my back. There's no sign of anyone as I wash up and brush my teeth in the large kitchen sink. Since I really don't have a room in the mission, I decide to sleep again in the courtyard along with everyone else. I find a place along the stone wall that's relatively wide open, with more than enough room for me to stretch out. I know that with Mike missing I won't be able to sleep, but I need to at least rest for a few hours. Sitting on the ground and looking out over the mounds of sleeping people, I finally begin to relax and plan my foray into Missing Acres.

As I lie down on my side and stare up at the sky, I hear a familiar voice whisper my name and feel a body lie down next to me. I recognize the strawberry scent and my whole body relaxes as a rough old green army blanket's been thrown over me. Within a few seconds I see my Glock dangling down in front of my face.

"Joe, if you want me to sleep next to you under the Mexican stars surrounded by over a hundred people, you need to put this somewhere else," Clare says, her voice sleepy. She punctuates her sentence with a long yawn. "I'm really sorry about what happened to Peter. And, Joe – we'll find Abby and Mike. Try to get some sleep."

I guess it's true that good things do happen in the midst of bad times. Just as I'm about drift off to sleep, I feel Fina step carefully over the both of us and sprawl out in front of me. The sweet scent of strawberries is quickly overpowered by wet dog smell.

Within a few minutes, I hear both Clare and the wonder dog fall into the rhythmic breathing patterns of sleep. I look up at the stars and wonder if Mike and Abby are also sleeping at this very moment.

Chapter 41

5:38 AM. THE MORNING comes quickly as the people sleeping in the courtyard begin to wake and attend to crying babies and hungry children. Clare and Fina are nowhere in sight. Maybe I just dreamt that Clare slept next to me last night, but the green army blanket and the scent of strawberries confirms her recent presence.

Getting up, I throw all my things, including the Glock, into my surf bag. My iPhone tells me that I have no messages as I walk into the kitchen to try and find a cup of coffee. The kitchen's filled with people cooking breakfast in large pots on both an old cast iron stove and in an adjacent fireplace. Señor Hugo's standing in front of the fireplace wearing a long green apron, stirring a pot with a large wooden paddle. He looks over at me and winks as I search the kitchen for coffee.

I spot Clare, this morning in jeans and a red button down sweater, standing in front of the cast iron stove, showing two youngsters how to flip pancakes without dropping them on the floor. The two little girls are mesmerized by Clare's expertise, and clap every time she flips one. She gives me a warm smile that almost forces me to go over to her and kiss her good morning. However, as I'm about to execute my plan, divine intervention takes hold of my arm and asks me to help set up the tables and chairs out in the courtyard. Father Ed can truly be persuasive when he uses his size as a point of negotiation.

We go out into the courtyard, pull tables and chairs from a large shed and set them up with assistance from many of the overnighters. With all the help, everything's ready and in place by 6:00. Even though

I'm in a rush, Father Ed persuades me to work at one of the serving tables with Señor Hugo and two beautiful Mexican sisters who live and work at the mission, Maria and Serena. These two sisters are both actually nuns – with husbands, brothers who farm over in the next village. At least, I think I have the story straight. Maybe they're married to God and the brothers are monks. All I know for sure is that they're both so nice to everyone, especially the very young and old.

When the crowds begin to thin out, Señor Hugo and the sisters send me back inside to get some coffee. In the kitchen, I find Clare scraping some leftover oatmeal out of a large stainless steel pot into an aluminum tray. She turns when I walk in, says hello and goes right back to work. With no one in sight I come up behind her, wrap my arms around her and kiss her on the left side of her neck. She lets out a small moan as she begins pushing her back into me.

As she turns completely around to face me, gunshots go off outside the mission, followed by frenzied yelling and screaming. I look for my bag on the floor of the kitchen, but it's nowhere to be seen. "My bag," I say. "It was right –"

Clare cuts in. "I locked it in my room – I didn't want any of the children finding the gun and possibly getting hurt," she explains quickly. We dash down the hall to her room, and find the door unlocked and wide open.

I go in slowly. I can see my bag stuffed under the bed, nearly hidden by three pillows. I pull it out and unzip it, quickly finding the loaded Glock. Grabbing the extra clip, I run back out to the courtyard and jump over the four-foot-high stone wall. Running along the outside edge of the building with Clare right behind me, we come up to the front of the mission and peek around the corner. There's a man lying on the ground holding his left foot above the ankle. Another man is running around him, waving a gun. There must be close to a hundred people, witnesses to this drama, most cheering for the man with the weapon.

Walking out into the open, my pistol pointing at the ground, I yell in English, "Drop the gun." The gunslinger seems to understand me and lowers the gun, but still holds onto it. He starts yelling at me in Spanish. The only words I can make out are "whore," "Carlos," "wife," "sleep," "kill," and maybe the slang for sex.

"*Caida de la pistola*," shouts Clare. "Drop the gun! *Es mas*. It's over."

The man lays the gun on the ground as I walk towards him. As I get closer, he begins to cry, then drops to his knees sobbing. A woman in the crowd comes over and holds him tight around his shoulders. I pick up the gun and stick it in my pants. Father Ed and Clare run over to the man squirming on the ground, holding his leg in pain. Señor Hugo calls out the names of four men who come running to help lift the man and bring him inside the mission. The crowd quickly thins out, and I'm left standing outside the front door with Señor Hugo.

"What just happened here?" I ask.

"The man with the gun suspected his wife of cheating on him last night with his best friend Carlos – the wounded man. As a result of his rage and poor aim, he shot him in the calf. What he just found out before he dropped the gun is that his wife, the supposed whore, had slept at his mother's home last night, in the next town over. I guess when he saw his mother and wife standing together over on the side, he had to believe it."

"Thanks for the explanation, Señor Hugo. By the way, your English is perfect."

"Joseph, please do me a favor and call me Diego. My English is good because I went to universities in America. And I lived in Australia for a while. That is where I met Darnell Houston, my business partner. Speaking of Darnell, I had a conversation with him last night concerning your missing friends. This is something we need to discuss, but not at this time. I also hear you have some interest in a broken statue?"

Walking to the parked multicolored bus, we see a tan Ford Econovan coming up the dirt driveway. Sadly, the unmarked van represents the first leg of Peter's final journey back home to family and friends. Señor Hugo looks me square in the eye and says sadly, "Peter was a good friend, even if he did work for the CIA."

Finding the Desperados business card in Peter's pocket after he died now makes some sense to me. I suspect they were friends. Peter's work here in Mexico obviously went beyond helping farmers grow more food, or for that matter Diego serving food at Desperados.

If the owners of Desperados knew that Peter was CIA, then I'm sure others knew as well. I also feel confident that Peter didn't die because of the accident – he was murdered by the thugs who drove his car off the road. They probably knew who he worked for, and he paid with his life. Maybe they weren't sure about Abby or Mike and decided to keep them alive.

Señor Hugo follows the Econovan around the back of the mission as I stand, out in the open, now with both a gun tucked in the back of my pants and one tucked in the front. The guns are bringing back some old memories – and are beginning to feel oddly comfortable. I know at this moment that the skills I used in the mountains of Afghanistan fighting the Taliban trumped anything I learned at Harvard Business School.

A feeling of acute déjà vu blows right through me, along with a sense of foolish machismo, as I see Clare waiting for me at the front of the building. Alone. This is going to be the moment I take Clare into my arms and, for the first time, kiss her solidly on the lips. My walk is steady with purpose, my ego inflated to match. She must notice my determination – and my guns sticking out of everywhere. Clare moves in very close to say something to me. This is it. This is our moment.

"Hey, water boy," she says in a sexy voice, "be careful with those guns before you blow your nuts off, or give people a real reason to call you a flaming asshole." She laughs so hard tears start rolling down her cheeks. I laugh with her while taking out both guns and placing them with exaggerated care on the ground. As I come up from the ground showing her I'm now empty-handed, I move in close, take her shoulders and kiss her gently on the lips. She pulls away for a split second, opens her eyes to look at me, then closes them and initiates an even more passionate kiss, the kind that includes open mouths and the swapping of spit.

After the second kiss, she starts to move away towards the front door of the mission. As I bend over to pick up the two weapons, Clare cups her hands around her mouth like a megaphone and yells back at me, "I hope I don't have to wait till the next time you have guns sticking out of your pants before you kiss me again!"

• • •

I WALK AROUND THE back of the mission in a bit of a daze, but I feel I should see if I can help by answering any questions for the folks who've come for Peter's body. However, the two men loading him into the van seem to know about Peter's employer; the questions they ask are few and very basic. Neither man solicits information about the accident, or asks if Peter was alone in the vehicle. They tell us that US government officials will "manage" his trip back to the States.

I wonder what Mike actually knew about Peter and Abby. Did he get caught up in a situation he knew little about? Were these two part-time CIA operatives, or simply informants? I hope to God we did our homework before we put Mike with these two.

Chapter 42

8:05 AM. In the courtyard, most of the Mission's adult overnight visitors are gone. A number of children are sitting on blankets in four different areas, learning how to read and write Spanish. Clare's nowhere to be found so I decide to try and call Jim and my mother to get updates; both are unavailable.

I feel I'm wasting time so I go into Clare's room, grab my bag from under the bed and throw it over my shoulder, then head back into the main house to find her. Walking down a long stone hallway, I come upon a pair of wide-open wooden doors. The smell of incense and burning wax invites me in, and becomes stronger as I stand inside the room and look around. It's the mission's chapel, with twelve rows of rough-cut wooden benches in perfect alignment facing the front alter. The sun's shining through its stained glass windows, and the flickering of over a dozen large yellow candles casts colorful shadows that dance throughout the room. In the last row of benches, I recognize the back of Señor Hugo's head bent down, his lips moving. If he hears me, he doesn't turn around.

Slipping out of the chapel, I'm heading to the main house when I hear an engine start up that can only belong to the mission's bus. Following the noise, I see the bus pull up to the front of the mission and stop. Clare jumps out and sees me walking briskly in her direction with my bag in tow. Fina leaps out of the bus and ignores me to chase a squirrel in the grass. Clare comes over to meet me with a questioning look on her face.

"Good morning, water boy," says Clare. "Where are you going?"

"I've been looking for you. I need to talk to you."

We go over to the bus, climb inside and sit down on the ends of the two front row benches, facing each other, knee to knee.

"Clare," I say in a near whisper, "I'm very anxious to find Abby and Mike. I need to borrow a vehicle. In all honesty – the first place I'm going is Missing Acres."

"And how do you plan to get through the front gate?"

"It's an hour drive from here. I'll have time to figure something out. You should know that Peter was CIA. More than likely, he was murdered – it wasn't an accident. I've also confirmed that Abby's CIA, and you've already figured out that Mike's not from some America university studying spiders."

"So who does that make you, Joe!" Clare shouts, tears welling up in her eyes. "Mike's no spider specialist, and you're more than just some damned water expert. That's it! I want the truth!"

I'm just about to respond when Señor Hugo comes onto the bus, a gun tucked into the front of his pants barely hidden under a grey Nike windbreaker. Taking the front seat, he turns and faces us. He's heard Clare's question.

"Joseph Dustan is a part-time DEA agent," Señor Hugo says. "He's here to find out if there is a link between the recent terrorist attack in Washington and the Mexican drug cartels. His associate Mike Lenoce is also with the DEA, and Abby works for the CIA. Both have been kidnapped – and are probably dead."

I feel Clare pull back from me after Señor Hugo's said his piece. What really hits me is that bullshit about Mike and Abby being dead. Who the hell is this guy and where's he getting his information? And where's my damned gun?

"Señor Hugo, I am in no position to confirm or deny what you've just said, and frankly, I really don't give a shit what you think. As I was just saying to Clare before you interrupted us, I need to borrow a vehicle to go look for Abby and Mike. So please do me a favor and let me finish our conversation. If you're still interested, you and I can talk later."

Señor Hugo stands up, nods and exits down the steps of the bus. I'm not sure what just happened, but it worked. I reach into my bag, pull out the Glock and tuck it in my pants under my shirt. By this time, Clare has moved a seat back from me with a bewildered look on her face.

"Clare, what Señor Hugo says is true. I do work part-time for the DEA. I'm down here to investigate a possible connection between the DC tragedy and the cartels, though truth be told, there's no solid connection that I'm aware of between the cartels and the attack in Washington. I did have a feeling that things would go downhill fast when that helicopter from Missing Acres came out to take pictures of me. I'm sure they ran it through their system and found out I work for the US government. How Señor Hugo knows who I am is beyond me at this point, but I plan to find out. But back to my first question. Can you help me get a vehicle?"

The inside of the bus goes eerily quiet, except for the sounds of Fina barking off in the distance, probably sitting outside the squirrel's hole expecting surrender. Clare looks at me with disdain and most likely feelings of betrayal. I have an idea that the only thing with wheels I'll be offered is an old yellow Columbia ten-speed bike that's been leaning against a tree since I got here. It's missing the handlebars and one wheel, which I guess technically makes it more of a unicycle.

I'm at work on Plan B when Clare leans over to me and says, "Joe, I can understand why you felt you couldn't tell me anything. It may have been a white lie to you, but it's still a big lie to me. The thing we had is over. Deception and relationships don't go together in my book. As for your request to borrow a vehicle to go in search of Abby and Mike, I'm truly sorry to say that we have none. Father Ed's taken the Jeep and as you know, I need the bus to get to the villages and give flu shots."

"Thanks for somewhat understanding," I say, "and I'm truly sorry for my deception. But, I do want you to know that there's no lying about the way I feel about you. I know I haven't known you very long or spent much time with you, but I do have strong feelings for you. I'll just leave it at that. I'm in the middle of a crisis. I need to find Abby and Mike, ASAP. I haven't heard anything from my counterparts and I've waited long enough."

I pick up my bag and walk down the stairs to see Señor Hugo standing at the rear of the bus talking on a cell phone. As I walk away from the bus, I hear its engine start up and move slowly away. Clare circles the lot and stops in front of the mission as the noisy engine puffs out black and blue smoke before it finally stalls.

· · ·

I FIGURE THE BEST thing for me to do is start walking and try to hitch a ride. I'm about a mile into my walk when I hear a very familiar sound behind me. I turn to see the mission's multicolored bus pull up beside me with the door open. Señor Hugo's in the driver's seat.

"It's a long walk to Missing Acres, and the locals don't trust Americans enough to give them a ride," Señor Hugo calls down to me. "Remember the Alamo! Jump in and we can talk on our way there."

"Get a move on, Joe! I have farm workers who need their flu shots," Clare yells from somewhere inside the bus.

I'm not sure what's stranger – getting a ride from someone who I suspect has ties to my father or a woman who told me less than an hour ago that our short relationship is over, but is still willing to put her life on the line to help me.

Señor Hugo smoothly shifts through all of the gears and the big ugly bus roars down the pot-holed, desolate road in excess of forty miles an hour. As I'm about to open my mouth and start discussing Plan B, my iPhone begins to vibrate. The secure text from Jim Carlone says that they are still unable to track the locator beacon in Mike's phone. He reconfirms that Peter and Abby are CIA. "Authorities stormed warehouse in Mexico City. Last known location of the black helicopter. Warehouse empty, no evidence. Meet at mission later to-day. Military getting ready to act in Columbia."

My Plan B's quickly becoming Plan C since we cannot determine Mike's location. Next stop, Missing Acres to give out flu shots – and learn anything I can thanks to Clare and Señor Hugo.

Chapter 43

AS WE MAKE our way to Missing Acres, we discuss different options to get me inside the perimeter and look around. According to Señor Hugo, the farm is over nine thousand acres and heavily patrolled 24/7 by highly trained and well armed security personnel. We all know that Clare and Señor Hugo will be allowed onto the property and that I will not. Clare's scheduled to be here today administering flu shots and Señor Hugo, a local businessman, has friends inside the farm. We finally decide that since Clare and the bus will get into Acres, that I should stay aboard and let Señor Hugo do all the talking.

I can't help but feel the tension between Clare and me, now that she knows more about my true intentions. She's pleasant enough, but speaks only when necessary. I'm sitting up front a few rows behind Señor Hugo, who reminds me to call him Diego. For whatever reason, I'm just not comfortable yet calling him by his first name. We try to have a conversation concerning the broken statue, but the bus noise is too loud, so I decide to wait for a more convenient opportunity.

About ten miles northwest of Missing Acres, we start to pick up hitchhikers along the road. Most of these folks are heading there for work since the rumor is they're hiring, though out of the twenty-seven people we pick up, the majority seem too old to work in the fields. Señor Hugo tells me that people who live beyond the local village are allowed to live at Missing Acres, or Acres, as he calls it, in dormitory housing while working there. Even with long days in the hot sun and back-breaking work, they're grateful for any opportunity to be employed.

11:27 AM. We pull up to the gate of Missing Acres. The bus is now over half full, and we are cleared to drive up to the main house with security vehicles in front and behind us. The main house is about a half mile from the gate via a narrow road bordered by thick rows of corn stalks that act as a natural fence. At the last crop row, our bus comes out into a large driveway with the main house immediately in view.

The white stucco, castle-like structure is surrounded by a small stream. A steel, one-lane bridge crosses over the water and ends in front of the building. The front door looks like solid oak that's been naturally weathered. The entire front of the house has only six windows, each at least twenty feet off the ground.

As we unload our passengers from the bus, yet another black Hummer starts across the bridge towards us. Flashing its lights and blasting its horn, it pulls in tightly in front of the bus, as if to prevent us from going anywhere. Four men dressed in military -uniforms jump out of the vehicle with automatic weapons pointed in our direction.

Clare and Señor Hugo immediately go over to them to try and calm them down. After a few minutes of shouting in Spanish, Clare asks everyone to line up in front of the bus for a quick inspection of legal papers and working permits.

As I come down the stairs, one of our hitchhikers begins to walk quickly behind the bus before breaking into a sprint heading for the one-lane bridge. I'm not sure if he thought he could hide in the fields, or make it back to the gate before someone caught up with him, but one of the men from the Hummer lifts his gun and is taking aim when Señor Hugo yells something to him in Spanish that causes the rifle to be lowered. It's at that moment I realize that this man doesn't just have friends here – he must have some connection and authority as well. Thank God he seems to be on our side and willing to help us.

Just as I'm lining up against the bus, another black Hummer comes out of nowhere and gives chase to the man running in the direction of the main gate. At the same time, the Hughes 500 that took pictures of me yesterday passes overhead, in hot pursuit of the running man, flying with its doors off and guns out. I have a feeling this situation won't have a happy ending after all.

Clare's walking with one of the men from the Hummer, trying to explain what we're doing here and why we picked up people along the way. As she's about to give up in frustration, Señor Hugo again steps in, speaking rapidly in Spanish. Trying to decipher what's said, the few words I can pick out are "sickness," "guns," "workers," "prevention" and "death." And two other words that really catch my attention: "Joseph" and "Dustan."

The guard walks quickly over to me and asks in broken English to see my papers. I reach into my pants pocket and pull out my passport and papers that allow me to work in Mexico for ninety days. As he reviews my paperwork, I can't help but think how hot he must be, dressed in black, with a black baseball cap pulled down over his short brown hair. The name of the farm is embroidered on the brim, with the white tiger embossed in the center. The man seems to be more than just a regular security guard. He's solidly built and has mannerisms a lot like mercenaries I've fought side-by-side with, over in the Middle East. He scours my documents, then pulls me out of the group while he makes a call on his cell phone. I can't hear what he's saying, but I can tell that the call's getting heated as the guard reads from my working papers.

When the call ends, another guard points his gun at me and tells me to move towards the parked Hummer. Leaning against the hood, I'm searched thoroughly by a third man while an assault weapon's pointed directly at me. When my pat-down's complete, I hear three quick gunshots emanating from the direction of the front gate.

As I'm being pushed into the back of the vehicle, the small helicopter appears again overhead and circles the bus once, before flying off towards the center of the compound. Sitting in the Hummer, I see Clare and Diego Hugo walking quickly in my direction.

"What's going on here?" Clare screams at the guards. "This man works with me and I need him released immediately. What the hell are you doing to him? I need to speak to your boss. I need to speak to Señor Amos, right away!" These are all valid concerns and great questions, but I doubt that answers will be forthcoming. A man who seems to be American and speaks good English pulls off his ball cap, tucks it under his left arm and walks over to talk with Clare.

"Move away from the truck," he says firmly. "This man has entered Mexico illegally. We are to detain him. Now, move away. Get back into the bus with Diego and you will be escorted to our medical building. If you do not follow my instructions, you will not be permitted on the property. Oh, and Sister Clare, Señor Amos is not here right now. Which makes me the person in charge. So shut your mouth and get moving."

Clare quickly reaches into the truck, touches my hand and whispers for me not to worry. I wink and tell her that once she's done administering the flu shots, I'd be more than ready to leave. Señor Hugo shoots me a look that tells me to be careful. As the two of them head back to the bus, an old red Dodge pickup pulls up next to the vehicle I'm sitting in. One of the guards points his gun at me in the back of the Hummer and tells me to get out and into the red truck.

While walking over to the pickup, I see the slumped body of the man who made a run for the front gate lying sprawled in the bed of the truck. From my vantage point, I can see that his head, blown away above his right eye, is dripping brain matter on the spare tire. Clare and Señor Hugo turn to watch me as I climb into the bed of the vehicle, sitting next to the body of a man who was killed moments ago. Clare's horrified at the sight. I give them a grim wave as a black Bell jet helicopter flies about thirty feet overhead, slowing dramatically as it makes its way somewhere within the compound.

As I'm mentally taking note of the general direction of the sound of the Bell's engines winding down off in the distance, I notice something shiny sticking out of the dead man's boot. Looking at the driver of the truck, I shift my weight noisily to see what it takes to get his attention. He barely moves, but does check his mirrors for my presence as we drive over the water, which to me now looks more like a moat stocked with alligators. As we hit a bump on the bridge, I fall over, grab the shiny object out of the boot and slip it between my right leg and the wall of the truck bed. The metal object turns out to be a Smith and Wesson six-shooter, fully loaded. While it's a good weapon to protect you from being robbed on the roadside, it's not so great going up against an army with automatic rifles.

The red Dodge pickup follows a fairly straight dirt road through the dense green fields. I have no phone, a gun with six bullets, and I'm riding in the back of a truck with a dead man. When we make a sharp turn, corn stalks beating the sides of the truck, I hold my breath and leap out. It's 12:02 PM.

Chapter 44

I'VE JUMPED OUT of lots of moving vehicles over the last ten years, including airplanes over Iraq and naval vessels in the Mediterranean. In my opinion a car or truck's still the most difficult, especially when you decide to do it at literally the last minute.

I considered it critically important to make sure that I landed behind the truck and on the road, so as not to leave one damaged stalk for someone to find. I've seen way too many of those movies in which an army quickly changes direction because some eagle-eyed private found a broken twig or a flattened blade of grass. The noise of the truck making its way on down the road tells me that my absence has yet to be noticed.

My immediate goal is to find the bus and retrieve my gun, the extra clip and my cell phone. I take off through the fields heading for a tall thicket of trees three hundred yards to the east. As I get about a hundred yards into my journey, I hear the motor of the red truck returning, getting louder off in the distance, and the engine of a helicopter being fired up somewhere near the main house. The troops have been alerted and are on the move, and are probably shutting down all possible exits.

I'm hustling as quickly as possible through the fields as the Hughes helicopter buzzes over me a few times, but is unable to track my movement. Reaching the protection of the tall trees, I come upon an old stone well that's located almost in the center. Tossing a rather large stone into it, I never hear it hit any water. I quickly climb up one of the larger trees and shimmy out on to a heavy branch, hoping it can support my weight.

Taking advantage of the good tree cover, I peer through the leaves in hopes of getting some idea where I am in relation to the main house, the perimeter, the gate and the mission bus. The main house compound is much larger than I'd expected, with covered walkways connecting it to other smaller buildings. I can see a grey hangar-type building behind the main house and can also see the black Bell helicopter being pushed into it by a small truck similar to those used to move airplanes onto taxiways.

Leaving the safety of the one branch, I move a little higher up the main trunk and try my weight on a thinner branch, only to have it give way. I manage to grab a thicker branch while almost losing my balance. From my new vantage point, I can now make out the bus parked outside an outbuilding with a large red cross over the doorway. It looks to be about a half a mile away from where I'm located and out in the open, which will give me ample opportunity to test my stealth skills, which are weak at best.

Starting my descent down the tree, I hear one gunshot quite close to my location, off to the west about a hundred yards. I freeze and wait for any other noise that might give me a clue if they're getting close or moving away. After about a minute, I'm back on the ground, listening again for any man-made noises. Just as I am about to move, I hear several voices and, looking above me, see and hear the helicopter now hovering above the trees. It seems that they've found my position, but are still unsure of my exact location. Best I can tell, no one's running towards me.

While I'm thinking I still have a chance to get away, bullets start to fly all around me. Shoot to kill must be the orders and if I don't move quickly, I'll be lying next to my friend in the back of the red pickup truck. I'm off in the opposite direction of the bullets, running through the fields, still trying not to disturb the stalks.

As careful as I am, I run right into a woman and knock her to the ground. She never makes a noise. I come back around and grab her right hand, trying to help her to her feet when the smell hits me like a ton of bricks. The silent woman is covered in mud and feces – and looks alarmingly familiar. I lay her gently on the ground and use my shirt to wipe her face the best I can as she begins to cry.

"Oh my God, Abby?" I say, "I'm so glad to see you. Are you hurt? Where's Mike?"

She makes noises, but nothing intelligible. Finally, she turns to me and opens her mouth. I look into her helpless eyes and sunken face and fall to my knees when I discover the reason she can't speak. Someone has cut out her tongue. Damn it, some inhumane monster cut out her tongue!

The shooting starts up again, forcing us to keep moving through the fields. At this point in the chase, I can't worry about knocking down stalks, since Abby and I are running side by side, cutting a path that the helicopter must find easy to follow as they are now shooting at us.

Bounding out of some tall grass, we fall into the deep muck of the river bank. Sprawling along the banks of the muddy water are alligators, close to fifty of them, all different shapes and sizes, watching us as we struggle to regain our footing and escape its sloppy hold.

The helicopter's coming straight at us, which I know won't give them a good shot. They'll need to circle around us for the shooter to get a better target. As they're about to fly over us at no more than twenty feet, I pull out the dead man's Smith and Wesson from my sock and get off two shots into the belly of the copter, right below the pilot. I cross my fingers and hope the helicopter wasn't modified with thick steel plates under the seats.

The chopper pulls up wildly and quickly spins out of control. The shooter, who hasn't anticipated the copter's quick, erratic movements, falls out of the open door into the river. One by one, the alligators along the bank start sliding into the murky water.

The Hughes 500 isn't going to fly far with a dead pilot at the controls. Within moments, it plummets into the fields a couple hundred yards from us, and bursts into flames. Abby turns to me with a quick smile and we're off again, heading towards the bus which we now see, moving away from the medical building at a high rate of speed. I pull Abby down to the ground and force her to look at me while I shout, "Where's Mike?" Immediately I feel like an ass. The woman can hear. She just can't speak. Trying to make herself understood, she comes out with sounds like "ell, el, kel." Finally giving up, she grabs a rock and writes in the dirt. "In the well." Next to that she draws a crude approximation of a well. Then she adds a pair of lines running into it.

"Mike's in the well? And there's some sort of tunnel?"

She nods an emphatic yes.

I can see the bus coming our way, but the road's on the other side of the river and we'll need to cross it. Having no choice, we jump in and swim for the other side, a mere twenty yards away. However, alligators that sat out the shooter's splash-down now show an interest in us. About half of them come sliding into the water in our direction. Boy, does a sight like that bring out the Olympic swimmer in both of us.

Abby and I scramble out on the other side near a fallen tree that gives us some much needed cover. As the bus gets closer, I jump out into the middle of the dirt road. Señor Hugo's at the wheel and hits the brakes the moment he sees me. I wave Abby over as the bus slows to a crawl, providing some additional cover from the main house as long as we keep moving alongside it. I can see Clare inside the bus, running to the front to open the door as the bus continues moving. Abby and I jump onto the bottom two stairs and I yell for Clare to close the door.

"Señor Hugo, listen to me," I say, panting, one hand on to the hand rail to balance myself, the other holding Abby upright. "Don't stop for any reason. Clare, find my surf bag and get a new shirt for Abby to wear. They've cut out her tongue. She can't speak. She needs medical attention right away!"

Clare runs up front with my bag and I ask her to open it quickly. Shielding Abby as best I can, I help her remove her blood soaked shirt. Just the act of removing her shirt is painful – cuts and bruises cover most of her chest and back. One of her nipples is blackened and charred, most likely the result of torture.

Clare gives her one of my Yankees t-shirts and helps her into it, and I ask Señor Hugo to lend her the dirty, old Nike hat he's wearing. Turning and reaching into my bag for a dry shirt, my cell phone, the gun and clip, I now notice that almost every seat on the bus is full. I put one of Clare's blankets around Abby's shoulders and walk her to a seat in the middle and settle her between two older women. Both of them look exhausted, their faces a study in blank stares – exactly what Abby needs right now.

We're getting close to the bridge and I need to get off. There's a building coming up on the right that looks like an old gas station, just before the bridge.

"Señor Hugo, slow the bus down so I can jump out at that filling station," I say.

"What are you talking about, Joe?" screams Clare. "You're not getting off!"

"Clare, I'm sorry, but I have to. Mike's here somewhere and I need to find him. Time's running out!"

"No, Joe! Please stay with us – stay with me."

"Clare, actually, I need for you to please get behind the wheel of the bus," says Señor Hugo in a quiet but determined voice, "so I can get off with Joe."

I give him a strange look as he brings the bus to a halt and quickly switches places with Clare, who is now crying openly. "I will explain later, but for now," he tells me, "I am getting off with you."

As the bus approaches the fueling area, I lean over, kiss Clare on the cheek and tell her I'll see her later. The door opens and Señor Hugo and I roll out onto the ground and hastily hide behind two large gas pumps as the two black Hummers come up behind the bus. Using the dead man's gun, I manage to shoot out one of the tires on the lead vehicle. The second one, right on its bumper, crashes into the back of the first. Our position blown, we need to move quickly, get inside the well and into the tunnel system.

Chapter 45

RUNNING BACK into the fields for cover, bullets whizzing over our heads, I can see the bus pass through the automatic gate and out onto the Mexican dirt road, heading north over the highway bridge towards the mission. They have been allowed to leave, which tells me that the people Missing Acres are after are still on the property.

I have no doubt that there are numerous security cameras in operation throughout the compound. For all I know they're watching us right now and setting a trap. Everything seems a little too quiet, so we decide to find a secure place in the field and formulate a plan. I try to use my cell phone but quickly find that my signal's being blocked. One of the many outbuildings scattered throughout Missing Acres must house some type of jamming device that renders communication devices useless.

• • •

2:08 PM. WE DECIDE TO use the remaining daylight to find the well.

Diego is relatively quiet as I go through a mental checklist, trying to determine our position in relation to the well. We hear numerous ground vehicles moving all around us, as well as a small Robertson R44 helicopter I can see buzzing overhead in a sweeping search pattern.

Diego and I are about to move away from the main house and head for the well when I feel the barrel of a gun pressed firmly into my back.

Turning around slowly, I see three men dressed in military garb, black masks covering their faces. Diego realizes I'm no longer behind him, and turns around to see the three men pointing automatic weapons at both of us.

There's no struggle or discussion as they march us out of the field towards one of the outbuildings behind the helicopter hangar. This structure is about twelve foot square and made of cement blocks, with a large grey door and no windows. It stands about ten feet high, and has a wooden roof covered by primarily broken asphalt shingles.

Diego handles most of the limited conversation in Spanish, but I'm fluent enough to know that we are about to be locked up in this building. Just before we step inside, additional men come over dressed like the rest, also with their faces covered. It's obvious to me that a few of our captors know Diego and seem to be apologizing to him. I have no doubt that if we decide to break out into a full run back to the fields, all guns will be aimed only at me.

As we approach the grey metal door, a strong odor of something dead causes my eyes to water. Leaning against the doorway, a short, skinny guy gives me a quick pat-down, but misses both the Glock and the six shooter in my boot. He does find my cell phone, but allows me to keep it. I guess he knows it's inoperable on the property so why bother.

A green Kawasaki ATV appears from the hangar, drives over to us and stops. An old, hunched over man with little hair and an unshaven face is barely able to lift two sets of chains out of the back and drop them on the ground. He nods at Diego, gets back into the ATV and disappears back inside the hangar.

Two of the masked men pick up the chains, walk over to us and begin fastening them around our ankles and wrists, then connect the ankle and wrist chains together with a three-foot steel cable. Based on my limited mobility, I decide it best to save my strength for later. Inside our twelve-by-twelve prison, one of the guards shoves me to the ground. Diego takes a seat on his own. The one thing that's entirely apparent is that these men are professionals and all business. Even though I shot down one of their helicopters and killed at least two of their counterparts, there seems to be no anger towards me – at least not yet. My guess is that someone must want us alive.

When the door's closed and locked behind us, the only light that penetrates the structure comes from a few small holes in the roof and cracks in the cement foundation. I walk around using the light from my Timex to see where the smell's coming from. In the corner, opposite the door, is a small pile that at first simply looks like pieces of wood and dirt. Upon closer inspection, however, I can make out two skeletons pushing through the decaying flesh of what look like the bodies of dead dogs. The two-foot-high stack of rotting corpses is so infested with maggots it looks like the pile is moving in the corner. Dog fighting's legal in Mexico. Something tells me these poor dogs are probably ones that lost.

Walking slowly back to the door, I see Diego sitting against the wall, his eyes closed. I have a few questions for him and, since we aren't going anywhere any time soon, now might be a good time to clarify a few things.

Chapter 46

5:03 PM. Any natural light we had is gone. Clare and Abby are probably back at Holy Spirit by now, assuming they didn't run into any further problems along the way. Diego is sitting in a corner, his eyes still closed, when we hear voices outside the door. He looks over at me and calmly says, "Shift change." The men outside the door are laughing; their cigarette smoke wafts in through the cracks in the walls. Their conversation ends quickly and footsteps are heard moving away from our cement prison.

"Diego, where do you know me from? Did we meet somewhere in Mexico while I was working on some water project? Did we meet in the States?"

"I really don't know what you mean by this. I have never met you, Joseph, not until a few days ago at the mission. Oh, and thanks for calling me Diego."

"When you got off the bus with me, risking your life, I figured it was time to call you by your first name. Look, something's going on here and I need you to tell me the truth, Diego," I say with exasperation. "Two days ago I was outside El Paraiso with Clare, Abby and Peter. We had lunch at Desperados and I spoke to your business partner, Darnell, who said you were at your restaurant near Cancun. The next morning, you're with Father Ed at Holy Spirit. Clare fills in some of the details and today we meet officially for the first time. But the truth is, I feel very strongly that we've met somewhere before." Having this conversation in the dark feels extremely awkward, but who knows when we might be interrupted.

"Less than a week ago, my mother received a box wrapped in plain brown paper with no information on it except for my name. We open the box and find what looks like a ceramic leg broken off a statue, as well as a large metal cross that has Holy Spirit Mission engraved on the back. Back at your restaurant, I see a statue of the three wise men on a shelf, among hundreds of other ceramic figures. It caught my eye because it was missing a leg. Once I got a good look at it, I was sure that the piece that showed up at my mother's apartment came from your statue. And I also believe that the cross once hung on the wall in the kitchen of the mission. Will you please tell me what the hell's going on? I want to know."

If Diego's surprised by my story, he certainly doesn't show it. I can hear him get up, stretch, and sit down again before he finally responds.

"Joe, I simply don't know what you're talking about," Diego says. "We have not met before, or if we did, I have absolutely no recollection of it. As far as the statue with the missing leg, I know exactly the piece you're talking about. As Darnell told you, I am a collector of religious statues. Most I have bought while traveling around Mexico. Many pieces have been given to me by people who know of my collection. Some even drop them off at the restaurant door when we're closed. I don't know where the statue of the three wise men came from, my friend, but I will certainly give it much thought."

I've been around enough to know that what he's telling me is one hundred percent bullshit. I think he has a good idea where the statue came from, and with any luck, I'll get to discuss it with him again some other time. Right now, getting out of this box and finding Mike are my top priorities.

I shine my watch's small light on my cellmate's face. "Okay, Diego, *mi amigo*, I'll accept your flimsy story for now, but I do have another question. What's your connection with Missing Acres? Obviously some of the guards know you quite well. They practically treat you as a friend. Most of them seem to have a certain level of respect for you. For all I know, they may even be afraid of you. They lock us in here and you fall asleep almost immediately and don't seem the least bit nervous. What's up with that?" Diego must be one hell of a poker player; his face barely reacts as I make this accusation. Instead of answering me, he turns and puts his right eye up to one of the cracks in the cement.

"Our guard is sound asleep in his chair outside the door," says Diego in a whisper. "The real security guards hate working at night. When the owner is away, they usually assign the job to one of the migrant workers. Many of these people work sixteen-hour days in the fields doing hard, manual labor, which almost guarantees they will fall asleep during their security detail. Unfortunately, if they are caught sleeping, they are punished."

"So tell me Diego, what *is* your connection to this place?"

For the first time, Diego finally appears uncomfortable. He looks around the room, then begins pacing by the door, glancing up at the ceiling from time to time. He bends down again, and again peers through the crack in the cement, then slowly pulls his head away. Then he turns to me and gives me a quick smile that borders on a smirk.

"Joe, we'll have time to talk later, I promise. For now, give me a boost."

I set my watch on the floor. It's feeble light gives us just enough illumination to work with. Even with the heavy chains around my wrist, I'm able to put my hands together and give Diego a lift up against the wall opposite the door. Reaching above his head, he removes one of the broken shingles from the roof. The weight of his wrist chains quickly tires his arms, and it takes six attempts before I see he's holding something in his left hand. I lower him back down and he shows me a set of keys. Quickly and quietly, he undoes his shackles, and then helps me remove mine.

"Joe," he whispers, "you are younger and stronger – and lighter than me. I will give you a boost back up to where I got the keys. You'll need to remove a few more of the shingles, then pull yourself up onto the roof. Stay away from the center, for it is very weak and lacks support. From the edge of the roof to the ground is less then twelve feet. You will need to jump. Quietly! Take these keys. You must unlock the door without waking the guard. With any luck, a friend of mine slipped something into his beer to help him sleep more soundly. Okay, maybe I do have a friend or two on the inside. Good luck!"

• • •

WITHIN TWO MINUTES, I'm up on the roof crawling along the edge looking for the best place to hit the ground. From up here it all looks the same – hard packed dirt. Finding another loose shingle, I manage to grab hold of one of the rafters and hang my body over the edge. I hit the ground with a soft thud, then check on the old security guard who's still snoring loudly.

I unlock the door as quietly as possible, but can't suppress the squeak of the door as Diego helps push it open from the inside. The sleepy guard opens his eyes, looks around – and goes right back to sleep. He never even notices that the door's slightly ajar – and that his two prisoners are now standing on the outside. I close the door and relock it. It's amazing how fresh the air is outside, after being locked up in that small room with those dead dogs for several hours.

As we're about to run back into the fields for cover, I grab Diego by the arm. "Diego, you seem to know this place quite well. Take your best guess and show me where you think they're holding Mike.

"I only know the basic layout, but I'll do my best. That I promise," he assures me. This time he grabs my arm and we're off running towards the hangar, using buildings and vehicles for cover.

Chapter 47

WHEN WE GET to the hangar, we find it unguarded. The black Bell helicopter is no longer inside. The area's stacked with 55-gallon drums of aviation fuel, along with an eighteen-wheel fuel tanker parked over to one side. The hangar also houses vehicles and agricultural equipment, including a half dozen large green John Deere tractors.

"The tunnels below the compound are used for moving equipment from building to building, in case of foul weather," Diego says. We both know these passageways are used for other things, like hiding things from satellites surveillance.

We sit on the ground underneath the fuel truck to get our bearings and plan our next move. According to Diego, there are several entrances into the tunnels, but we aren't near any of them. The closest entrance is in the main house, which is presently occupied by security personnel and therefore our last choice. We end up going with the tunnel entrance that's farthest from the main building.

Diego and I leave the hangar and start running along the side of a dirt road that will lead us to what Diego calls a communications hut, about a half mile away. Diego is in remarkably good shape. He looks like he could run a half marathon.

6:07 PM. A light rain begins to fall and we quicken our pace. As we approach the communications hut, I see a single yellow bulb shining down on two men sitting under a metal overhang outside playing cards. The way they're dressed, they look like farm hands impersonating security guards. Neither is wearing a mask.

Numerous air conditioning units sit on the roof of the building and two large generators are purring away in a smaller cement block building attached to the hut. One side of the generator building's open, which probably allows for good air circulation and easy access to conduct maintenance on the units.

Diego and I circle the building through the fields, finally taking cover behind a tan golf cart as the two men start shouting at each other, which I quickly realize they have to do to be heard over the noise of the generators. Figuring the ruckus will provide a distraction, we slowly crawl away from the cart and over to a row of blue drums marked "diesel."

As we're about to move closer to the hut, one of the generators begins sputtering and shutting down. A loud beeping noise and the flashing of red lights coming from the open-walled building means that one of the generators is running out of fuel and will need to be refilled.

Peering over the top of the diesel containers, I see the two men walking in our direction, one pushing a hand truck used for moving the large drums. Diego points out a security camera over the door of the communications hut that follows the men as they approach the line of blue drums. The rain begins falling harder and both men begin cursing in Spanish, then leave the hand truck fifty feet from the barrels and run back to the metal overhang. With their backs to us and the camera tracking their movements, we're able to run inside the generator room and over behind the unit that's still operating.

"Diego, do you have something sharp, like maybe a knife? We need to cause a problem for the generators, something that'll keep these guys busy so we can get inside the communications hut. Oh, and by the way, I think this building's generating some type of jamming signal that renders cell phones and GPS useless."

Diego grins and pulls a red Swiss Army knife from his pocket and hands it to me. It's the big version with all the cool accessories – screwdrivers, tweezers, the always handy cork screw. While I'm not planning to open wine anytime soon, I have a suspicion the corkscrew may come in handy. Diego tells me nobody ever wanted to mess with the Swiss because their enemies knew that each soldier had one of these knives on their person.

Using the smallest and sharpest blade I can find, I make a tiny slit in the gas line located far under the tank. Trying to find and repair it is guaranteed to drive these guys nuts. I repeat the process on the other generator. Once I make the cut in the line of the second unit and feel the cool liquid on my hand, we leave the open room and move back out into the rain.

"Joe," whispers Diego, "let's circle around the hut and come up behind the two men. We need to find a flashlight. Once the generators run out of diesel, we'll probably be in total darkness. It will make it that much harder for them to refill the tanks."

Just as Diego finishes his sentence, generator number two begins to run rough, accelerating up and down. Within thirty seconds it stops working altogether and the area's plunged into both darkness and silence, though we can hear plenty of Spanish expletives from outside the communications hut.

Just then, I trip over something on the ground and fall onto the table where the two guards had been sitting a few minutes earlier, knocking their cards all over the ground. If they've heard anything, they don't show it by reappearing with guns drawn. Now that I think of it, I never saw *any* weapons with them when they came out the first time to pick up the 55-gallon drum of diesel.

"Diego," I whisper, "I think the men left their guns behind. Keep your eyes open."

A few moments later, Diego says he's found a flashlight.

Crawling along the ground and searching for anything that looks like a weapon, I feel my cell phone vibrate in my pocket. The power outage must have temporarily shut down the jamming device. I pull the cell out of my pocket and begin downloading information as well as uploading my position.

Wrapped around the leg of the metal table, I find a leather holster with a handgun inside which I immediately confiscate. Diego and I slide along the ground and inside the unlocked door of the building.

The room's dark and because it has a dirt floor, the air smells dank and musty. We can hear electronic humming in the background. Looking around the room with my Timex light, I see a large plate of glass off to the side of us with dim red lights blinking behind it.

The silence is broken when one of the generators comes back on line, causing the plate of glass to vibrate. As it comes up to full speed, the lights in the room begin to get brighter, and red blinking lights now turn green. It's safe to assume that the communications jamming equipment's back on line. We douse our light.

Within a few minutes, we can see that the red and green lights are part of an elaborate computer hardware processing system, banked together in four rows ten feet deep. The glass wall is one side of a clean room housing the computer equipment. I can't help but think about how cool and, yes, clean the air must be in there.

Moving against the wall and away from the glass, we both hear the whine of a security camera sweeping the room looking for anomalies – and intruders. Just as it's about to point in our direction, the working generator begins to run rough again, causing the lights to blink wildly, then turn off completely as it shuts down for a second time. The security guys must have only partially filled the tanks and the cut fuel lines are bleeding the generators dry again.

The camera in the room is still operating, but now in complete darkness. Two green lights on top of the camera sweep over to the opposite side of the room from where we're hiding, then freeze in one position. My iPhone begins to buzz again as we crawl along the dirt floor to a small hallway behind the bank of computers that leads to a hole in the floor.

Chapter 48

Directly above the metal ladder that drops into the hole is a camera pointing down the hatch. Even with the building in total darkness, except for some minor emergency lighting and flashing red lights, the security camera should be able to at least pick up shadows. I point out to Diego that the camera has a blind spot directly behind it that could possibly hide two grown men. Even with the blind spot, we'll still need a brilliant idea to get us down the ladder without being picked up by any of the cameras.

"Joe," whispers Diego, "any minute now one of those generators is going to start running again and the lights will come back on. Let's at least get into the blind spot. Then I will tell you my plan."

We crawl quietly along the floor hugging the wall behind the camera. It's logical to think that we aren't being seen since the camera hasn't moved out of position. We reach the spot Diego had in mind for us.

"Joe," he says, "when the lights start coming back on, I want you to get yourself near the top rung of the ladder. When you see me reach up and shine my flashlight directly into the lens of the camera, you need to scramble down the ladder and into the tunnel as fast as you can. This should distract the people monitoring the cameras. With luck, they will turn away for a few seconds, allowing you enough time to get into the hole. If I think there's enough time, I will be right behind you. If not, I'll wait for the next opportunity."

"Great idea, Diego," I say. "Thanks. I'll wait for you in the tunnel."

Before I've barely finished the thought, the lights begin to flash back on and I'm onto the ladder. Diego stretches his arm up to the camera, positions the flashlight directly over the lens and hits the on switch. He says, "Go!" and I'm already halfway down the ladder before the lights stay on for good, radiating a beam of filtered light into the tunnel.

I hear Diego's voice from above, but I can't make out what he's saying, when the flashlight falls past me and onto the ground where I now stand. Moving a few steps into a tunnel, I test the flashlight against a mold-covered stone wall, and am happy to see that it still works.

Making use of the time till Diego can join me, I open my iPhone to read the latest two texts that await me. The first one's from Carlone, who says they're waiting for a helicopter to take them to Holy Spirit Mission. The second is from my mother and quite confusing. "Need to talk to you ASAP. I may have found out something about your father."

Somewhat stunned by my mother's message, I start moving back towards the shaft when I hear a single gunshot go off from above. Seconds later, a body falls through the hole and onto the dirt floor at my feet.

Chapter 49

SHUTTING OFF THE flashlight, I grab Diego's feet and hurriedly pull him away from the ladder and the spying eye of the camera. He fell about ten feet onto soft ground and seems to be all right.

"Diego, are you okay? What happened? I heard a gunshot."

"Somebody came through the door," says Diego hoarsely. "I saw his reflection in the clean-room glass. The camera turned in his direction. An English-sounding voice speaking in broken Spanish asked if anybody was in there. When the camera was pointing away from the ladder, I jumped down without touching any of the rungs, hoping not to make any noise. It felt like I fell about twenty feet. I may be a little sore, but I'll live."

"Are you sure you're all right, Diego? You took quite a fall."

"Yeah, Joe, I'm fine. I landed on my side. My ribs are a little tender, but I'm ready to get going. I think it could have been even thirty feet."

"Come on, Diego, thirty feet?" I joke with him. "Ten, maybe. Does that fancy knife of yours have a tape measure?"

He shoots me a look of disdain that in itself feels familiar. We move away from the ladder just as a bright light comes spilling through the hole and onto the ground where Diego was lying moments ago. From where I'm standing, I can see the upside down face of a man peering into the shaft, casting large shadows with his flashlight. After a few seconds, he gives up and the bright light from above is gone, soon followed by the slamming of a door. We've somehow managed to go undetected – so far.

We're now heading down a long, unlit cement-lined tunnel. After about three hundred yards, we come to a fork where tunnels branch off in opposite directions. Diego, who's in the lead, veers to the right, walking briskly toward a dim light ahead. As we get closer to it, we find a locked steel door on our left with a small window about three-quarters of the way up. No light comes from the window.

Using the flashlight to look through the glass, I see a room filled with drums of chemicals stacked on wooden pallets three high, up to a point about a foot from the ceiling. The labels are in both Spanish and English. Skulls and crossbones have been stenciled all over the drums in bright orange. The English markings read "AGRICULTURAL FERTILIZER." We both think it odd to find fertilizer stored below ground in such great quantities, considering the numerous out-buildings on the property that sit much closer to the fields.

The intel I read on the bombs that went off in Washington indicated that they were homemade, and that the main ingredient was ammonium nitrate, a chemical compound of nitrogen and calcium carbonate which is found in agricultural fertilizers.

As Diego and I walk another twenty yards, we come to an intersecting hallway that's at least fifty feet wide. This area contains several forklifts, industrial battery chargers, wash sinks and more pallets of fertilizer stacked to the ceiling. Down the hallway, we can hear the whine of an unseen camera, along with voices – including one that sounds familiar. It stops us dead in our tracks.

Not knowing where the camera is, we lie down along the wall and listen again for the source of the electronic buzzing noise. It's fairly dark but for a faint yellow light coming through an open door about fifty yards down the unlit corridor. Just as we are about to move down the hallway towards the voices, Diego touches my shoulder and points up to one of the garage-style doors off to the left of us. Above the door is a constant green light, mounted on top of a security camera that's slowly sweeping both hallways in a 180-degree arc. Knowing there's no avoiding the camera, we stand up, look directly into the lens and smile.

Just as I think we've won a temporary victory, a long, horrifying scream from the lit room down the hallway echoes through the tunnels. I know this scream, and it sends shudders through me, making me nauseous. Pulling the Glock from my boot and breaking into a sprint, I pray it's not too late.

Chapter 50

Even though I spent time in Special Forces and conducted several extractions in Afghanistan, North Korea and Iran, all that experience goes out the window at the sound of Clare screaming. Diego is somewhere behind me as I burst through the open door to see an older women with no teeth and a middle-aged, obese man tying Clare's arms to what looks like an old dentist chair.

Clare's limp body is strapped down. Several car batteries sit on the floor nearby, in a wooden box with jumper cables coming off it. Clare's sweater has been ripped open; the other ends of the cables are attached to a metal band strapped under her breasts.

I wait for no explanation. As the fat man and the toothless woman turn to me, I fire off two shots, hitting them both on the forehead, dropping each of them to the ground with their eyes still wide open.

Diego grabs a large pry bar from the ground and smashes the two security cameras to pieces as I gently remove the jumper cables and straps from Clare's body. She has a rapid, intermittent pulse, but I cannot revive her. I wipe some blood off her arms with my t-shirt and re-button her red sweater as best I can.

With alarms blaring in the background, Diego waves me into a small room off to the side. There's blood all over the walls and ceiling. Decaying body parts litter the floor beside a make-shift bed with springs and coils exposed. Only adding further horror to this room of horrors is the sight of Abby strapped down, naked, on her back in the middle of the bed. Her lying there, broken and battered, reminds me of a recurring nightmare I have, from my time in Pakistan, where I saw a woman get pushed and run over by a train. I was around long enough to see her body after the police managed to pull it free from the train's undercarriage. Poor Abby looks about the same. Most of the right side of her face is caved in, and both her legs and arms have been broken in too many places to count. She has a clear plastic tube coming out of her left arm on the underside of her wrist, carrying a green-yellowish liquid, mixed with Abby's blood, which drips out the other end and onto the stone floor. The puddle has a sweet smell, most likely ethylene glycol, one of the main ingredients in antifreeze. I can only hope she died long before they got to any of this shit.

I ask Diego to check on Clare while I cut the straps holding Abby to the bed frame and wrap her in a stained white blanket I find in a cabinet above a blood-spattered sink. I place her over my right shoulder and carry her into the main room where Clare's beginning to wake up. We have to get moving. Security knows our whereabouts and will find us shortly.

"Diego, we're basically trapped. I'm sure the way we came in must be heavily guarded," I say quickly. "Do you have any ideas?"

"I saw a blue print of the tunnel system in Tomás's office several months ago. I have little memory of it, but I believe most of the outbuildings are connected underground. We need to keep going forward until we find some stairs or some other way to get the hell out of here."

Clare's starting to come around, spitting out words that make no sense. She certainly recognizes us, but looks utterly distracted and confused. She starts to lift herself off the table, using the wall beside it for leverage. Her balance is off as she slips slowly back onto the table. I lay Abby's wrapped body down gently, go over and look into Clare's eyes.

"Can you hear me? Clare, can you hear me?"

She pulls away from me in fright and tries again to stand on her own. I reach down, slide one hand under her left elbow to help lift her and she begins to scream. This time she forms a pair of coherent sentences.

"What are you doing? Don't touch me!"

"It's okay, Clare. It's okay. I won't touch you, but we need to get out of here. Can you stand?"

She looks across the room and sees two bare, bloody feet sticking out of the blanket on the cold ground. Clare again uses the wall to balance herself, sliding her feet down till they reach the ground. She's standing tentatively as the lights throughout the room and hallway began to flicker. Thank God for small miracles. The two men above ground have yet to find the cuts I put in the gas lines of the generators.

Within a minute, the alarms go blessedly silent and the lights go off, pitching us into complete darkness except for our flashlight. Shining the light on Clare, I see she's standing away from the wall now, still keeping her balance but shaking dramatically. I follow her eyes down to the ground where she's staring at the vague shapes of the two monsters who'd been torturing her less than five minutes ago. She looks back over at me and manages a weak smile.

As I lift Abby's body over my shoulder, we hear men shouting in both English and Spanish that gets louder as they make their way in our direction. Diego leads the way as I take hold of Clare's hand. Her first steps are tentative, but pretty soon she's moving with a will. We pick up the pace considerably when we hear gunshots, and bullets whiz by us and ricochet off the cement walls.

Chapter 51

CLARE DROPS MY hand and begins running closely behind Diego. Abby and I aren't far behind them. We need to get some distance from our pursuers while the lights are still out. Diego has our only flashlight, which has grown noticeably dimmer as we come to an intersection.

We take a hard left into a section of tunnel to avoid the flying bullets. The cement floor here is wet and begins to slant downhill at about a thirty-degree angle. The further we go, the more slippery the floor gets. Small streams of water are now flowing under our feet. At the same time, we can see what we hope is moonlight in the distance. I can make out storm grates overhead. I realize we're in a large drainage pipe.

The floor dips suddenly and I lose my balance, falling hard to the ground. Looking ahead, I see the dim flashlight and two figures moving in the shadows that bounce off the walls. I still hear voices behind me and a few gunshots, but thankfully they seem to be coming from farther and farther away. My body's starting to ache as I regain my footing and move Abby's body to the other shoulder. The lights have begun blinking back on behind me when I feel a bullet ring by my right ear.

I pick up speed as I continue down the dark, sloping drainage shaft. I finally see Clare and Diego's silhouettes in the moonlight at the end of the tunnel, about twenty-five yards ahead of me. Stopping to shift Abby's body again, the two figures disappear – followed by Clare's screams. In moments I know why.

Slipping again in the muddy water, I begin sliding on my back down a steep decline, holding Abby's lifeless body cradled in my arms. Stars are in front of me as I plunge out of the drainage pipe and into the open air, freefalling into the darkness below.

Chapter 52

Within a few seconds, I hit the rushing water below, with gunshots and bullets flying all around me. The moonlight fades in and out as fast-moving clouds above shield its rays, but I can see the river open up in front of me. Abby is floating behind me as I hold on to her right hand, struggling against a strong current not to let go. Up ahead, I see the old highway bridge we drove over to get to Missing Acres and, to my great relief, two familiar figures standing on the river bank. As I get closer, Diego steps back into the water and pulls me to the bank, with Abby in tow. I'm finally able to stand in the water and catch my breath.

"Thanks, Diego." I can barely get the words out. "Is Clare all right?"

"She seems better, but she is still very shaky. I'm sure that long fall out of the drainpipe into the river didn't help. Her speech is slow and a little slurred. The good news is that she certainly found her voice before we hit the water. She has also been mumbling about the mission bus being at the top of the hill on the other side of the bridge."

Diego helps me carry Abby up the muddy bank of the river. I notice Clare looking up at a grove of trees on the opposite side, where lights can be seen reflecting off the ground. We agree that we must move quickly to prevent capture – and probable death.

"Clare," I whisper, "can you hear me?" She continues staring at the opposite bank. "Clare, where is the bus?"

She finally turns to face me with a trace of a smile. Her hair is stuck to one side of her face and her clothes are covered in mud. As she moves towards me, I notice she is limping. Looking down, I see that she's wearing only one shoe and on the wrong foot. Clare put her arms around me and places her lips near my ear to whisper, "Thanks." Knowing Clare is okay and hugging me helps me to get my second wind. It's 8:08 PM.

"The Hummers forced us off the road on – on the north side of the bridge," Clare whispers to me, slowly and with a slight stutter. "They emptied out the bus and lined us up against one side. Three people were – were shot dead. Everyone else ran into the woods as fast as they could. Abby and I were kicked to the ground. Our hands and feet were tied and sacks put over our heads. They started to rip off our clothes. I think they would have raped us, but a vehicle pulled up. We were forced into the trunk at gunpoint. I think that's when I lost my shoe."

Clare begins crying softly on my shoulder, exhausted at the effort of telling us even that much. My only wish at that very moment is to stop time and hold her, but a bullet bounces off the rock in front of us, bringing us crashing back to reality as the three of us hit the ground.

I turn to Diego. "The bus is on the north end of the bridge. We're on the south side. We have to cross the river, using the bridge for cover."

From where we're standing, the water doesn't look too deep. Wading across is our only option. The clouds begin to thicken, increasing the darkness, which is to our advantage. We can still hear gunshots off in the distance, but none of the bullets are hitting the water near us.

I tell Clare and Diego to start crossing, that I will meet them on the other side with Abby. Diego nods in agreement, takes Clare's arm and they begin moving across the river. Clare keeps turning to look back at me, until their shapes vanish in the darkness.

Sitting on the riverbank in several inches of mud, I decide to try and call in some help so the Holy Spirit bus can make it safely back to the mission. As I dig into my pants pocket for my phone, I see Abby's body peacefully floating down the river.

Chapter 53

I CAN'T ALLOW Abby's body to be lost somewhere in Mexico. She needs to get home so friends and family can mourn her death, have proper closure. It takes only a few minutes to catch up with her, but now I'm passing below the bridge and find myself caught again in strong currents. With the help of the faint moonlight, I see that the river gets very close to the opposite shore before turning sharply away in the wrong direction. It's my last chance.

Wrapping Abby's body under my left arm, I swim the best I can, using only my right arm and kicking frantically towards shore. While my swimming technique is certainly questionable, I finally make it to shallow water and stagger the last several yards to shore.

Still clutching her body, I fall face down into the pebble-strewn mud, nearly exhausted, where I lay until I feel someone tapping on my shoulder. "Joe, it's me," says Diego. "I'm surprised you made it. I saw you caught in the currents and lost you in the darkness. Clare is at the top of the ridge, waiting for us. I think the water woke her out of what looked to be a drug-induced stupor. She is now very angry and talking revenge. The good news is that the bus is right where she left it."

"Thanks, Diego," I say in a hoarse voice. "I owe you one. I need to call in reinforcements so we can all get out of here."

• • •

I'M HAPPY TO SEE that my iPhone is still working and has a strong signal, but my battery level is down almost two-thirds. Now out of jamming range, I get Jim Carlone on the phone in less than a minute. He's still at the Mexican Embassy with my mother, waiting for a US Army helicopter out of Mexico City.

Jim tells me that it looks like thirteen different drug cartels in Mexico, Central and South America are all tied into the terrorist action in DC. Battle plans are being drawn, and Missing Acres is definitely on the hit parade.

Still no word yet on Mike. I'm giving him an update on Abby, and he's responding when he stops talking in mid-sentence. He pauses, regains his voice, then patches me into someone at the Pentagon. Using my phone as a homing device, they get a fix on my location and tell me that help is on its way, without committing to any timeframe. I tell Jim and the person on the other end at the Pentagon that the multicolored bus will need cover to get safely back to the Holy Spirit Mission. They're both giving me a verbal thumbs up when I have to interrupt them.

"Jim, this place is beginning to crawl with security people," I tell him. "I see flashlights across the water. They're searching the woods and river banks."

"Joe, hold on. I have to take another quick call."

Carrying Abby on my left shoulder and hanging on to the phone in my right hand is quite taxing as I climb a small hill. It's so dark now that I can't see Diego in front of me, but I can hear his footsteps crushing down the small brush.

"Joe? Joe, are you there?"

"I'm here."

"I just got confirmation that the unmarked Bell left a private airport outside Mexico City several hours ago and is heading in your direction. We have an AWACS aircraft headed your way to track the helicopter and the bus."

"Thanks, Jim," I say, out of breath.

"Hang on. Your mother needs to speak to you. She says it's an emergency."

My phone begins beeping, letting me know the battery's getting ready to die. I'm hoping that my surf bag's still on the bus – it has a fully charged battery inside a hidden pocket.

"Joe, can you hear me?" Mom's voice comes through. "About your father – after you told me about the piece of broken statuary, I went home and went through my father's photos when he was working at the embassy in Mexico City. I remembered a photo of me standing in between my parents, holding their hands at a state dinner when the vice president came to visit. I found it. This was right after Christmas and, sure enough, the VP had his arm around my mother and was holding a wrapped box under his other arm. While we were changing places during the photo shoot, I accidentally bumped him and he dropped the box on the floor. I remember hearing something break, but I didn't find out what it was till the next day."

"My father was in his office with the VP when I came in to get a book from his library. They were both laughing at a statue sitting on my father's desk. When I went around the desk to see what was so funny, I saw a hot glue gun lying on a piece of cardboard. My dad saw my curiosity and turned the statue around to me so I could see what they were laughing about. It was a statue of the three wise men. The piece that broke off was a leg. We were laughing at the fact that either my dad or the VP glued the leg back on backwards. They left it that way. My father kept it on one of his filing cabinets, even after the holidays. He said it helped him laugh during difficult times."

"Okay, Mom," I say as I sit down on the ground to hear the rest. "Are you sure it's the same one?"

"Joseph, as you know, the night you were born, an explosion in the embassy parking lot killed your grandfather. Several days after his death, I was packing my things to go live with my Aunt Lillian in Maryland, and went into my father's office. People from the embassy had all his personal items packed to be shipped to my aunt's, until I had a place of my own. Don't forget honey, I was only sixteen and now had no living parents. Sitting in my father's old leather chair, I noticed that the statue of the three wise men had fallen behind the filing cabinet. I couldn't reach it, and I didn't have the strength to move the cabinet, so I just left it there. I remember looking down behind the wall of the cabinet and thinking of how the leg got glued on backwards. But, when I looked more closely at the statue, I could see the leg had broken off again, and I burst into –"

My phone dies and the noise of a helicopter off in the distance sets me running across the dirt road.

• • •

9:03 PM. I FIND THE BUS, Diego and Clare sitting inside. Clare quickly comes over to me with a clean white sheet for Abby. I wrap Abby's body, carry her back outside at Clare's suggestion and place her gently into the luggage compartment beneath the seats.

As we walk back up into the bus, gunshots erupt all around us, blowing out the back window. Clare throws herself to the floor and begins searching under the driver's seat for something. Sitting back up in the driver's seat, she inserts the screwdriver into the ignition and fires up the engine. Within seconds, the bus lurches forward, out of the ditch and onto the main road, with Clare grinding all the gears in the process.

Chapter 54

THE BARRAGE OF bullets keeps coming as the bus rolls along at close to seventy miles an hour, swerving all over the road in an effort to avoid the craterous potholes. Sometimes the gunshots let up behind us, but we know it's only a matter of time before they catch us.

Running to the back of the bus, I find my surf bag under one of the seats covered in shards of glass. As I crawl down the center aisle on my hands and knees towards the front, bright lights from behind suddenly illuminate the inside of the bus. A new round of bullets pierce and tear the rear seats off the floor. Lying on the floor about three rows from the front checking my Glock, I see that Diego has somehow managed to take over the driving from Clare, though I can't imagine how. I can see Clare's reflection in the rearview mirror. She's lying on the floor near the stairs, loading shells into the sawed off double barrel shotgun. She has shards of glass in her hair and a few scratches across her left cheek.

It's painfully obvious that we are outgunned and outmanned. We have a very small chance of ever making it back to Holy Spirit unless we can somehow turn the tables. Diego screams for us to hold on tight. I grab Clare around the waist but forget to hold on to anything else as Diego takes a hard right off the main road.

Clare and I are thrown around as the left wheels of the bus come off the ground. As soon as all tires are back on the ground, we run to the back of the bus. The emergency door has been completely blown away. Within seconds, the back of the bus is again lit up by the lights of what I can now see are two vehicles following closely behind us. Clare and I take cover on the floor behind one of the broken seats. I shout instructions to her and she nods in agreement.

"Diego, Diego," I yell at the top of my lungs. "Stop the bus! Stop the damn bus!"

Diego slams on the brakes, causing the bus to fishtail slightly, but he's is able to keep us straight. The vehicles behind us react too slowly, however, and come up close behind the bus, putting them within firing range. Lying on our bellies, Clare takes out the lights of the truck on the right and I blow out the windshield and lights of the other.

"Diego," Clare screams, "Go! Go! Get us out of here!"

The bus lurches forward before I can grab anything to keep from sliding headfirst out the emergency door onto soft dirt. My head is spinning as I miraculously roll between both pursuing vehicles with barely a foot to spare, dropping my gun in the process. I don't think any of our pursuers can have seen me; no one slams on the brakes to come back. The headlights on the two SUVs are completely out, but I can still hear the roar of their engines. Scrambling along the ground on my knees searching for my gun, I hear a chopper pass overhead in the direction of Missing Acres. It must be the Bell coming home.

I find the gun in a mud puddle and move off to the side of the road near a small stand of trees in an open field. I can now see the bus coming back in my direction, the two vehicles following closely behind. Diego and Clare are searching for me, running in wide circles, as one of the rear tires of the bus blows out, sending it veering over the side of a small hill.

When the Hummers come by the trees I'm hiding behind, I unleash two quick shots, taking out the driver of one and a tire on the other. The vehicle with the shot driver goes over an embankment and is lost from sight. The SUV with the flat tire keeps rolling towards the stopped bus. Running as fast as I can to the bus, I hear two blasts from the shotgun and watch the second Hummer catch on fire and blow up.

When I reach the bus, I shout for Clare and Diego who both respond quickly to my voice. They're standing outside the bus, watching the SUV burn, looking like they've just about reached the ends of their ropes. Our only means of transportation back to the mission has a rear flat tire. Every window's been blown out except the windshield. Our ammunition consists of five shotgun shells and thirteen bullets for the Glock. Our flashlight is almost out, but at least I'm able to find a spare battery for my cell phone. It's 9:33 PM.

The good news is that we have a spare tire. Diego and I set to work changing the flat as Clare rummages through the inside of the bus looking for anything that could be useful if we're attacked again. Changing the tire on the bus is definitely a two-person job. As we struggle to loosen the lug nuts and lift the tire off, the bus teeters on an old car jack meant for a much smaller vehicle. Every time Clare, inside, moves near the back of the bus, the jack starts swaying seriously and one or the other of us yells at her to stay put in the front.

Clare gets off the bus and heads back to where we're working. "Stop yelling at me," she yells at us, slapping her hand on the side of the vehicle under the blown out windows. "Is my tire changed yet? Don't make me call the auto club." The levity feels good.

What a scene it must be, Diego and me wrestling this large, heavy tire that knocks me over when it finally comes off the axle. Diego's kind enough to break my fall as the blown tire rolls over my foot, grabbing my arm as we both fall into a puddle of mud and break out now into truly hysterical laughter. Clare runs over to us, fearing we're hurt, shining the flashlight in our faces, which only makes us laugh even harder.

"Are you guys okay? Is anyone hurt? What's so funny?" she wants to know, but when she gets a good look at us, she joins in laughing herself. The three of us are close to total exhaustion. I think we're beginning to crack.

"You two sure are an ugly pair," says Clare. "I'm walking back to Missing Acres. I'm gonna knock on the door and get some real men to help me change this tire."

She keeps the fading light on our faces as we start to get up. She goes from shaking her head at us to studying our faces with new interest. "You know something? You do look a little alike. The bone structure in your faces. And your eyes are almost identical. Maybe you *are* related."

Diego and I look at each other and bust out laughing all over again.

"So tell us, Diego, are we related?" I say, gasping. "Enquiring minds want to know."

Diego stares at me and is about to speak when we all hear a small pop. A whooshing sound passes a few feet over the top of the bus, followed by an explosion off in the woods. We hit the ground as the next pop and whoosh comes by us, with a fiery tail. That one smashes right into the front of the bus, which comes off the ground and flips on its side.

I grab my surf bag off the ground and the three of us go running into the woods as the third shot from a portable missile launcher hits the bus dead center, causing the gas tank to explode. The flames are too hot to even try and rescue Abby's remains from the luggage compartment. Her ashes will now become part of the Mexican landscape, a place she loved dearly.

"Sleep tight, Abby," I say quietly. My Timex beeps, telling me it's 11:00 PM.

Chapter 55

Hiding in the woods, away from the burning bus, we see three vehicles coming down the embankment. One SUV turns in toward the bus while the other two move in our direction, shining spotlights into the woods. The three of us find an old stone wall and hide behind it for protection.

We lack fire power – the shotgun was left on the bus and I only have thirteen bullets for the Glock. I barely have enough time to formulate a plan when all hell breaks loose. Bullets spatter the wall in front of us.

The only viable option I can think of is to run deep into the woods until we come to the river and follow it away from Missing Acres. Since I'm the one with the gun, I tell Clare and Diego to get moving and to meet me on the river bank north of the bridge. Clare gives me a full kiss on the lips before Diego drags her away into the woods. Watching them scramble down the hill, I can't understand how Clare can still smell like strawberries after all she's been through.

The three security vehicles meet up at the edge of the woods and drop off several men who walk with flashlights along the perimeter. I'm already on the move when I see two figures climb over the wall where we were hiding only moments ago. My plan is to circle back to the smoking bus to draw their attention away from Clare and Diego. It ends up working too well. As soon as I sprint out into the open, shots are fired and two vehicles start heading my way at high rates of speed.

Just when I think my luck is about to run out, I hear a faint but familiar sound overhead. Lying on the ground behind the blown-off bumper of the bus, I reach in my pocket, pull out my iPhone, push the on button and touch the GPS icon. The signal is fluctuating, but along with a steady green light which I hope means I have enough power to mark my location.

I hear a sharp pop and a whoosh that goes over my head and crashes into one of the SUVs, disintegrating it on impact. The bad guys aren't the only ones with rocket launchers. Thankful for the distraction, I jump up off the ground and fire three shots at one of my pursuers, an easy target as he stands out in the open watching the SUV burn. Falling behind the skeletal bus remains, I hear another pop and whoosh that blows the cab off the next SUV, sending it deep into the woods. Based on my experience in the Middle East, I know my friend in the sky will now be returning home. I hear the humming getting closer. I hope the camera is on as I lift my head towards the sky and do a quick military salute as the remote-controlled drone passes overhead at about fifty feet.

I end my show-boating by replacing the empty magazine with the fresh one – ten bullets left to take out the remaining SUV and occupants. Needing a place to hide, I slide myself into the remnants of the still burning bus frame lying on its side. The last black Hummer is circling the area, looking for anyone still standing. From what I can see, there's a driver and a single passenger in the rear seat of the vehicle. A third person is walking in my direction with an assault weapon. I lose him in the darkness.

If this is to be a fair fight, I'll need the element of surprise to take out the man walking toward the bus. However, the surprise is on me as the barrel of a gun is pressed into the back of my head. Someone's yelling in Spanish. I slowly and carefully raise my hands over my head.

Just as I'm about to drop my gun and turn around, an inverted bus seat breaks free from the metal structure and comes crashing down a few feet off to our right, catching us both off guard. Almost in unison, we jump to our left to get out of the way of falling debris. Knowing that this will be my only chance, I turn and fall to the ground and am able to get three shots off at the man behind me. My first two shots miss by a mile, but the third one catches him in the leg, and the force of it pushes him back into twisted metal still red from the heat. As he falls backwards, one of the supports from the seats comes straight through his back and out his chest. Death comes quickly as his face goes from a look of surprise to one of peace. I try reaching for his assault weapon, but it's buried under red hot debris.

I'm forced to crawl on the ground along the burning bus frame to get clear of the wreckage and out into the open. With seven bullets left and two enemies that I know of out there, it's time to finish the job. It's still relatively dark so I will again try for the element of surprise. Climbing under one of the burned-out bench seats, I wait as the Hummer moves in closer to my position. I am thankful that the doors have been removed, allowing me to see that both occupants are still aboard. Jumping out of my hiding place, I run full speed across ten feet of open ground towards the vehicle with the Glock in my right hand.

Leaping up onto the running board, I shoot the rear passenger through the left side of the head and pull the driver out of his seat and onto the ground, using his body to cushion our impact. As we tumble in the dirt, his legs get tangled in the undercarriage and he's dragged behind the Hummer as it careens down the embankment and into the river, stopping in the mud in about a foot of water. When I get to the truck, I find the man face down in the muddy water, dead.

I jump into the truck, throw it into reverse and am able to rock it out of the mud and up the embankment. Once back on solid ground, I push the dead guy out of the back seat, then take the time to drag his dead body into the woods and out of sight. Coming back by the bus, I notice that even with all the shooting and explosions, the luggage compartment is still closed and still intact. I find a pry bar on the rear floor of the Hummer and use it to force it open. I reach in, pull out Abby's body, still tightly wrapped in the white sheet, and gently place it in the back of the SUV, promising her that this time she will make it back home.

Driving along the deserted road in my newly acquired vehicle with my lights off, I notice two figures trying to hide at the last minute behind a pair of trees. I slow the vehicle to a stop.

"Anybody need a lift?" I call over to them. "This thing may not be good on gas, but it certainly has enough room for the two of you."

"Oh my God, Joe, is that you?" yells Clare.

Diego walks towards the idling Hummer. Clare runs up behind him and jumps into the front seat, slapping on her seatbelt. Diego falls into the back seat, sprawling across its entire length.

"I need a ride," Diego says, exhausted. "You both know I'm too old for this shit, right? Thanks for the ride, man. Thanks for the ride."

Clare looks over at me and says in a deep voice mimicking Diego's, "Yeah man, thanks for the ride. And Diego, you're right, you are too old." Her laughter ends in tears.

Both Diego and Clare are sound asleep before we even hit the end of the third mile. Its 3:03 in the morning and the full moon, now beaming without a cloud in the sky, illuminates the beautiful landscape. The Hummer has a full tank of gas, and we're traveling at over forty miles an hour. At this rate, I figure we should pull into Holy Spirit in time for breakfast. The occasional jarring from potholes in the road is not enough to wake my passengers. They sleep soundly as my thoughts turn to Mike. Finding him is now my top priority, no matter what it takes. I know he's a survivor. He'll find a way to make it. He knows I'm looking for him. Hang on, buddy. I'll find you.

• • •

THE ROAD BACK TO the mission is quiet, except for a few people out walking or already at work in the fields. The only other vehicle I see is a flatbed truck, overloaded with people of all ages, probably migrant workers heading out to an industrial farm for hard work and little pay.

Our newly acquired SUV is loaded with extras including multiple packs of Orbit gum, maps, five grenades, and a case of bottled water, two large bags of Lays Natural potato chips and a Fiona Apple CD. The strangest item I find in the glove compartment, however, is a set of four ticket stubs to a Washington Redskin's home game back in December. "Schnell" is handwritten on the back of one. Does Schnell play for the Redskins?

We pull up to the side entrance of the mission at 5:11 AM. I turn off the engine and climb quietly out of the vehicle, letting my two passengers sleep. Opening the back compartment door, I carefully lift Abby's wrapped body, carry her over to a small flower garden and lay her on the ground.

Father Ed looks up startled as he turns around to find me looking down, watching him pull weeds. He stands up, comes over to me and gives me a hug that literally takes my feet off the ground.

"Joe, I'm so glad you made it back in one piece," says Father Ed. "We've been worried about you. Is Clare okay? Where is she?"

"Clare's sleeping in a borrowed SUV parked out front. She seems all right, but she's gone through a rather traumatic event. She was drugged, maybe tortured, and practically killed at least a dozen times. Unfortunately, Abby *was* tortured and killed, back at Missing Acres. She's over there," I say, gesturing to her body.

Sighing deeply, Father Ed goes over to the body and kneels down heavily besides it, pulling out his beads and offering prayers. I walk back to the SUV and find that Clare has unbuckled herself from her seat and is just stepping out. She's steady on her feet, and her face lights up as I approach her. Throwing her arms around me, she holds on tight while whispering another thank you in my ear, only retreating when we hear excited voices coming up behind us. Turning around, I see my mom and Jim Carlone running towards us. As they both give me a hug, I can feel my body start shutting down from exhaustion.

"Joseph! You have no idea how happy I am to see you," cries my mother. "I've been stranded here, unable to get in contact with you, not knowing what happened. It wasn't until I received a photo of you saluting the drone they sent to help you that I knew you were still alive."

"We tried to get better air support for you at Missing Acres," Jim adds in frustration, "but as you know that didn't happen. The drone was the quickest and best option we had."

"Jim, have you heard anything about Mike," I ask anxiously. "I wasn't at Missing Acres long enough to know if he was still there. Before Abby was killed, she told me he was in the tunnels. The last time I saw him, he was with Abby and Peter, and now they're both dead."

"No word yet," Jim says, his voice cracking. "We're confident that he was at Missing Acres at one point, but we don't know his whereabouts at this time." Jim's choking up and my mother squeezes my hand tighter every time Mike's name is mentioned.

I reach behind me to draw Clare into the conversation. "Mom, Jim, I'd like you to meet Clare Atwater. I think you both know that she works here at the mission with Father Ed."

"Nice to meet you both," says Clare softly, her voice tearful. "Joe has certainly made things very exciting since I picked him up at the airport several days ago." My mother walks over to Clare and gives her a long hug, which causes them both to start crying openly.

As they finally break apart, I can hear Diego waking up in the back seat of the Hummer. He clears his throat a few times, then slowly climbs out of the vehicle and begins to stretch. We all turn to see this man, covered in mud and blood stains. I run over to him, telling him to sit down quickly.

"Diego, are you okay? You have blood all down the front of your shirt."

He looks down at himself with a worried look and runs his hands along his body, but finds nothing out of the ordinary. Looking into the backseat of the SUV, I see that blood has soaked into the fabric at some point, but clearly it isn't Diego's. Rewinding my brain back a few hours, I finally remember that I shot a guy in that backseat before jumping out with the driver.

"It's okay," I say. "It's not your blood. You're fine, Diego."

The five of us talk for a few minutes about what went on during the last twenty-four hours, but as I see that Clare is starting to shake again at the retelling, I change the subject as quickly I can. At the same time, it's obvious to me that my mother is in deep thought. Her eyes have glazed over, but she does her best not to block us out entirely.

Fina the wonder dog comes charging over and jumps up on Clare, almost knocking her over – the best medicine you could want. Clare kneels down and allows Fina to lick away all her tears. This is the first time I see her smile since getting back to the mission. Fina certainly has a way of bringing happiness to Clare. It must be that unconditional love thing, that ability animals have to break down barriers and allow us to feel good again.

My mother has mentally rejoined our conversation – the way you can tell is that her eyes are blinking more regularly and the corners of her mouth have begun to turn up. I've known this about her since childhood. She steps into the center of our small circle and reaches out for Diego's hand.

"Hello, Diego," she says.

"Hello, Caroline."

"It's been almost thirty years since I've seen or heard from you," my mom says, smiling. "I never knew what happened to you over all those years. Besides the blood on your shirt, you look well. The mustache and graying hair threw me a bit. The last time I saw you, I don't think you'd even started shaving."

"Caroline, the years have been very good to you. You are as beautiful today as when you were a young girl attending formal dinners at the Mexican Embassy. However, you are wrong about neither seeing or hearing from me over the past thirty years. I have attended conferences in Washington when I knew you were the keynote speaker. For a few years, when I lived in DC, we both shopped for our groceries at that same small store off of Groveland and Lincoln. For most of Joe's life you heard from me on a yearly basis. Right around his birthday."

Standing there in silence, I'm not sure what shocks me the most: the idea that I'd been fighting along side my father over the last twenty-four hours – or the recently replaced mission bell breaking from it's restraints and crashing through the roof of Holy Spirit.

Chapter 56

Tuesday, January 29, 2013 / 6:20 AM
Holy Spirit Mission

THE DAMAGE FROM the bell breaking loose isn't as bad as first feared. It's limited to a small section of roof and the inside wall of the bell tower. As a result, the kitchen pantry now has a skylight. The three brothers, *los tres amigos*, responsible for rebuilding the tower are already discussing how they will get the bell back up in place. They tell Clare "no worry," that the bell of Holy Spirit Mission will ring again *muy pronto*, very soon. Father Ed takes charge, shouting out orders in Spanish to anyone who will listen.

Walking into the courtyard, I see my mother and Diego talking alone under an old apple tree. The conversation looks serious, so I think it best to stay away. Finding a shady area near the courtyard wall, I set the alarm on my watch and lay down using my surf bag as a pillow. I hope my dreams take me off to find Mike, tell Clare how I feel – and give me the courage to speak to my father.

• • •

8:10 AM. I WAKE UP FEELING somewhat refreshed and ready to continue my search for Mike. I am pleasantly surprised to find Clare sitting next to me drinking a cup of coffee.

"Good morning," she says. "Did you sleep okay? I came looking for you an hour ago and found you here hugging your bag with a smile on your face. I hope she was worth it."

"No question. 'She' was you. I don't dream about just anybody, you know. I need a shower and something to eat. Is the kitchen in working order?"

"The roof and wall have been repaired temporarily and, believe it or not, the three *amigos* already have the bell back up in the tower," Clare reports. "And your mother wanted me to tell you that she and Mr. Carlone went back to Mexico City for an urgent meeting. They'll be back around four. She asks that you stay here till they get back. She said they hope to have more information concerning Mike's whereabouts, as well as an update on 'the operation,' whatever that means."

"I overheard them talking about Missing Acres, and Tomás Amos, the farm manager – that someone is tracking his movements. I've met Señor Amos who, if you ask me, is one very strange man, but he's always been good to the community and to our mission. He wears a half mask over his face. They say he was in a fire when he was younger. His speech is sometimes slurred, but I've never had a problem under-standing him. Needless to say, my opinion of Missing Acres has changed – a lot. But I don't think Señor Amos knows about all of the things going on. Even after all I've been through, I can't think he's involved. I may be naïve, but he's no monster. I assume the operation your mom was talking about must be the real reason you came here. Maybe we can discuss it later. Anyway," she said, quickly changing the subject, "go take a shower. I'll make something for breakfast and meet you back here in about twenty minutes."

"Thanks. Do you happen to know where Diego is?"

"Darnell, his business partner picked him up about half an hour ago. He told Father Ed he had some business to clean up."

Walking down to the showers with a YMCA towel over my shoul-der, I think about my next move. I need to get back to Missing Acres once more to search for Mike. I'm sure the military will be taking out specific cartel targets, and Missing Acre's definitely on the list. The whole issue with my father has to wait. He hasn't been part of my life for thirty years. Another week won't make any difference.

Fina's waiting for me outside the shower building. When I walk past her and into the men's side, I find that Fina isn't the only one waiting for me. The smell of strawberries quickly awakens my senses.

Chapter 57

As I WALK PAST the shower doors, trying to follow the elusive scent, one quickly opens and a hand grabs my sleeve. I'm pulled inside the room and the door closes hard behind me. At first I think I must be dreaming, seeing Clare standing three feet from me in a very small towel. Where I come from, we call those towels face cloths.

She says hello and drops the "towel" to the ground. At that very moment, the only thing that goes through my mind is that, okay, maybe this does happen in real life and not just in the movies.

Clare's body is amazing, and yet it's her face I'm drawn to. She has a look of happiness, vulnerability and sadness all wrapped up together. She's been through so much since I showed up, and now I'm the one who's shaking. I wrap my arms around her and she begins to cry, then pulls my shirt off over my head and leans in to me. Her naked body against my skin banishes my worries. My knees are starting to get weak, now thinking of nothing else but her. I pull away slightly and kiss the tears off her cheeks. Her taste and smell are intoxicating.

My romantic state of mind is interrupted by the sound of Fina breaking into relentless barking. Clare stiffens and pulls away from me.

"Dear God. I'm sorry, Joe, but I've gotta leave."

"What are you talking about?" I say, almost panting. "Please, stay a little longer. I apologize if I said or did anything wrong."

"It's not you, it's Fina." Fina?

"Don't worry. She'll calm down soon enough."

"Joe, Fina's my alarm. It means that Father Ed's in the area. And getting close – her bark's getting louder."

JAMES K. ZAVEZ

"Clare, Clare are you in there?" we hear Father Ed shouting over Fina's barking.

"Yes, Father," Clare responds quickly. "I'll be right out. Quiet, Fina!"

"Thanks, Clare. I need your help back at the main house. We have about twenty-five people waiting to get vaccinated and then back to work in the fields."

"I'll be right there. I'll meet you in the courtyard. Quiet, Fina!" she yells, then laughs softly and bends down to pick up her clothes. Her naked backside is so sexy and for a moment, I forget about what just happened. She turns her head back to me, catches me staring and just smiles.

In the last forty-eight hours, Clare has really changed me. Whether it's her words, her touch or her marvelous ass, she's someone I never want to be without. Watching her get dressed only excites me more, both mentally and physically. She steps back to me in her bra and panties and begins kissing my chest and running her hand over my groin. Closing my eyes, I feel her do incredible things to me with all parts of her body. Erotic sounds and the smell of strawberries fill the small space as I begin to breathe rapidly.

Hearing someone bang on the door and yell hurry up in Spanish forces me to open my eyes. Clare is nowhere in the room and I'm done with my shower. It must have been a dream, nice ass and all.

"I'll be right out! *Voy a sacerlo!*"

• • •

WALKING BACK UP the hill and over to the courtyard, I can see a line of people moving slowly into the back of the main house. Father Ed's voice is blaring out directions in Spanish from inside, and Clare is standing next to a table writing down people's information. She's the most beautiful thing I have ever seen, in her red New Balance running shoes, well fitted jeans and my grey Hampton Beach t-shirt.

Chapter 58

10:05 AM. I'm loading my bag into the "borrowed" Hummer. The battery in my iPhone's been recharging all morning, complements of a 12-volt outlet in the vehicle. I stow the Glock in the glove compartment, then send a text to Jim informing him that I'm on my way back to Missing Acres, that I need to make one more attempt to find out what happened to Mike before we call in the heavy artillery.

All the local villagers have left and the mission is noticeably quiet. Fina's sleeping in the Hummer's driver's seat, only opening her eyes to let me know when I'm making too much noise. The sky's a heavy grey, and the air is stagnant. The temperature's 82 degrees.

I check all the fluids and gas in the SUV and determine that I have enough to get me to Missing Acres and back. My supplies consist of two flashlights, six bullets, one iPhone, Diego's Swiss Army knife and a borrowed cell phone sealed in a ziploc plastic bag. My head's still spinning, thinking about Diego's and my mother's private conversation, but I need to put those thoughts aside so I can finish my mission: find Mike. The clock's ticking and I'm way behind. The sweet scent of strawberries hits me once again. No one has to tell me that Clare is standing behind me.

"Excuse me, Joe, where do you think you're going?" she asks sweetly. "I need a ride to a town outside Sayula de Aleman, to pick up our new old bus. And I've nominated you as my designated driver.

"Clare, Clare, Clare. You know there's nothing I'd rather do than give you a ride, but I need to get back to Missing Acres and look for Mike."

The words "Missing Acres" hit a nerve with Clare. She stands silent for a moment before slamming her thoughts right into me.

"What the hell are you talking about? How can you even think of going back, after all we've been through. Do you think you can knock on the door and ask politely to search the property? Are you crazy?" She sits down on the ground and begins to cry. Fina wakes quickly, gives me a dirty look and jumps out of the driver's seat into her lap.

"Clare, you have to understand," I say quietly. "Mike is a friend of mine. He's got a wife who loves him dearly waiting back in Washington for news. She's already devastated – they lost a year-old baby less than a year ago. I can't tell her she's lost her husband too. And Jim Carlone's crushed – he talked Mike into joining his group less than a month ago. I'm Mike's only link now that Abby is dead. I can't leave any stones unturned. Right now our military's formulating a plan that may wipe Missing Acres off the map if we can turn up a solid connection between them and what happened in DC."

"What you're saying," Clare responds equally quietly, "is that I have no say. That I'm supposed to understand all this? Don't forget how close I came to joining Abby in the tool shed." She gives me a long, hard look. "All right, listen. I realize you need to go, but please do me one favor – take me with you. I need to pick up the bus anyway, and the garage isn't that far out of the way. We can figure it out on the way there."

I'd had a strong feeling that once Clare knew where I was headed, she'd want to go, which was why I was hoping to leave earlier without saying anything. The episode in the shower clouded my thinking. While I don't regret what happened, I need to get focused and down to Missing Acres. Now. I go over to where she's sitting and sit down in front of her.

"Okay, Clare, you win," I say, taking her hands in mine. "You can go – on one condition. Please promise me that you'll be reasonable and stay safe at all times. I have some history – and training – when it comes to dealing with bad guys. You have to let me take the lead. And you must listen to what I say. This is a very dangerous situation. If I'm ever to propose to you, one beautiful day in the future, it might be a good idea for us to get back here alive. If we somehow become separated, you must *not* look for me. I want you to promise me that you'll come back to Holy Spirit Mission and wait."

Clare jumps in my arms with such force that I almost roll over backwards. Fina, not sure who's attacking who, stands over us, barking at us both.

"I love you, Joe!" Clare exclaims. "I need to get a few things. I'll be right back."

She jumps up and runs up the hill towards the mission's front door before I have a chance to respond. Fina gives me a quick look, tilts her head, then jumps back into the Hummer.

Probably the right thing for me to do would have been to leave before Clare came back, and I might have done just that if she hadn't told me she loves me. After closing the hood on the vehicle, I hear Clare yelling my name and look up to see her and Father Ed approaching the SUV.

"Father Ed has asked if he can join us on the ride to Sayula de Aleman," says Clare, a strange look on her face.

"Joe, I need to get away from the mission for a while after all that's happened," says Father Ed. "I can help Clare check out the used bus and drive it back if needed. I've put the sisters in charge during my absence, and I pity the fool who doesn't listen to what they say. You need help from the A-Team."

"No problem, Mr. T," I laugh. "We can use all the help we can get!"

"What's the A-Team? Who's Mr. T?" says Clare, bewildered. "I don't get it."

"I'll explain on our way," says Father Ed. "It was just a hokey TV show, back in the early eighties about soldiers of fortune who were sent to prison by a military court for a crime they didn't commit. I remember every episode," Father Ed says, grinning proudly.

Times like these, I wish I had my iPod. I'm not interested in hearing about the A-Team or why Mr. T wore twenty pounds of gold in every show. It might be fascinating to some, but not to me. I take a large brown bag from Father Ed and place it in the back of the Hummer. It's long and heavy, like a bag of baseball bats. Maybe it's filled with religious items or food for the poor – or maybe it's for something else.

Father Ed climbs in the back next to Fina. Clare's up front, telling me all about this new old bus they're getting, through a friend of Darnell's. Hearing his name returns my thoughts to Diego and how he might be my father. Something's irking me, something that just doesn't seem to fit in this compelling father-and-son story. Over the last twenty-four hours, I've been in a life and death struggle with Diego. You'd think he might have told me then. Either of us could have been killed – a confession would have been appropriate. Or maybe that only happens in the movies.

• • •

DRIVING DOWN A NEARLY deserted highway, our conversation bounces back and forth between the A-Team, Fina needing a bath, the color of the new old bus and the man behind the mask at Missing Acres, Tomás Amos. Since Clare and Father Ed know little about Señor Amos, we skip over that subject and talk about what happened in Washington.

With very little traffic this morning, I find it strange that a white Ford Expedition has been behind us now for almost ten miles. I think it's safe to say we're being followed.

Chapter 59

Our trip to Sayula de Aleman is relatively uneventful except for our friends in the Expedition behind us. When there's enough space along the side of the road, I pull over to let them pass us, but it always ends up behind us again within ten minutes.

11:35 AM. We get to the shop where the bus is located – "Joe's Garage." So there really is such a place.

Three older Mexicans are at work under the hood of a bus – the bus we're here for, it turns out. From inside the bus, a young kid screams in our direction in Spanish. I'm able to pick up "cable broken," "fuse box, " "shit" and "your mother is a pig," which starts two men under the hood to laugh loudly, while the third quickly runs up into the bus and starts what looks like a mock fist fight with the kid. Father Ed quickly boards the bus, breaks up the one-sided fight and carries the kid out by the back of his shirt.

I stay with the Hummer, watching for our friends in the Expedition and checking messages as Father Ed brokers a peace between young and old. A black, military-style Hummer belonging to a powerful local family is easy to spot and report to those who need to know. It's time to get the hell out of here.

"Joe," says Clare, "it turns out the bus won't be ready until six tonight. The accelerator cable snapped and they've sent someone to Vera Cruz for the parts and some fuses they need for it. We're stuck here for a while."

Running a quick calculation in my mind, I figure Missing Acres to be about sixteen miles east of our present location. I hate to strand

Clare and Father Ed, but my need to get to Missing Acres grows more urgent with the passing hours.

I take a deep breath and look Clare in the eye. "Okay, Clare – I'm going over to the farm and try to find a way back into the tunnels. I know the river's one option, but I'm hoping to find another way."

Clare returns my gaze with equal seriousness. "We have at least six hours until the bus is fixed," she says calmly, "so I'm going with you. Father Ed says he has friends in the area he'd like to visit in the meantime."

I shake my head. "Clare, this is both crazy and dangerous. I would rather you stay here till I get back. I can't put your life at risk, not again."

"I appreciate your concern, really, Joe, but it's my life and I'm going. I'm not asking you, I'm telling you. So please get Father Ed's bag out of the back so we can go. You have no choice!"

The look of determination on her face tells me I'm not going to win this argument. Father Ed comes driving around the corner in an old, rusted-out '67 Chevy Nova, belching clouds of blue smoke every time he hits the gas.

"I've borrowed this from the shop and I'm going to visit friends. Let's meet back here at six o'clock," Father Ed shouts over the noisy Chevy.

"Okay," yells Clare. "See you at six!"

Fina decides to stay at the shop, having found a comfortable spot under a shady tree for a siesta. She even has a yellow cat, stretched out lazily on a branch above her, for company. She gives us one sleepy, unconcerned last look as Clare and I drive away.

As soon as we're back on the main road, the white Ford Expedition reappears, about fifty yards behind us. Just before the metal bridge that leads over to Missing Acres, I begin to slow down and pull over. Since we're now being followed, it makes no sense to split up. We slow to a stop, but the Expedition picks up speed, quickly closing the gap between us. I tell Clare to check her seat belt and brace herself.

I manage to get the Hummer moving again, just as the Expedition hits us from behind on our left side, shoving us along the edge of the road towards the bank of the river. Their plan, obviously, is to not allow me back on the road and over the bridge, but rather to push us off the side and into the river.

Gunning the engine causes the white Ford to bounce off us several times, but it's still pushing us inexorably towards the river. As we continue to play bumper cars, the front of their vehicle gets hooked on our rear bumper and the two vehicles become locked together. This is when the shooting starts. They blow out the rear windows of the Hummer and begin ripping holes throughout the interior. With little time and no defense, I tell Clare to hold on, and throw the Hummer into heavy duty four-wheel drive mode.

As our wheels dig in, I put the accelerator pedal to the floor and our train bolts forward. I hold the wheel steady as the Ford, hooked behind us, breaks heavily to try and stop our forward momentum.

"Clare," I yell, "grab the wheel and hold the accelerator pedal to the floor. Try your best to keep us straight! Aim for the cliff above the river – don't try to get over to the bridge."

I jump into the backseat and grab our bags. I pull out a gun and shoot two quick bullets through the black tinted windshield of the Ford. As I climb back into the front seat, I can feel the vehicle behind us going out of control. Now we're swerving left and right.

"Clare, take your foot off the gas and let go of the wheel. I have it."

We're some three hundred feet from the edge when I click on the cruise control at forty-two miles per hour and put the tilt wheel all the way up. Smoke and the smell of burning rubber fill our vehicle as I pull Clare over to my side and prop open the driver's side door. Jerking the steering wheel to the right, we jump out of the Hummer about ten feet before the edge. We have just enough time to hit the soft ground and I have enough time to wave at the boys in the Expedition and holler "Choo choo, assholes!" as it follows the Hummer over the cliff.

Lying on the ground entangled in my surf bag, we hear the explosion and see thick black smoke coming from below the cliff.

"Are you okay, Clare?" I ask as the adrenalin slows its mad dash through my system. "Did you get hurt? I'm sorry, but that was our only option."

She doesn't say a word but rolls over and kisses me. I can taste the dirt on her face. Boy, how I love this woman!

Chapter 60

THE EXPLOSION OF the two vehicles has surely alerted the troops at Missing Acres. From where I'm standing, I can see the roof of the main house across the bridge.

The rain's beginning to fall heavily as we start down the river embankment, trying to find a reasonable place to cross. Clare pulls out her Red Sox baseball hat from her bag and puts it on, pushing her hair behind each ear. Just as we're about to walk below the bridge, we hear a car coming down the road behind us, beeping its horn a few times.

Clare and I duck behind a large cement block as the car slows and pulls over to the side just before the bridge. Squinting through the heavy rain, I recognize the car as the one Father Ed drove away in over an hour ago. The '67 Chevy Nova, with its one working headlight and no muffler, creates a steady booming that echoes off the walls of the river valley. If two exploding cars weren't enough to attract attention, the noise from the Chevy is.

I tell Clare to stay put as I draw my gun and walk up behind the car. As I approach the driver's door from the rear, the car shuts off, the door opens and Father Ed lifts his bulk out of the squeaky front seat. Hearing me behind him, he turns around to see me pointing my gun in his direction.

"Joseph, it's me," says Father Ed. "Please, lower the gun!"

"I'm sorry, Father. What are you doing here?"

Before he can answer, the rear passenger-side door on the opposite side opens and a man steps out. Standing in the downpour wearing a black rain poncho and a blue cap on his head, I recognize the outline right away.

"Hey, Diego – or should I be saying, 'hey, Dad'? Please excuse me, but I'm a little confused and I really don't give a shit. All I know for a fact is that I have to find my friend before this place turns to dust!"

"Call me whatever you want," Diego says sharply. "We need to talk, but again, now is not the time. Do you have some sort of a plan, Joseph?"

"Funny you ask since I'm working on one as we speak. Why are you here, Diego?"

"To help you find your friend and put an end to this drug madness. Mexicans and Americans can no longer turn away from this problem. We must work together to eradicate both the production and consumption of illegal drugs. I think America finally has a president who's willing to shoulder some blame and responsibility for the daily tragedies taking place on both sides of the border."

"Agreed. But my concern right now is finding Mike before the cavalry shows up. I'm not sure if he is still here. This farm manager, this Tomás Amos, sounds more like a comic book character than an actual person. To find Mike, I suspect I'll need to go through him."

"Tomás is no, as you say, comic book character. He may cause pain for some, but he also provides comfort for many. He is a local hero and well respected within the Mexican government. Tomás provides food, jobs, shelter and protection in this community. All that said, I leave it to you to try and judge him. Joe, you need to remember that Tomás is not the owner. He runs the farming operation," Diego says seriously.

"Look, Diego, I'm not sure what your connection is with this place and you know what? Like I said, I don't give a shit," I say, spitting out my words. "And let me tell you something else. There's reason to believe that your admirable friend Señor Amos was in Washington DC during the terrorist attack."

The mention of Tomás being in DC during the attack causes Diego to suddenly avoid my eyes – even though I made it up. Back in Washington, Mom and I both saw someone wearing some kind of a mask in the back of the helicopter. I remember Clare also told me that Tomás Amos wears a mask. What are the chances?

Once I finish my verbal assault on Diego we move away from politics and the blame game and get serious putting together a plan to get into Missing Acres. Diego has friends on the inside who will help us gain access to the property, but if the shooting starts, we're on our own.

Unfortunately, the plan includes going back across the river and back into a drainage pipe. The fence is open due to building repairs, but the tracking security cameras and motion detectors are in operation 24/7. Diego says we have a forty-five second window in which to slip through the open fence and not set off any alarms. Once in the tunnel, we'll head back to the area where Clare and Abby were being held. Clare had mentioned that she'd seen numerous rooms behind large grey steel doors with very small windows.

Clare and Father Ed will come back in three hours and pick us up here, in spite of the fact that Clare has tried hard to convince me that she too should go, but we hold firm to our decision that Diego and I are the A-Team. Saying goodbye to Clare almost breaks me in two as tears start to run down her cheeks.

"Joe, I *need* to go with you," she says, her voice steely, but soft as velvet too.

"And I need you to stay behind with Father Ed and use my phone to make contact with my mother and Jim. It's useless here, and they need to know where we are and what we're up to. The farther you get away from Missing Acres, the stronger the cell signal becomes. I need *you* to do that for me. The numbers are all programmed into the phone. All you have to do is push one button to get you through. Please, do this for me. I love you, Clare. *Please.*"

After giving Clare a quick tutorial on how to use my phone, I hug her so tight I think I hear wheezing. When I finally give her some air to breathe, she whispers in my ear, "Joseph Dunstan, you better plan on coming back to me. I never really loved anyone in my life until you came along. I always felt comfortable being alone, but now that I've met you, I'm terrified of it. You come crashing into my life and make me feel crazy about losing you."

'Don't worry, I'll meet you back here in three hours. I feel the same way about losing you. I guess that makes us both a little bit crazy. You want to hear crazy? The other night I decided to burn my life-long membership card to the 'He-Man Woman Haters Club.' My heroes, The Little Rascals – you know, Buckwheat, Spanky and Alfalfa – they're probably turning in their graves right now, God bless their souls."

I let go of her, all but one hand, when I hear Diego calling my name from beneath the bridge. The rain has slowed to a light drizzle and the sun pops through the clouds from time to time. With another short kiss, I finally relinquish Clare's hand and head down the small embankment under the bridge. I turn once more to see Father Ed standing next to Clare waving to me before I disappear from their sight behind two large cement bridge supports.

Diego's waiting for me. We head down the slope to the edge of the water. Its 12:11 in the afternoon when we step into the warm river water – and feel the ground shake as two Navy Super Hornets fly about ten feet above the bridge, making a wide circle over Missing Acres.

I hear a sharp swish, followed by a small explosion somewhere inside the compound. A few seconds later, the cell phone I borrowed from my mother begins to vibrate in my front pant's pocket. Finally, someone's been able to take out the communications jamming equipment for good. Go Navy!

Chapter 61

Diego and I start our journey across the shallow part of the river, out in the open without the protection of the bridge. We hope the bombing of the jamming equipment is enough to keep prying eyes away, at least for the time being. When we get to the opposite shore, I remove the cell phone from the bag and turn it on, send Carlone a short message as a test and get an immediate response. Not sure if this phone is secure, I send another text telling him to call my cell, knowing that Clare will pass the details to him.

As we walk through the thick brush on our way to the drainage tunnel, Diego fills me in on the history of Missing Acres. Juan Delgado, he tells me, had been leasing the property from the Mexican government for over twenty years. Several buildings once stood on the grounds that housed those considered mentally incompetent to live within society – the misfits, homeless, retarded and handicapped, as well as people who disagreed with the government.

The name Missing Acres comes from the actual deed to the property. Per the agreement, Señor Delgado had leased ten thousand acres, but when he had the property surveyed, the acreage totaled just over ninety-four hundred. Juan went back to the government, only to learn that the missing six hundred acres consisted of unmarked mass graves. The Mexican government reduced the cost proportionately, and gave Delgado access to some no-interest loans to expand his farming operation and pay for the property. Many people still come to Missing Acres to be near friends or relatives they believe to be buried in those rocky six hundred acres. Diego, however, thinks there's more to it and goes on at some length about rumored secret medical experiments and tunnels that people lived in while being exposed to deadly viruses.

"Tell me, Diego," I ask him, "what is the significance of the white tiger? I have seen this tattoo on people's necks, as well as on the sign on the gate."

"Please understand, Joseph, that this is pure speculation on my part, based on things I have heard," Diego prefaces his answer. "When Pablo Escobar was killed in Columbia in December 1993 in a shootout with government officials, it was said that they found a baby white tiger with black paws in the back seat of his car. It's widely known that Señor Escobar had a zoo on his property, with all types of exotic animals including rare white tigers. The story quickly passed into folklore and caught on. Members of a number of drug cartels started using the white tiger as a symbol of power and purity, supposedly to symbolize the power of the cartels and the purity of their product."

"So tell me, Diego, why would a woman in her early twenties living in the United States have that tattoo on her neck?"

"Again, I have heard that people with this marking are somehow tied into drug trafficking by either moving or selling. The tattoo is supposedly put on their necks as a warning that they belong to a particular cartel that requires obedience and loyalty. If you're captured by an opposing organization and they find the tiger, you may be killed. They say that if you are disloyal to the cartel, your mutilated body will be found as a warning. Why do you ask?"

"A friend of mine with that tattoo was found dead several days ago. When she was discovered, most of the bones in her body had been broken and a big chunk of her neck had been removed exactly where the tattoo was. But she never knew she had the white tiger on the back of her neck, Diego. I spoke to her myself."

"It's a terrible thing," says Diego staring sadly at the ground. "How did we ever become so mean and cruel to one another?"

Chapter 62

IT'S ABOUT A half-mile jog from the bridge to the construction site where the fence is open near an unoccupied guard shack. Diego and I count six cameras sweeping the grounds in specific patterns covering every square inch. Low clouds and fog still hover over the property, but the rain has ended, leaving behind numerous mud puddles. We speak to each other only when necessary. This certainly isn't the time for any further father-son discussions. Diego knows I have a job to do and that I'd be grateful for his help, whoever he is. When this is all over and we find Mike, we'll have plenty of time to pose for family photographs.

12:59 PM. Our forty-five second window to bypass security happens at 1:00. Diego says that we are not to use our watches, but rather listen for the bells to start ringing at a small church outside Jaltipan, located about two miles from us. I get a little nervous waiting for the bells to chime since my watch now says 1:02. When they finally toll at 1:05, we scurry out of the bushes, up past the guard shack and into the fields.

Diego knows of an old ventilation shaft that hasn't been used for years except by many of the younger workers who go down there at night to smoke a little pot or make out. Tomás, the farm boss, has never bothered to have it sealed and probably never will as long as everybody is at breakfast and ready to work at 5:00 AM. It takes us close to an hour to find the shaft, located in a far corner of the property covered by old branches and cornstalks.

Once the debris is cleared away, you're greeted by the smell of urine and stale smoke. I climb down an old, rusty ladder into a vertical shaft about three feet in diameter. At about ten feet, my boots hit the ground. I can see a large tunnel that disappears into the darkness. I think I hear voices, but figure it's my imagination. Flashing my light around the tunnel, I see several old mattresses, newspapers, shoes, clothing and waxy remnants of candles long since burned. Bending over to check the date on one of the newspapers while waiting for Diego, I hear loud voices from above.

"Joe, someone is coming and I must hide," Diego calls down to me. "I'll meet up with you as soon as I can. If you turn left or right in the tunnels, put a mark on the wall so I will know which way to go. *Buena suerte*, Joseph. Good luck."

Somebody is yelling in Spanish down into the shaft as I break into a run into a semi-dark tunnel large enough to drive a truck through. I use my flashlight only when absolutely necessary, and soon notice the floor sloping upward towards a fork in the road. I stop to get my bearings, scratch a mark on the left side of the wall with a rock and head off in that direction.

After a few minutes, I come to a doorless room on the right. Shining my light in, I see stacks of army cots on one side and antiquated looking medical equipment on the other. The dust is deep, suggesting that this room hasn't been disturbed in quite some time.

Making another mark on the wall, I go right into a series of rooms that all open into the tunnel. Some of the rooms have doors, some don't. I quickly check them for any signs of life, but it's more of the same, just quantities of old furniture stacked to the ceiling.

Looking ahead now, I can see some stray light leaking out beneath a garage-style door into the hallway. This part of the tunnel has new cement floors and is less musty smelling. Just as laughter explodes from behind the garage door, it suddenly begins to open. I draw my weapon and try my best to disappear into the shadows.

As the door terminates at the top, I hear a diesel engine start up, then grow louder as a forklift comes over the threshold carrying two surface-to-air missiles. The vehicle turns in the opposite direction from where I'm crouched and proceeds slowly down a long, brightly lit corridor.

The door begins closing. Without thought, I roll into the room à la Harrison Ford in "Raiders of the Lost Ark." From my vantage point, I can see that the room is void of people. Banks of LCD monitors cover the left wall. Surface-to-air missiles are stacked three on top of each other, six rows deep, on the right. Two empty missile cradles explain the load I saw a few minutes ago moving down the tunnel.

Looking up at the banks of monitors, I'm able to view different locations throughout the compound. Two of the fourteen monitors set my heart racing. In the first, a wood-paneled room, a man sits in the center, his hands tied to a steel chair. In spite of the brown sack over his face, I can easily tell it's Diego. The other monitor features an empty '67 Chevy Nova parked outside the main gate of Missing Acres – with two Mexican police cars parked alongside it.

Chapter 63

My BRAIN STARTS firing on all cylinders as I hear the garage door start to open again as well as several voices laughing on the other side. The only place to hide is behind the stacks of missiles. It doesn't appear that they know I'm inside the storage chamber, as the laughter continues when they enter the room. Wedging myself into the corner of the wall behind the SAMs, I take out my Glock and get ready if shooting is required.

Three ex-military types come into the room, all with close-cropped hair, dressed in camo from head to toe, and they speak better English than I do. The current topic of conversation seems to be a local whorehouse where all the "bitches" are infected with HIV and "still have the balls to charge high prices." One of the men with a Boston accent says that he knows of another place that enslaves kidnapped teenagers who are more than eager to please. However, he finally admits, this place is a hundred miles north, which would require additional time off for the men. I make a mental note of the name and location of this illegal operation, thinking we might want to have a drone check it out.

As the men continue talking about their local nightly adventures, I resume watching the security television monitors flip through locations throughout the farm, hoping to see Clare. The video on each screen holds for about two minutes before it moves onto the next location. Once again I see the room where Diego is tied to the chair with the bag over his head, but now my eyes move on to the location on the next monitor, which looks alarmingly familiar as the camera pans a room with missiles stacked to the ceiling. What really catches my attention is when I see a glimpse of myself jammed between the wall and the missile cradle system. Oh, shit!

One of the men, wearing dark glasses, spins around and begins scanning the room; the other two men follow suit. Knowing my cover is about to be blown, I get off one shot, hitting the man in the glasses. The bullet splits his shades in two at the bridge of the nose, killing him instantly.

For a quick second, I have a crazy thought that no one in his right mind will shoot at someone hiding behind a stack of missiles. How wrong I am, as bullets begin flying and ricocheting off the missiles and walls. Most of me is well protected behind the strong metal cradle system, but it's only a matter of time before either I run out of bullets or something detonates one of these missiles and I become the first man to walk on the moon in the twenty-first century.

Looking across the floor to the open garage door, I estimate about a forty-foot sprint out of the room back into the tunnel system. Since the two men firing at me have made no mention of surrender and are probably quite pissed at me for killing their friend, getting out of here alive is a weak option. How would this work in a movie? I look frantically for some type of latching device that will release the missiles, freeing them to roll over the enemy allowing me to escape. Unfortunately, no such device exists.

My next idea: at least cause some confusion. I fire two quick shots at the LCD screens on the monitors and glass starts flying. Which leaves me with only one bullet left in the Glock. I run through half a dozen near-impossible escape scenarios and, with a mental groan, pick one. As I'm just about to launch what I've already labeled my suicide mission, I hear shotgun blasts and see my two enemies hit the floor, still firing aimlessly as they lay dying in their own blood.

After a few seconds, the room goes quiet, except for a voice echoing in at me from outside the tunnel. "Joe, are you in there?" the disembodied voice calls. "It's me, Jim. Are there any other shooters in the room?"

"It's all clear! Nobody in here except me, three dead guys and several dozen missiles."

Jim runs into the room holding a shotgun in his right hand. I slide up against the wall, dusting off fragments of white cement from my clothing. That's when I see that Jim is not alone.

"Thanks for saving my life, guys," I say with utmost sincerity. "Oh, and Father Ed, I too always thought those commandments were a little too strict in our line of work. You know like 'Thou shall not kill'?"

Chapter 64

Then it hits me. "What happened to Clare?" I shout, still standing under the blown-out monitors. "I saw the Chevy parked in front of the gate. No occupants, two Mexican police cars parked along side it."

"Relax, Joe," whispers Jim. "She's with your mother and four Mexican government officials, trying to set up a meeting with Juan Delgado. We're not even sure if he or Tomás Amos is on the property. Clare called me on your phone with the update. We met an hour ago a few miles from the bridge."

"Listen to me, but please don't tell me to relax," I say, but I do lower my voice. "It's hard to be calm with Mike missing and Diego tied to a chair with a sack over his head in one of the buildings. The two women I love are trying to meet with two madmen, including one who quite possibly wears a mask. It's gotta be the same bastard I saw in the helicopter the day of the attack in DC. They need to know this! Damn it, doesn't Clare remember she was a prisoner here just twenty-four hours ago? Am I suppose to feel better that she's with government officials? Listen to me, Jim, you just rescued me from a room filled with surface-to-air missiles. Anybody worried yet? Before you both got here, two SAMs were transported outta this room, destination unknown. And last, but certainly not least, two days ago I see 'Father Ed' celebrating mass and Holy Communion. Two minutes ago he shows up carrying a shotgun and assault rifle. Did I miss anything?"

"Okay, you're right. Don't relax. Stay on edge," Jim says, as close to hysterical as I think I've ever heard him. "Let me tell you what I got.

We now know for certain that Mike's been moved to South America. The four so-called 'Mexican government officials' with Clare and your mom are actually Army Special Forces – our guys. There's a small army within striking distance, ready to destroy this place very soon. We need to find Diego quickly! The initial warning strike will be at 3:00 PM. The final raid comes thirty minutes later. To be completely honest, this roomful of SAMs comes as a most unpleasant surprise. We need to find the launchers before 3:00! And let me finish by saying that Father Ed's more like a minister than a priest, technically speaking. He's also been working undercover for the DEA in Mexico for the last twenty years." Father Ed gives me a nod and walks out into the tunnel.

"Sorry for my outburst, Jim, and – thanks," I say, mollified. "Okay, listen. We need to find out where Mike was taken and get Diego out of here. Oh and Jim, do I still call him Father Ed or just Ed, now that I know his seedy background? I gotta tell you, buddy," I whisper, "I knew there was something fishy about him. I just hope we know everything."

Moving rapidly through the maze of tunnels, the three of us check every room for any clues Mike might have left behind. All we find are more missiles, guns, pallets of fertilizer and bomb-making parapher-nalia. I know Diego is somewhere above ground – sunlight was coming through a window in the room where he's being held.

After about ten minutes, we finally come to the end of a long corridor where we see rubber tire marks on the cement that look like they were made by the modified forklift I saw carrying the missiles. Unfortunately, it's a dead end: in front of us, a large aircraft hangar door defies our best efforts. The three of us are all on the verge of hernias, having tried desperately to open it.

There appears to be no way past the hangar door except possibly through some large metal grates covering drains in the floor. Since I'm the smallest, I quickly get out Diego's Swiss Army knife and start removing the six heavy-duty screws holding one of the grates in place. The cover, thankfully, is relatively new – the screws aren't rusted and come out easily. Lifting the grate off the drain, Jim shines a flashlight into the hole. "The pipe looks like it opens up below, but it'll be a tight squeeze when you first climb in," he tells me.

The vertical pipe, about two feet in diameter and eight feet long, drops into a larger tube running horizontal that looks to be about five feet in diameter. The hope is that the system is interconnected and that I'll find another drain cover on the other side of the hangar door. If that much proves to be true, I'm not sure how I'll climb up eight feet and unscrew the drain from below. Time to channel MacGyver.

With the vertical section being as tight as it is, I take everything out of my pockets before climbing into the hole. With no flashlight and going down feet first, I feel a little claustrophobic until I fall the final five feet into the large open area below.

Just as I hear the drain cover being moved back in place, a gun goes off overhead where I just left Father Ed and Jim. Seconds later, a flashlight bounces off the top of my head onto the cement floor. My gun, another magazine and Diego's Swiss Army knife quickly follow. Fortunately, the gun bounced off my shoulder and not my head like the flashlight, since that probably would've knocked me out cold. I hear a blast from a shotgun above and I think I hear Jim yell, "I'm hit." I slam the new clip into the Glock and place it in my boot opposite the plastic wrapped cell phone.

Crawling quickly through the pipe, I'm pleased to see that it does in fact head in the direction of the hangar door. Light filters down through several drain grates that lie ahead, and I can hear the sound of machinery. Not hearing any voices, I stash the knife in my back pants pocket and, contorting my body as tightly as I can, I climb up the vertical drain shaft that should lead to the room on the other side of the door. The fit being so tight, I'm able to pull myself up a foot at a time, then do what it takes to expand my body against the wall, giving myself a few seconds to rest.

After a few minutes and with little energy to spare, I get to the top of the drain with my face about six inches from the metal grate. The first thing I notice is that this drain is not the same type as the one I climbed down. Lifting my right arm above my head, I feel around the grate to see if I can find any screws or bolts holding it down. Not finding any, I push up slowly on the grate and to my amazement it lifts easily out of position, but before I can even begin to appreciate this piece of good luck, I develop a severe cramp in my right arm, leaving me with no choice but to quickly slide the cover as quietly as possible along the floor.

I wait a few seconds in silence to verify the absence of voices or clicking of guns. Feeling confident that I haven't been detected, I climb up and out of the drain hole, and lay out on the floor on my stomach to catch my breath, but before I'm able to take the first breath, the room lights come up to full power and the barrels of guns are poked into the side of my head.

The next thing I know, someone's placed a coarse bag over my head, tied it at the neck and I'm lifted to my feet and forced to walk. The good news is that nobody checks me for weapons. The bad news is that my gun has slipped out of my boot – I can feel that it's only loosely being held in place by my sock. The faster and farther we walk, the better the chance that the gun will fall out onto the floor and get someone's attention.

Two people are holding me, one on each side. With the barrel of a rifle jammed into my back, we start walking. I've counted two voices, and have to assume the presence of a third.

Feeling my gun begin to slip out of my sock, I stop suddenly and fall to the ground, taking the guy on my right with me. This frees my hand long enough to grab the gun before it can hit the ground. I turn quickly and fire three blind shots behind me.

The guy on my left lets go of me completely as I squeeze off another four bullets at the unseen person to my right. As I get off the last remaining three shots, the empty gun is knocked out of my hand and I hear it clattering along the cement floor.

Unable to untie the sack on my head, I tackle the guy behind me, who is quite large and smells oddly like incense. We scramble along the floor, his light punches connecting and mine not so much. Somehow I have to even up this fight.

Reaching into my back pocket with my left hand, I pull out Diego's Swiss Army knife. Working as quickly as I can, I opt for any one of its numerous blades or tools and tuck it into the palm of my right hand.

At this point, I'm desperately hanging on to the stranger as he continues to swing me around and use me as a punching bag. Since I can't see a thing, I need to get as close as I can to this person and try to use my sense of hearing to sort things out. The opportunity comes in a split second when I hear him take a deep breath. Feeling his acidic exhale on my face, I swing my right arm around as hard as I can and stick the knife into the side of his head.

He starts screaming and releases me. Ripping the sack from my head, I see the face of a man racked in body spasms, trying desperately to pull the knife out of the left side of his temple. When he finally pulls it free and drops it, I see it was the cork screw I jammed into his head. Bits of brain matter are caught inside the screw.

The large man is now lying on the cement floor, struggling to breathe as blood rushes out of the hole in the side of his head. He will die here, and it will be a slow death. He'll have plenty of time to fully feel his own pain, and think long and hard about his betrayals.

"I hope you enjoy your journey to hell, *Father* Ed," I say through clenched teeth, as his eyes flutter and his body starts to convulse. "May you never rest in peace, you traitorous bastard!"

Chapter 65

As I QUICKLY WIPE off the corkscrew on Father Ed's shirt, I hear Jim banging and yelling from the other side of the closed hanger door. Running like a madman, I search desperately for a switch that will open the door between us. After a few frantic minutes, I finally locate a large red button hidden under a stainless steel table. The moment I hit it, the door starts to roll up, followed immediately by the sound of sirens blaring and lights flashing in the corridor. Needless to say, if no one knew we were here, they sure do now.

As soon as there's enough space between the floor and the receding door, Jim crawls under it. His left thigh is bleeding, and he's holding a full roll of industrial wipes against the injury.

"Jim, are you okay?" I ask him. "What the hell happened?"

"Our good friend Father Ed turned out to be a double agent, it seems, and he shot me in the leg, that son of a bitch! Once you disappeared down into the drain, we heard voices coming down one of the corridors that bothered me a lot more than Ed, though. As they got louder, Ed yelled to them in Spanish saying everything was under control and that the hangar door needed to be opened right away. Thank God for high school Spanish. Anyway, not feeling good about this new state of affairs, I took the safety off my gun, but it clicked a little too loudly. Father Ed – just plain Ed – turned on me with a sawed-off shotgun and told me to drop the gun. Just as I was about to, the lights flickered and the door began to open, which caught the bastard off guard, and gave me a chance to fire off a couple of quick shots and run for cover down the dark hallway. Unfortunately, my shots didn't connect with Ed, but I caught a few pellets from his shotgun. Then, for some reason, he stopped pursuing me and ran in here with his two buddies and closed the door. He must have thought he'd killed me."

"That's probably about the time I came up through the drain hole in the floor and was ambushed," I say, having to shout over the alarm. "Fortunately for me, I had Diego's trusty Swiss Army knife. Anyway, Jim, we gotta get outta here! This place is gonna be crawling with security personnel in a matter of minutes. Are you mobile enough, or do you need me to carry you?"

"Look, asshole, I'm fine! I'll probably end up carrying you out of here!"

"Only if I'm in a body bag," I shout, slapping him on the back. "Thanks, buddy!'

"But I'll tell you one thing, Joe, no way I'm carrying Ed out of here. He can be buried with the rest of these murderous thugs."

• • •

I DON'T KNOW IF it's just me, but every time I feel I'm getting a few steps ahead, bad shit starts to happen. The minute we head out into the tunnel again, shots start pinging and ricocheting off the walls. We run back into the room for cover and quickly hit the switch to close the door. It's time for a new plan if we're going to get out of here before this place gets leveled. Looking in all the cabinets, closets and under every table, we can't find one thing to help us in our escape. With all the banging on the other side of the door, we know it's only a matter of time before they get in. I throw Jim a roll of black electrical tape I found in one of the cabinets and slip another in my pocket.

"Jim, wrap your injured leg with this, tight. Our only option out of here is up," I say, pointing to the ceiling.

While Jim rewraps his thigh, I move a large wooden stepladder over into the middle of the room. It's a ten-foot ladder; the ceiling's about twelve feet. Climbing into the overhead ventilation system *should* be easy. Pulling out Diego's Swiss Army knife again, I remove six slotted screws, then accidentally drop the vent panel, which smashes on the cement floor. Putting it back in place after getting inside the shaft is now out of the question.

As Jim climbs up the ladder and into the ceiling, I hear the hangar door begin to lift. Leaping off the bottom rung, I race over to the table and hit the switch, causing the door to close again. As soon as I take my hand off the switch, it begins to open. Those sons of bitches have found a way to short out the door and open it from the other side.

The good news is I still have the master control. The bad news is I now have to hit the damn thing every time the door starts to open. Keeping my hand on the switch only works for about ten seconds before it starts to open again, so taping it down isn't an option. Because of this, one of my hands is in constant motion. I scream out my dilemma to Jim and tell him to get moving, that I'll catch up. Doing the calculations in my head, I have about thirty seconds to release the button, climb the ten foot ladder and get myself into the overhead shaft. After that, men will be scrambling into the room, firing their weapons and chasing us up the ladder in hot pursuit. I need to buy us a little more time.

I look around the room and see three items that will help us in our escape. Taking my hand off the switch, I run quickly over to Father Ed's body and collect his weapon, then run back to the switch. The door opens about six inches before I'm able to close it. Releasing the button again, I scramble over to one of the cabinets and grab a heavy box of nuts and bolts about the size of a brick. Running back to the table, I hit the switch, closing the door this time before it can go up even a few inches. Taking the roll of tape out of my pocket, I sprint about six feet over to an old Hysol fork lift, quickly wrap the throttle control in the fully squeezed position, and turn the steering wheel all the way to the right. Having taken more time than before, I'm forced to jump out of the way as stray bullets begin to fly in under the door before I can hit the red button. I catch my breath for a few seconds. It's now or never.

I hold the heavy box of nuts and bolts in my left hand while keeping my right hand on the red switch. Eying the gun on the stainless steel table in front of me, I release the switch, grab the weapon and run over to the forklift. Dropping the box of bolts onto the accelerator pedal, the forklift jerks forward and begins moving to the right. I dodge to the left and jump up to the third rung on the ladder.

I'm at the top of the ladder as the door starts to open yet again. Stopping, I fire off two shotgun blasts in that direction. The out-of-control forklift's moving in circles that grow wider with every turn, hitting a few of the men clamoring into the room as they fire wildly at shadows. I climb into the ventilation shaft, then slip the shotgun back down by my leg and aim it at the wooden stepladder below me.

Firing my last two shells, I blast away the metal hinge assembly, causing the ladder to fall over and hit the ground in two pieces, rendering it useless.

My location's been given away. I quickly scramble up the ventilation duct as stray bullets penetrate the metal shaft in numerous locations. Thankfully, it soon connects with another horizontal tunnel where I find a flashlight left behind by Jim and can now move faster through a maze of turns, directed by small arrows drawn with Jim's blood.

Chapter 66

AFTER CRAWLING through the tunnel for over ten minutes, I finally catch up with Jim, looking exhausted and taking a much needed break.

"Hey, thanks for waiting for me," I whisper.

"Somebody has to save the day," says Jim. "I don't know if you've noticed, but I think we're under the main house, maybe close to the basement level. Can't you smell bread or something baking?" I could. "I'll guess that this shaft connects to the main house somewhere near the kitchen. It probably leads to the basement where the blower units and air filters are maintained."

"When did you become such an expert in ventilation systems, Jim?"

"You don't remember? I spent a few summers working with Mike in his family's plumbing, heating and air conditioning business. We installed several of these really large systems. Let me tell ya, it's hard work. Shit, you were probably surfing those two summers."

We go about another hundred feet, then see light up ahead. Our flashlights go off and we move slowly towards the light. Looking out through vent holes, I see what looks like a dirt floor in a windowless room. I can also see two men standing by some creaky looking stairs, conversing in Spanish and lighting up cigarettes. Smoke fills the small room as a door at the top of the steps opens suddenly and a body is thrown over the railing, hitting the packed dirt below. The two men lift their heads, share a quick laugh, and continue on with their conversation. The groaning body starts moving slowly along the ground away from the two men, who take little notice, drop their unfinished cigarettes, and walk up the steps and out the door. The lights go off and the door is bolted shut.

Knowing we are running out of time, I kick off the vent cover and hear it hit the ground below. A man is murmuring in both Spanish and English. I recognize the voice. Turning on my flashlight and jumping down to the floor, I shine the light in the man's face, thankful he is still alive.

"Diego! Diego, can you hear me?"

He nods, but has trouble getting out the words. He seems to recognize who I am, but remains incoherent. I go back over to the ventilation shaft and help Jim climb down onto solid ground. We can hear muffled voices and footsteps from the room above, which quickly fall silent as a siren goes off somewhere in the compound. Within seconds of the siren, the feet are back on the move, doors slamming and voices shouting.

It's 3:00 PM. The first wave is about to hit. Numerous explosions can be heard outside as I move up the stairs and kick a hole through the door. Reaching through, I unbolt the door and push it out into a deserted room with a lone chair that's been knocked on its side in the center. I recognize the wood panel right away, thanks to those video cameras in the missile room. The only noticeable difference now is that the roof's been blown off. Right on schedule, the drones have hit their targets. As I know, this is to be followed by a far more severe follow-up attack in half an hour.

Its 3:03 and we need to move fast. I first have to check the whereabouts of Clare and my mom using my cell. Unfortunately, my calls go unanswered and right into voicemail, but I have no time for messages. As I pocket my phone, Diego stumbles up the stairs into the room, slips to the ground and stares up into the sky where the roof once was.

"Diego," I yell across the room. "Can you hear me? Can you walk?"

Diego again nods and tries to stand up. I run over to him to help him get back on his feet.

"Clare and your mother are gone," he says in a slurred voice. "Government officials evacuated the place of all workers. Clare and your mother boarded a government vehicle and drove out of here a while ago. I know this first-hand. I was hiding behind it near the fence when it moved away, exposing my position. This undercover shit is not for me. Before I was able to hide again, a group of security people tackled me, beat me up and hauled me into the house."

"Jim, Diego, we need to get out of here right away!" I shout. "Diego, did you see any evidence that Mike was here?"

"Yes! Yes! My friends who work here told me about a man and woman being brought here a few days ago and held down in the caves, or underground tunnels as you know them. The woman would have been Abby. The man must have been your friend Mike. We know what happened to Abby, but according to my contacts, Mike has been moved to somewhere in South America. The reason is unknown. Maybe leverage. I'm sorry for your friend." Jim and I are saddened to have Mike's being moved reconfirmed – but at least we can hope he's still alive.

• • •

IT'S 3:18. WE HAVE only twelve minutes until the big dogs are sent in to finish the job. Leaving the main house with Diego walking slowly and Jim, even more slowly, I look for any type of vehicle that will help us get away quickly, but there are none to be found. Diego suggests that we look over by the hangar for a truck or maybe even steal a helicopter. I took a few flying lessons in the Navy and know I could get one into the air – but the fact is, I have no experience with the landings.

It's 3:23 when we get to the hangar and find the black helicopter being towed out into the open. Diego and I are immediately surrounded by a group of security types all pointing assault rifles at both of us. Jim, following a few hundred feet behind us, sees our predicament and jumps out of sight behind a parked red dump truck. The guards throw us to the ground, empty our pockets of almost everything and then tell us to stand again.

• • •

AT 3:25 THE ROTORS begin turning on the helicopter and a man in a long, thin black coat wearing a mask over the right side of his face walks up to our small group. He stares at Diego, then smiles oddly at me, but says nothing. Tomás Amos.

Amos tells the guards to handcuff us and get us on the helicopter. Our new traveling companion spits in Diego's face and says something about "disgrace" and "brother" in Spanish. Diego doesn't answer back, just looks over at me after wiping his face with his shirtsleeve. As we're pushed over to the helicopter, I see Jim crouched down inside the dump truck. I hold up four fingers to let him know that he's got four minutes to get the hell out of here.

As we're about to be pushed up and into the helicopter, sirens go off all over the compound again. The security assholes behind us force us against the door opening and tell us to stand. Within a matter of seconds, we see a roof on an outbuilding a hundred feet from us begin to slide open, followed by a high-pitched, electronic whizzing sound – a high-tech elevator system lifting two surface-to-air missiles above the building's roofline. Small streams of white smoke trickle from the back of both. My guess is that the SAMs are identifying their targets and will soon be taking off.

A diesel engine starts up, followed by a series of loud back-fires and I see the dump truck start to move, fast, in reverse. Jim backs the truck right into the wooden structure with enough force to tilt both missiles towards the ground. Their electronic guidance systems cannot react quickly enough – both missiles fire from their launch pads, skim barely above the ground and crash less than five hundred feet away. The truck reverses gear and starts to roll forward, just as Diego and I are forced into the revving helicopter. Two big, American-looking guards force us onto a bench seat and re-cuff us to a bar that runs the length of the seat above our heads.

The 3:30 PM alarm goes off on my Timex bringing a smile to my face as the helicopter lifts off the ground. Two Navy Super Hornet jets streak right by the front of our windshield, navigating a few hundred feet above the ground. From where we are, we can see their bombs launched one by one, followed by a series of steady explosions.

The black helicopter is forced to fly very low, out through the back of the property, down a small slope and out over the river. Just as we are about to pass under the bridge, I see the red dump truck crossing it, heading in a more friendly direction.

Diego and I both look at each other, smile and lean back into our seat. I'm thinking perhaps this is the father-son moment. But then again, maybe not. Looking up towards the front of the helicopter, I can also see the half-masked man using the rear view mirror to observe what is taking place in the back between Diego and me. Tomás Amos seems to be studying me. Which really gives me the creeps.

Chapter 67

THE BELL 430 skims over the mountainous terrain, trying desperately to outrun whatever's chasing us. We're flying so close to rocky walls inside valleys that I think for sure it's only a matter of time before the pilot makes an error and we become part of the scenery. Diego and I, our hands cuffed to the steel bar above our heads, slide back and forth along the bench seat.

Directly across from us, two men who look American and speak very good English, are in a heated discussion concerning the upcoming Super Bowl and pay very little attention to us. Both have semi-automatic rifles lying across their laps, which they hold tightly due to the gut wrenching maneuvers of the helicopter. The tall blond man sitting across from me, who looks better suited to be a professional surfer than a paid mercenary, has two percussion grenades attached to his belt and a Colt 45 tucked into his pants. The other guy, opposite Diego, has no visible weapons, but looks strong enough to lift a house off its foundation. He seems very nervous with our erratic flight plan, grabbing his stomach every time the helicopter acts more like a rollercoaster than a modern flying machine.

Diego slips in and out of consciousness as we whip though mountain passes that allow us but a few extra feet on each side. We are so close to the valley walls, I'm sure if I look hard enough out my side window I'll see birds building nests in the rocky landscape. The security guys change topics and are now talking about Guatemala. Perhaps that's our destination.

The ride starts to smooth out. Apparently, whoever was chasing us must have given up. Diego's eyes are now wide open.

"Tell me, Joe, what happened?" he whispers. I have to strain to hear him. "For whatever reason, I've been unable to keep my eyes open for very long. It must be from the drugs they pumped into me while I was strapped in that chair. The last thing I remember was being loaded into this helicopter after a truck crashed into the building housing missiles. I think I saw the same truck crossing a bridge."

"Don't worry. You didn't miss much except a bout of motion sickness. We've been flying up, down and sideways through mountain passes trying to elude our pursuers, who by the way have stopped chasing us. I think I overheard that our final destination is Guatemala."

The men sitting across from us remain engrossed in their own discussion, only glancing at us from time to time. The masked man, Tomás Amos, continues to watch us via the cabin rearview mirror. He is sitting in the co-pilot seat, and throughout all the abrupt speed and altitude changes, didn't get too involved. He has a Bose headset on and when he turns toward the pilot, his lips move a mile a minute. He must be communicating with someone on the ground, getting the latest updates on all the shit that's coming down on the heads of the cartels. Finally he turns and closes the door between the cockpit and the main cabin.

"Hey, Diego, are you related in some way to Tomás?" I say cautiously. "I thought I heard him say something about you being a disgrace as a brother. That was about all I could translate."

Diego goes quiet, and drops his eyes to the floor. He doesn't owe me any kind of explanation, at least not now. If he's related to the masked phantom in some way, I'm sure I'll find out sooner or later. The thing that bothers me the most is that, if Diego is my father and Tomás is his brother, I guess that makes the strange-looking man sitting in the co-pilot seat my uncle.

Just as I'm about to search for my happy place, alarms go off in the helicopter, followed by a strong dip down and to the right. We have company, and this time I can see it with my own two eyes.

Chapter 68

THE TWO IDIOTS sitting across from us finally stop talking about football and Guatemala as two Army AH-64 Apache helicopters flank us on both sides. Throwing on their headsets, they begin conversing with the pilot and co-pilot while gripping their assault rifles in preparation for an air war they stupidly think they can win. The Bell 430 is a top notch piece of flying machinery, but no match for the Apaches.

The blond-haired surfer goon gets up, goes into a cabinet above his head and takes out a portable missile launcher he quickly assembles. As the other security goon loads a Stinger missile into the launcher, both doors on the right and left side of the Bell automatically open.

An immediate rush of air into the helicopter forces it to dip hard to the left, causing the surfer goon to almost fall out the door into the great beyond, but with his feet planted firmly back on the floor as the helicopter quickly levels, he hits the trigger and the Stinger shoots out the open right-hand door. Its hot plume of smoke exits out the left.

The pilot in one of the Apaches sees the oncoming missile and banks his chopper almost straight down, eluding the missile as it overshoots its target by a hundred yards. The mercenaries quickly reload the launcher, but by the time they're ready, the two Apaches are nowhere to be seen. The pilots in the Apaches are probably talking to someone in charge, letting them know that they've been fired upon. Their commanding officers will either decide to call off the Army helicopters or continue with the pursuit and fire only if fired upon again. I figure we'll know their decision shortly.

A few minutes after the launch of the missile, the Bell turns sharply to the left and over on its side giving us a good view of the ground below. As it begins to right itself, I can see one of the Apaches flying below us, off to the left. The air war is on, and we will certainly be defeated if and when the orders come to shoot us down. The fact that the helicopter in which I'm riding in is firing Stinger missiles at Army aircraft doesn't bode well for our chances of survival.

As soon as we begin to level off again, the two American goons are up out of their seats in preparation for another shot. Diego is fighting to stay awake and conscious as we play this cat and mouse game. He looks at me from time to time, drool foaming down the left side of his mouth. I can only hope that whatever they used to drug him with back at Missing Acres doesn't kill him.

• • •

JUST AS I RETURN MY gaze to the front, both doors open up on the Bell and another Stinger's launched. This time the cabin fills with smoke for a few seconds, but clears out quickly with all the air rushing in through both open doors. Looking out the right side window, I see the missile heading directly for one of the Apaches, which makes a quick down maneuver into a river canyon and disappears from sight. The Stinger harmlessly hits the water and explodes. The doors on the Bell 430 close and the guards quickly strap themselves back in their seats.

We continue on in level flight for about ten minutes when all of a sudden the helicopter begins climbing rapidly and then quickly descends. The cabin lurches to the right at an almost forty-five degree angle to the ground. I use every muscle in my body to try and stay seated, simultaneously using my legs to keep Diego's limp body pushed against the back of the seat, leaving some slack on his cuffed wrist. With our crazy flight pattern, it would be easy for us to break our wrists since we're not strapped into our seats.

It's been a while since I saw the two Apache gunships, but something outside is making our pilot very nervous. The only positive aspect of his erratic flight plan is that ten of the twelve screws holding the steel security bar in place over our heads are vibrating loose and backing out. All I can think is, thank God the person who installed this bar didn't use Loctite on those fasteners. With only two screws holding the overhead bar tightly in place, we may have a chance after all if I can wake up Diego.

The helicopter's leveling off again when the alarm begins to ring in the cabin. The two shit-heads across from us unbuckle their restraints, open the overhead bin and again pull out the missile launcher and another two Stingers. It's the same routine: one goon positions the launcher on his shoulder while the other loads a rocket. The doors open with the same loud whoosh, and the air again forces the Bell to lose stability until the pilot is able to regain control. And again the noise wakes Diego out of his drug induced stupor and he looks over at me.

"Stay with me, Diego," I say loudly. "Don't pass out! I need you!"

I look at the wall above the right side of my head hoping Diego's eyes will follow suit. He tracks my line of sight and I am relieved to see that he too sees that the security bar has loosened. He winks at me to let me know he understands.

The goons are waiting for their target when all of a sudden a military jet appears on the left side of our helicopter and slows to try and match our speed, a Navy Super Hornet that's teasing the pilot of the Bell into battle. The security guys launch the Stinger at the jet as it drops chaff, leading the Stinger on a merry chase to a dead end.

This time, as the two assholes are reloading the launcher, the Hornet comes directly at us on our left side. It's packing a pair of AIM-9 Sidewinder heat-seeking missiles under each wing. Our pilot must be very nervous at the sight of the Navy jet bearing down on us. He puts the helicopter into a hard right turn, heading to the ground fast for cover. It's too late for an accurate shot, but the trigger-happy mercenary hits the launch button anyway. Before the Stinger can leave the cabin, I kick out my right foot as hard as I can and catch him on his left kneecap. Losing his balance, the goon's now standing on one foot with the launcher pointing straight up. The Stinger releases and crashes through the metal skin above the left door.

Immediately, the cabin begins to fill with white-hot smoke. Taking advantage of the fact that both goons are now off balance as the helicopter dips and rolls to the right, I nod one, two, three. On three, Diego and I both yank down hard on the security bar above our heads. It breaks easily, hitting poor Diego in the head before I can grab it with my cuffed hands. Holding the bar as a weapon, I push the surfer security guard into his friend behind him, with enough force to knock one of them out of the door of the helicopter. I'm not sure who's screaming the most, the goon who's freefalling back to earth or the one who's still hanging on to the bar but leaning dangerously backwards on the threshold of the open door.

While this is certainly a problem for him, the bigger issue is that I'm the one holding the other end. Diego's right arm is wrapped securely in a fastened seat belt, while his left hand holds the bottom of my pant leg. I give the remaining American mercenary a "so sorry" look and let go of the bar. He balances for a few seconds in a position of almost perfect weightlessness, till the black helicopter takes another dramatic, sharp turn to the left, forcing the guard out the door, where he bounces off the bottom of the fuselage and into the helicopter blades. If Diego wasn't still holding on to my pants, I would have gone out the door with him and been ground up through the blades, only to be identified later by my pearly whites.

Chapter 69

T HE BELL'S FILLING with smoke amidst the noise of non-stop alarms coming from the cockpit. The helicopter's still tilted heavily to one side and our speed continues to dissipate. The Stinger, having gone off inside the cabin and punched a hole through its skin, has made a major contribution to its slow death.

Diego straps himself into a jump seat and stares out the open door as I quickly look for our things. Lifting up the seat where the two goons had been sitting, I find both my empty Glock and the plastic wrapped cell phone. I also grab the Colt 45 and the key needed to remove our handcuffs. Unlocking Diego's cuffs, I hand him the Colt. He still looks a little out of it, but at least he's managing to keep his eyes open.

The Navy Super Hornets are flanking us on both sides, waiting for us to die. In front of us, I can see the masked man and the pilot through a window in the door between the main cabin and the cockpit, slumped over. I try to open the closed cabin door, but it's locked. Ramming it twice with my shoulder, I finally succeed in forcing the locking mechanism to break. The door blows open towards me; a rush of air mixed with smoke and glass fragments knock me to the ground. Most of the helicopter's windshield is gone.

Crawling on my hands and knees through the smashed-open door, I find the pilot slumped over, with a long shard of glass protruding from his left eye. This will be his last flight for sure. Tomás is sprawled over the control console. Shards of glass cover the back of his body, making it look like he's been caught in a snowstorm or has a severe dandruff problem. I grab the neck of his jacket and pull him back into his seat, and notice he's still breathing. The mask on his face has slipped to one side exposing his melted skin covered with grafts.

I've had enough flying lessons to recognize good news when I see it, that we are on autopilot. The bad news: all systems are failing, and multiple red lights are flashing all over the console. I try to wake Tomás with no luck, so I scream to Diego for help. He comes right in, making the sign of the cross as he views the mess in the cockpit.

"Diego, do you know if Tomás knows how to fly this thing?" I yell urgently.

"No, I don't know!" he screams back at me over the alarms and air noise.

"We need to get the pilot out of his seat and into the back! Can you help me?"

Diego nods and helps me carry the pilot to the back, where we lay him on the floor. When turned on his side, we can see that a long, spike-like piece of glass actually went into his eye and clear out through to the back of his head, tearing a hole in the seat cushion we just laid him on.

"Diego, listen to me! We're on autopilot, but not for long since all systems are failing. Oh and by the way, we have nobody to fly this thing except me. I had a few flying lessons in the Navy taking off, but I was shipped to the Middle East before I could get my first landing lesson. You might want strap yourself in – real good. I'm gonna try to land this thing before it does it on its own. Either might have the same result, but I like my chances a hell of a lot better."

Diego hurries to the back cabin. As I belt myself into the pilot's seat, I pull the wrapped cell out of my pocket and read a text message from my mother through the plastic. "Found Mike alive!"

Before I have a chance to celebrate, the light goes off below the autopilot switch and the Bell 430 pitches nose down sixty degrees, screaming towards the ground.

Chapter 70

T HE VALLEY FLOOR is coming up quickly as I grab the controls and reduce engine power to try slowing our momentum. Alarms continue sounding and smoke now trickles out from under the console by Tomás's feet. The LCD control panel isn't operating, so my speed and height are unknowns which can only be judged by sight and the flow of air through the broken windshield into my face.

I manage to muscle the machine from impact and keep our altitude at about twenty feet, the ground skimming under the Bell. I hear Diego yelling "fire" from the back as I look for a place to attempt to put us on the ground. For all too many reasons, the helicopter will not climb. The sight of a large stand of tall trees on the horizon causes me great distress, to say the least.

Flying an aircraft in the open air is one thing, but flying around obstacles is another, especially in a machine that is no longer controllable. As I come up to edge of the trees, I hear my Navy flight instructor, Captain John Calla, screaming in my ear, "Altitude's your friend! Pull up! Pull up!" Using whatever strength and coordination I have left, I manage to take the Bell to an altitude at which I think we'll clear the trees. I'm about to pat myself on the back when limbs of trees come crashing through the broken windshield, followed by ugly twisting metal sounds coming from just below my feet.

Pushing the control stick hard to the right, I manage to avoid a head-on collision with a mighty oak that's probably two hundred years old. Swinging the flying machine back around the way we came, I now see what that crunching metal sound was all about. Scattered along the tops of several thick trees are pieces of the Bell's undercarriage including our most critical component, the landing gear.

• • •

THE HELICOPTER'S ROLLS ROYCE engines are dying quickly as she tilts heavily to the left. I cannot bring her under control. The altitude is down to about ten feet and the forward speed is just enough to keep it from falling out of the sky. I remember something called autorotation, but sadly realize my flight lessons were in an airplane. It's time to ditch.

"Diego, come up front quickly!" I scream, as he stumbles through the cockpit door. "We have no landing gear. I'm going to try and put us down in the river up ahead. Hold on tight, but be ready to get out once we hit the water!"

"Okay, Joe!" he says, crossing himself several times, then kissing our masked copilot on the top of his head. Tomás is still unconscious and strapped in tight.

The river's about a half mile ahead. Already I can see whitecaps, which suggest that the river is moving quickly and possibly shallow. The plan, if you can call it that, is to get us over the river, then shut down the engines. If I remember what I read once in a flight manual, this should stall the bird, causing us to lose lift and drop us gently into the water. Needless to say the word "gently" is mine, not the manual's.

My plan, unfortunately, is rapidly falling apart. Our altitude continues to drop and the chopper blades are coming very close to striking the ground. How I can possibly level the Bell to prevent us from cart-wheeling into the water? The need for a solution comes more quickly than anticipated as the engines begin thumping and the rotor blades slow dramatically. However, the abrupt loss of engine torque allows me to level the Bell just before we hit the water.

I cut the fuel to the engines as the black Bell helicopter begins to list to one side and water starts filling the cabin. The rotor blades come to a screeching halt as the engines seize. The water in the cabin actually helps to stabilize the helicopter and causes it to act more like a boat.

Now we're moving quickly down the river. Large trees hanging over the banks are looming far too close to the dead rotor blades for comfort. In the sudden silence, the only sound I hear is that of the rushing water.

"Joe, we need to get out! Now!" Diego screams. I understand his urgency. The cockpit's rapidly filling with river water that's now up to my knees. "I think this is the Usumacinta River, which separates Mexico and Guatemala. It has many winding turns and waterfalls, Joe! We need to get Tomás!"

I follow Diego back into the main cabin and out to the side door just as the rotor blades catch on one of the trees and the Bell pivots a sudden ninety degrees. River water quickly fills the cabin. It's official: the helicopter is now sinking.

The rushing water knocks Diego off his feet and sweeps him outside, but he manages to grab a flimsy piece of broken metal hanging off the Bell. "Joe, I can't hold on!" he yells back at me. "I'm losing my grip! I will meet you on the Mexican side of the river. Don't forget Tomás! You need to help Tomás! I hate to be the one to tell you this, but – *he* is your father!"

Diego lets go and is gone but his last words echo in my head.

● ● ●

WADING UP TO THE front of the barely floating Bell 430, I unbuckle Tomás Amos from the co-pilot's seat. He starts to mumble as I make my way back to the main cabin with him over my shoulder and sit him down in one of the jump seats. The water is up to our waists, and our forward speed is increasing, telling me the river is getting narrow and that we may be approaching some falls.

Looking hastily through all the cabin bins, I fail to find anything that will float, but I do find a length of yellow rope. Abruptly, the helicopter comes to a sudden stop. Water continues to fill the inside, and I'm knocked off my feet and halfway out the door, holding on to a belt that's attached to the bench seat. The seat itself begins to give way under the sheer force of the rushing water.

Rolling onto my back, I can see the rotor blades are caught on some massive tree limbs and are bending quite dramatically under the incredible strain. I know it's only a matter of time before they snap and my short career as a river boat captain will start again.

Pulling myself back into the helicopter, I see a frightening sight. The river ahead has disappeared from view – or should I say dropped from view. Diego's short geography lesson quickly comes to mind, and I begin slapping Tomás's face in a frantic attempt to wake him up. He starts to stir, but his one good eye remains closed. Looking out the door and up at the trees, I get an idea that goes something like this: Tie a weight to the rope I just found. Throw it over a tree. Hook it on a limb. Tie Tomás and myself to the rope. Watch the helicopter disappear over the waterfall. Somehow get to shore.

Who am I trying to kid? This bullshit's the stuff of stuntmen and Hollywood special effects teams. As I look for a weighty object to act upon my far-fetched plan, the rotor blades snap and the fuselage begins its final journey towards a watery grave.

Time for a new plan.

Chapter 71

CHECKING THE RESTRAINTS on Tomás, I quickly wade up front to see how close we are to the falls. Because of all the water in the cabin, the Bell fuselage is heavy and scraping the bottom of the river. I look through the broken glass of the windshield and see open air as we again come to an abrupt stop. Investigating further, I see that the nose of the Bell 430 is caught between two large boulders sitting at the very beginning of the falls. Straining my neck to look out the gaping hole that once was a windshield, I look straight down a steep bank of water shooting over the falls to an outcropping of rocks – which looks to be rocky for at least a half a mile.

Because we are now temporarily stuck in one place, the remainder of the cabin fills quickly and we begin to sink even deeper into the river. The water level has now risen to Tomás's neck, which causes him to simultaneously wake up and panic as he begins choking on water now splashing on his face.

Paddling my way out of the cockpit and into the cabin, I release his restraints. His body begins to float with the current that's coming in through the cabin doors and exiting out via the broken cockpit windshield. He says nothing as I grab hold of his arm and pull him against the current back into the main cabin. There I tie one end of the yellow rope around his waist and the other end over my shoulders and under my arms. While under different circumstances, this action might qualify as a father-son type moment, my only goal right now is to keep the man alive long enough to find out what his role was on the terror attack in Washington.

The cabin is almost completely filled with water as I hear the sounds of scraping metal resume outside. Peering out the door, I can see that one of the boulders holding us in place is now starting to give way. As the fuselage begins to turn, I try to jump from the cabin onto a small island of rocks, only to fall short into some deep water. Since Tomás and I are roped together, he of course also falls into the water, face first, and gets caught in a strong current that starts dragging him towards the edge of the falls, taking me with him.

I manage to wrap my arm around the remaining piece of landing gear. It's enough to stop our movement over the falls, but again the Bell's fuselage begins to move, grinding along the rocks and tearing metal as I hold on for dear life. Looking for Tomás at the end of the rope, it's clear that he's actually gone over the falls. I can only hope he's hanging in mid-air, as opposed to mid-waterfall. I'm hampered by his dead weight at the other end of the rope as I struggle against the current, grabbing any handhold I can find on the Bell's underbelly.

Unfortunately, one of the large rocks holding the helicopter in place chooses this moment to give way and we commence racing to the edge of the falls, only to once again get stuck, this time in the river's muddy bottom. As the water continues to pound the Bell, the helicopter begins to flip, almost standing straight up and pivoting on its nose. With both arms still wrapped around the damaged landing gear, I'm dragged up and out of the water about ten feet, just as the helicopter starts a slow backwards somersault over the edge of the waterfall. I have just enough height and slack in the rope to be able to jump down onto another small rocky outcrop and brace myself before the dead weight at the other end forces me to dive onto the ground and dig my feet into the mud. I take Diego's Swiss Army knife out of my pocket and pull out the largest blade, ready to cut the rope if it somehow gets tangled around the helicopter as it goes over the edge. It is only a matter of seconds before the demolished Bell 430 disappears from sight and explodes somewhere on the rocks below.

Sitting on my butt, leaning back with my legs buried deep in the river mud, I start to try and reel in Tomás. No luck. I move my position on the small island to see if there might be a better way to increase my mechanical advantage. I slip on some moss-covered stones and fall into the water, where the current knocks me against a series of small rocks and branches. I've heard all those stories about crazies who've jumped into the Niagara River and gone over the falls with no protection, not even a pickle barrel, and survived. I only hope that some day I'll be able to swap stories with those survivors.

As I finally go feet first over the waterfall, I feel the weight of Tomás's body below me and, at the same time, see two Super Hornets streaking across the sky above me. Go Navy!

Chapter 72

AFTER FEELING LIKE I've been falling for a very long time, my chest hits the water with such force that my breath is knocked out of me and I almost black out. My feet quickly find the ground under the water and I use all my remaining strength to push myself back up to the surface. Making my way over to a shallow part of the river, I struggle to catch my breath. My whole body starts to shake as I throw up what little I have in my stomach.

Nearly exhausted, I'm finally able to get to shore, where I again start pulling on the rope to see if Tomás is still attached. Seeing his arms fluttering in the water tells me I caught something I won't be throwing back in. This is no catch and release program.

Taking the rope from around my shoulders, I wade back into the water to help Tomás get to shore. His mask is gone and now I understand why he wore it in the first place. The whole right side of his face is scar tissue. Where his right eye once was, there is a hole, now filled with river mud. With his shirt torn practically off him, I can see that most of the right side of his body has been badly burned and left upholstered in scar tissue. Crawling up on the soft ground, he looks defeated. Maybe even ashamed.

"Do you know?" he asks in raspy English.

"Yes, Diego told me."

He hits the ground exhausted, the burned side of his face buried in the mud. His left eye closed, he begins to mutter again in Spanish.

He mentions my mother's name, something about an explosion, and something about forgiveness.

• • •

IT'S 7:51 PM. DIEGO'S missing, and I'm lying on the shore of some Mexican river just below a beautiful waterfall, ten feet away from someone who is supposed to be my father. I think of Mike, my mom, Jim and Diego as I slip into the sleep of absolute exhaustion.

I guess only in dreams can I admit who I miss the most: Clare. I pray in my own way that she is okay, and that I will see her again soon. My dreams take me back to the Mission's courtyard where Clare and I held hands, talked a lot and slept next to each other, without any kind of funny business. Drifting through my memories of being with Clare, I'm reminded that we haven't yet gotten into any funny business. I think I hear her crying out to me telling me to wake up.

When I feel the barrel of a gun poking me on the side of my head, something tells me my sweet dreams are over and that a new nightmare is about to begin.

Chapter 73

MY LEGS AND ARMS are chained together, making it quite difficult to walk, never mind keep up with my new captors. When I fall behind, the barrel of a rifle pressed into my back reminds me to keep up. There's no sign of Tomás in the group. He either escaped or was taken earlier.

Most of my new, Spanish-speaking friends look to be under the age of twenty. A few might be close to thirty. Ten men and two women, all dressed in camo, all wearing American baseball caps representing a good cross section of teams from both leagues. While their outfits look old and tattered, their baseball hats look new and spotless. All the men are clean shaven, which tells me that the home base is close by and that whoever's running this outfit cares more about appearance and not so much about uniforms.

• • •

AFTER WALKING SOME TWO hours through the dense forest, I begin to smell smoke coming from the direction we're heading. I haven't had anything to eat in over twenty hours. Just the smell of smoke makes my mouth water.

It's 5:22 AM. Surely these people know it's time for breakfast. I certainly do. We break into a small clearing with several dull green, Quonset huts and a paddock full of horses. The source of the smoke:

five individual small fires burning beneath some sort of metal netting. Eggs, tortillas, fish and some kind of meat are cooking on top. Against the wall of one of the huts are hundreds of cases of Poland Spring Water.

Two of my young captors sit me down on what looks like an old telephone pole which has u-shaped metal bars bolted along the front. The youngest boy of the two unlocks my chain, strings it through the metal bar, then snaps the lock shut again. They say very little, but keep smiling throughout the entire lockup process. Neither of the boys has any weapons that I can see. The firepower seems to be reserved for the older members of the group. It's hard not to notice guns sticking out of the front of their pants. I jump quickly into my not-so-fluent Spanish before the boys go off to do something else.

"Niño's! *Cerdos, hombres, me hambriento! Comer*, food. *Comda. Por favor?*"

Both boys turn around to look at me. The older-looking one, who has long black hair, speaks good English.

"Mister, we are not boys nor pigs, but men. You are hungry, yes, and food will be brought to you soon. Good news. We have found your *amigo!*"

Hearing some commotion off to my left where all the Poland Spring is stacked, I see Tomás, covered in mud, walking slowly between his two captors. His mask has been replaced by some very large white sunglasses, the kind Elton John would have worn back in the seventies. Unfortunately, the glasses cover only a portion of his face, which causes all the people in camp to stop what they're doing and stare at him until he's forced to sit on the pole a foot away from me. He has the same chain set-up as I do, and sits quietly as they pull the shackles through the metal bar. While many would see this as potentially another father-son type moment, we talk very little.

"So what happened, Tomás?" I ask him. "I woke up with a gun pressed to my head and you were gone."

"I left during the middle of the night, to avoid capture. These people know of me, and do not like me too much."

"Who are they?" I say in a whisper.

"They are an offshoot of a group that calls themselves the Ejercito Popular Revolucionario – the EPR for short. They are a socialist revolutionary group. The EPR has strong support from the people in southern Mexico. They have been fighting a guerrilla war with the Mexican government for many years. I'm not exactly sure who our captors are, but I will venture a guess that they are somehow related to the EPR."

Before I can say another word, the two boys come back over to us with two large plates of food. I can honestly say that I haven't had this much food since I've been in Mexico. They smile and unlock our chains to give us full use of our hands to either eat or kill each other, if and when the time comes.

"Why do you think they unchained us?" I ask in a whisper.

"Joe, you must understand that the Mexican people are respectful and have a long proud heritage. Most are not garbage like me. They are honorable, hard working people like your Uncle Diego, trying to support their families in an unfair world. Missing Acres has employed thousands of Mexican migrant workers over the years and not one has ever stolen from me."

"So why don't you tell me about the torture rooms," I shoot back quickly. "I've seen those rooms scattered throughout your underground tunnel system. And the rooms filled with pallets of fertilizer stacked to the ceilings. And the SAMs, and the portable Stinger missiles. Most people won't steal if they understand the consequences." I pause. "Diego is my uncle?"

"Yes, Diego is your uncle."

Our conversation ends as quickly as it began. We anxiously dig into our breakfast while slowly moving down the pole in opposite directions enjoying our freedom from each other. My thoughts quickly turn to figuring out a way to get out of here. We are being closely watched by our captors as they go back and forth to the food tables to refill their plates or replace a lost fork.

I decide to test the seriousness of our captors by standing up and starting to walk over to one of the tables where bottled water is laid out. I am quickly intercepted by the two boys.

"*Agua*, water," I say in a non-threatening tone. "*Por favor?*"

"*Si, si*," they both say in unison.

"Help yourself," says the older one with the long black hair. "Take one back for your friend."

"*Gracias, amigos*, but he is not my friend," I say loudly as I walk back over to my seat on the log and toss the bottle of water over to Tomás.

Sitting on the pole still unchained, I see a medium sized tan dog run out of the woods and over to one of the food tables and start begging for scraps. A tall, heavyset man wearing an L.A. Dodgers hat over his hairnet comes out from behind the table and lays down a large plate of food for the dog. From where I'm sitting, I can't help but notice how much this dog looks like Fina, back at the mission. It could be Fina's twin, that affectionate dog with the awful breath that slept between Clare and me on the ground what seems like a lifetime ago. I guess it must just be a common breed of dog in Mexico.

Thinking back on Fina, revisiting our smelly times together, it takes a moment to realize I'm hearing voices approaching, growing louder as they are about to come off the trail and into the clearing. Two female voices, one male. I could swear I recognize both female voices, but honestly have to assume I must be hallucinating. But as they walk out into the clearing, I find I'm not.

There before my eyes are Clare and my mother, followed by my new-found uncle, Diego Hugo. Small children come out of nowhere, screaming in excitement, running up to Clare to hug her and hold her hands. She glances over and sees me standing next to the pole, and just smiles.

My mother walks quickly over to meet me with tears in her eyes, then sees Tomás sitting on the ground with his badly disfigured face, in the pair of cheap sunglasses. Giving Tomás a weak smile, she throws her arms around me.

It certainly feels nice to be rescued.

Chapter 74

DIEGO TELLS ME that when he got washed out of the helicopter and into the river, he managed to grab hold of a large tree limb that was caught on a pile of rocks. From there, he was able to swim to a shallow part of the river and make it to shore without getting caught in any strong currents that would take him over the falls. He witnessed much of our drama in the helicopter, including when we went over the falls, and apologizes several times for not being able to help.

I purposely ask him to repeat the going-over-the-falls scenario a few more times. Every time he retells the story, Clare squeezes my left hand and Mom squeezes my right. Basically his version goes like this:

On his way out of the flooded helicopter, Diego grabbed a floating plastic bag and stuck it in his shirt. When he got to the shore, he opened the bag and found the cell phone given to me a few days ago. After he saw Tomás and me go over the falls, he climbed up a hill until he was able to get reception. He got a hold of Jim on his way to Columbia who passed the call on to Clare who was at Holy Spirit with my mom. Clare, knowing the area well, made calls to a few people who contacted a few other people. Once permission was given and certain things verified, Diego called Darnell, who got hold of a helicopter, and picked up Mom and Clare at the mission, then found Diego – who I now need to get used to thinking of as my uncle – about five miles from here. Darnell stayed with the chopper as the three of them and Fina the wonder dog just walked into camp.

"I spend time in this area a few months each year working with Doctors Without Borders," Clare explains. "I have a lot of friends in Mexico. The group that captured you is really more of a social club than a band of revolutionaries. They thought you were spies sent by the Mexican government. I convinced them you weren't. They are good people."

"Jim wants me to thank you for all that you did, and apologizes for not being here," my mother says quietly. "He flew down to Columbia to bring Mike home. Prior to a bombing raid on the Sanchez cartel in Columbia, Special Forces went in to clear the buildings and found an underground prison filled with over two hundred people. Most were skin and bones, except for one big white boy who still had his baby fat. He was identified as Mike Lenoce, but then he got lost during a gun battle with cartel mercenaries. The next day, he was found by Columbian police drinking a beer in a hotel bar. A call was made to the US embassy in Columbia, and Mike was promptly picked up and taken there. We think he'd been tortured, but we'll know more when Jim gets back."

After all that's happened over the last several days, hearing about Mike is my breaking point. My eyes start to well up as I remember how he saved my life more than once while fighting in Afghanistan. During my three tours in the Middle East, the only time I truly felt like a liberator of some sort was when I was with Mike. I have clear memories of us walking into a village after a shootout as the women and children ran out to greet us, clapping their hands and thanking us. Mike would pick up the children and start singing some old Bob Seger song that certainly wouldn't have gotten him on American Idol, but seemed to calm us all down.

Chapter 75

WHILE TALKING QUIETLY with Clare, I see my mother and Diego sitting with Tomás under a large tree. Fina is sleeping on my mother's lap. Diego and Tomás do most of the talking.

We are being picked up back at the drop-off location at noon, about two hours from now. We have a five-mile walk through the woods, so the plan is to leave the camp in about thirty minutes. I figure this should give us enough time in case we get slowed down along the way.

The problem in my mind is what to do with Tomás Amos. He's wanted by the United States government and is to be put on trial along with forty-three drug kingpins who've been captured over the last two days. I'm prepared to take him with me back to the States, but our temporary captors have their own ideas. They say Señor Amos is worth a large ransom to his boss, Juan Delgado.

I try to tell them that Señor Delgado has been captured and is probably on his way to the United States. The boys in the camp tell me that Amos and Delgado have millions of dollars hidden away somewhere that might buy him out of this situation. The chances of taking him with us are slim to none, outnumbered and outgunned as we are. The only weapon I have is Diego's Swiss Army knife. When I was captured and searched by members of what Clare calls a "social club," they took the Swiss knife from me, only to give it back after checking out all the different tools. They all laughed when one of my captors found what he assumed were remnants from the last bottle of wine still on the corkscrew. If they only knew.

It's hard for me to keep Clare's attention since children keep running over to her, grabbing her hands and leading her off somewhere. The quasi leader of the "social club," a young man in a St. Louis Cardinals hat, comes over and sits next to me to let me know that we cannot take Tomás with us. He's too valuable and not a good man, he says. I explain to him as best I can in my broken Spanish that serious people from the United States will come looking for him, and that his group needs to be careful if this happens. As he shakes my hand and thanks me, I hear a pop, see his eyes open wide and feel wisps of his blood hit my face as he rolls off my shoulder and slides down to the ground. There's no way to save him. I can see that a large chunk's missing from the back of his head where his hat had just been.

Chapter 76

PANIC BREAKS OUT across the camp with the sound of gun shots and small explosions in the surrounding woods. The children vanish as I run over to grab Clare and find cover. Diego and my mother have already hit the ground, and I catch a glimpse of Tomás running off into the woods. The two boys that gave me breakfast an hour earlier toss me a gun and tell me to run.

Clare and I hurry over to where my mom and Diego are hiding behind a cement block fireplace. The gun battle in the woods continues as we make our move down the trail. Diego picks up two guns from the ground, keeping one and handing the other to my mother. I'm not too preoccupied with survival to take notice of the odd sight: my mother, of all people, cradling a shotgun.

We're on the move, with Fina leading the way and gun shots exploding all around us. The trail is empty with the exception of a few members of the "social club" who provide cover for us as we run for our lives. I have no idea who's shooting at us – all I know is that they're wearing government uniforms. If the uniforms are for real, we probably have very little time to get out of here before other government forces join the fight. Clare and Diego lead the way. My mother and I bring up the rear.

I manage to get a few shots off at the uniforms behind us, but as our limited firepower decreases, the shots from behind us increase. Just as my mother and I make a turn around a grove of small trees, she falls, hit, to the ground. I quickly pick her up and carry her behind the relative cover of the trees as blood starts to soak the lower left leg of her jeans. Ripping off a piece of my shirt, I push her pant leg up and wrap it around her calf to staunch the flow. Her face is scraped up from hitting the ground, but her determination to get out alive is apparent as we stand together and start moving.

After a few minutes of navigating the overgrown trail, I feel a sharp pain in my right shoulder that causes me to trip over my own feet and hit the ground. I've been playing the odds since I got here and have finally taken a bullet. My mother stumbles with me and as one, we fall into some thick brush. Knowing our forward progress is now dramatically diminished, I lie on my stomach, hold the gun in my left hand and tell my mother not to move.

Within a half a minute, two men in government uniforms come running in our direction. Neither see us lying on the side of the trail and are just about to trip over us when I shoot the first guy in the hip and catch the second in the neck. As they fall into the grass and begin crawling in pain, we move as quickly as possible and almost immediately run into Clare and Diego who've doubled back to look for us. Clare rips off her UCONN sweatshirt and wraps it tightly against the blood coming from my shoulder.

"There is a first aid kit on the helicopter!" shouts Diego. "Come! We must hurry!" Diego helps my mother as they take the lead, with Clare and me following close behind.

I'm beginning to feel a little lightheaded as we break out into the clearing. We can see the chopper coming towards us through a river valley about a half mile away. Lying on the ground waiting anxiously to be picked up, I see Tomás come out of the woods, walking slowly in our direction and I find myself wondering if what I see is real. He kneels down next to his brother and says a few words. Then he sees my mother holding her leg where my shirt is wrapped tightly around it. He goes over to her, whispers something in her ear and then stands up. He waves goodbye to me and runs back into the woods.

The helicopter's about to land when three men in uniforms break out of the woods and fire on it, forcing it back into the sky. Clare grabs my gun as I roll up against her. The first shot is perfect, taking down the guy closest to us. Looking down a small slope, we can see the helicopter land about a quarter of a mile away.

"Clare, Mom," I shout, "you need to start moving to the helicopter! Diego and I will hold them off! Go! Now!"

"Joe, I can't walk, never mind run!" my mother screams.

"Diego, get them out now!" I scream wildly.

Diego throws me his gun, picks up my mother and gently rolls her onto his shoulder, and starts running for the chopper. Clare comes back with tears in her eyes, saying she won't leave me. I'm stuck. I can't get up by myself, but I need to convince her to leave. As I fire the next to last bullet, I see Diego and my mother getting into the helicopter.

The two remaining men firing at us take cover behind some large rocks. While I'm still trying to tell Clare she must go, both come running out from behind the rocks towards us. I hear a single shot and see one of them go down about fifty feet from us. The other one is all but ten feet from us when I get off a shot that shatters his right knee-cap, forcing him to hit the ground hard.

Breaking out of the woods and running towards us, I see a familiar face hidden behind large, ugly white sunglasses. He and Clare lift me off the ground and begin to carry me down the slope to the helicopter. A new round of shots start popping behind us as Diego reaches out and helps Clare into the chopper, and Tomás rolls me onto the floor. As the helicopter begins to lift, I see Tomás back away, screaming the words "I'm sorry" at me, and the wonder dog leaps into Clare's lap.

Diego says nothing as he watches Tomás duck and run around the front of the helicopter as it begins to rise, and continues racing down the slope towards the river. Just as we fly over the edge of the river, I can see Tomás Amos holding the white sunglasses against his head as he jumps off a hundred-foot cliff into the water below. The helicopter banks hard to the right. The last thing I remember seeing before passing out, is the top of my father's head bobbing above the white foam.

Chapter 77

I WAKE UP a few hours later in a field hospital somewhere inside Guatemala, managed by Doctors Without Borders. It's decided that, since we aren't sure who the men in government uniforms were, staying out of Mexico for a while may be a good idea. Clare has a close friend here who allows us in and even removes a few bullets free of charge.

My mother and I are rolled out of the large white hospital tent in wheelchairs to join Diego and Clare, who are sitting in folding chairs. We have lots to talk about, but the conversation begins to slow when we get to the part about boarding the helicopter.

"You know, Caroline, this is the second time Tomás tried to save your life," says Diego sadly. "The first time was the night you were born, Joseph," he says to me. "Tomás had just gone into the Mexican military when he heard of a plot to blow up foreign embassies in Mexico City. This was in the early years of drug trafficking and the cartels in those days didn't like other countries getting involved in Mexico's business, especially if it meant losing money. Tomás became very nervous and called on me to help. While I worked in my uncle's food store during the day, I infiltrated a few drug rings at night, trying to find out about these rumored bombings of embassies. I must say that I stumbled on the plot to blow up the US embassy quite by accident. Unfortunately, the time was not set in stone, so an anonymous call to the authorities only helped keep the place well guarded for a week or two. The night you were born, I got a call from a girl I knew who told me to stay away from the US embassy.

"Again I tipped the authorities, but it was the story of the boy who cried wolf – they had no interest in what I said and told me to stop wasting their time. Caroline," he said, directing his gaze back on my mother, which is when I realize that this story is meant for both of us, not just me. "I was worried for your safety and watched the embassy from across the street, but no one came except for a few cars going into the embassy's parking garage. I told Tomás about the possible bombing threat and he managed to get away that night. My brother and I, we took up positions across the street from the embassy and watched every little bit of movement near the building. I remember the weather that night – all lightning and no rain.

"Tomás knew you were about to give birth, and he was so worried about you. He became very agitated and decided to go up and see you, or at least tell your father what he had heard about a possible bombing. I can still see him running across the street, going down into the garage. A few minutes later, there was a loud explosion that collapsed most of the garage, onto itself, and onto Tomás. I made a quick call to the authorities, then ran into the garage and was able to find my brother lying under a car, severely burned.

"Knowing I could not take him to the hospital, I brought him to my new friends who worked for the traffickers. They thought he was responsible for the bombing and took him in and fixed his body the best they could. I went back to work in my uncle's store and cut my ties with the traffickers. I visited Tomás for about a month after the bombing where he was recuperating at a Catholic monastery outside Mexico City. One night I went to see him and was told he was gone."

"That explains why back at the camp he told me he was sorry for not being able to save my father," says Mom, who's been preoccupied, trying to sort through confusing memories.

"With all due respect, before we submit his name to the pope for sainthood," says Clare, "we need to remember what happened to Abby.

I was in the next room when they tortured her. I've barely slept since. Awake or asleep, I can still hear her screams."

Clare kneels down on the ground next to my wheelchair, covers my hand with hers and drops her head in my lap. Her sobs, vibrating through my body, remind me of what was done in those tunnels below Missing Acres. My mother stares straight ahead, watching Fina chase a lizard through the tall grass, but after listening to what Clare has just said, she tries to say something herself but ends up crying instead.

"He is my brother," Diego says in a flat tone. "Please know that he is not the monster you think he is. Is he somehow involved in illegal drug business in Mexico? Maybe. Did he approve of torture or conduct any torture? No. You need to understand that Tomás did not live at Missing Acres. He lives outside Cancun. I know that for a fact, person-ally, because when I visit our restaurant in Cancun several times a year, I stay with him. He asked me to buy a condo in his building, but I refused, not wanting to get involved in his business in any way. It was Tomás who found me at Missing Acres tied up in a chair with a sack over my head. He had no idea what was going on there, you must believe me. In fact, he felt I betrayed him because I didn't inform him that his only son was in Mexico having lunch at my restaurant."

Diego breaks down and begins crying heavily, shaking from head to toe. My mother reaches out and takes his hand as he falls to his knees. A nurse comes over and asks if he's okay and if we need any-thing. I tell her we need a few drinks and a nice long vacation. She smiles and says she'd be more than happy to join us as she helps Diego back into his chair.

Diego sits quietly for a moment, then bursts out, "The one thing you must remember is that it's my fault, not my brother's, that he has this life. That night thirty years ago, I should have brought him to a regular hospital, instead of to my friends in the drug trade. Don't you see? It's my fault." But he puts up his hands to stop anyone from answering. His is a rhetorical question, one that he has to live with. He's not looking to any of us for an answer.

The four of us go silent as we watch the sun set over the Pacific. It's a reminder to me that in twelve hours, more or less, the sun will once again rise over the Gulf of Mexico and we'll begin a new day. I guess we can only hope that the next day is not as bad as the one before. Having hope gives us the opportunity to begin again. To start fresh, recreate, make peace with the past and move on. We don't need to dish out or beg for forgiveness if we can't forgive ourselves. Nobody gives us the life we have. We choose it. We can either build it into something special and worthwhile, or destroy it.

What I've learned over the last several days is that we have the power in ourselves to reconstruct our lives and make them better. I think of poor Natalie, losing her final battle with addiction. I am honored to have known Peter and Abby, both of whom died for something they strongly believed in. My thoughts race to Mom and Clare and how lucky I am that they both survived this ordeal and are sitting here with me. It's hard for me not to tremble thinking that I almost lost my dear friend Mike. I do take some comfort knowing that when Mike and I do slip our earthly bonds and sail off into the next life that we will always be part of each other's soul. No forces in the universe could ever break up two great friends. Unfortunately, it sometimes takes great battles to remind us what's really important.

• • •

I'M NOT SURE HOW my father will fit into this equation. I'd like to believe he is part of the life reconstruction phase. Diego feels guilty because he thinks he set Tomás down the path his life has taken. My mother is trying hard not to get buried in all the sadness that's transpired over the last several days. Clare is wrestling with both the life she chose, and concerns that she might lose that choice by loving me. Before coming to Mexico, I chose a life that fit me well. Going over a raging waterfall, my new-found father attached to me by a rope, almost ended my life. My experiences here in Mexico over the last week certainly have brought my life to an abrupt if temporary halt. Finding Clare through all the bad stuff gives me hope to start over, enjoy every minute of each and every day, and remember what's really important in life.

As we watch the last of the sun dip into the sea, we know we are lucky to be alive and feel a spiritual moment overtake us as Diego bows his head and slowly recites a Mexican prayer in Spanish. I look to Clare for translation and she just smiles. There is a silent moment at the end of the prayer when we all make the sign of the cross together. My mother completes the prayer in a strong voice, in English.

"In the Name of the Father, Son and the Holy Spirit."

We take each other's hand and all chime in with the "Amen."

My mind drifts over to one of the large medical tents where I can hear music wafting out through the open flaps, the familiar sounds of Jeff Buckley taking his sweet time playing the guitar intro, then finally singing the words to "Hallelujah," a great old song written by Leonard Cohen.

Chapter 78

Good Evening. Fourteen days ago Washington DC came under attack by an unknown terrorist group that killed 977 people and injured over a thousand. After this cowardly act, I authorized every security agency at my disposal to double-check every piece of data and triple-check all evidence.

We set up five teams, headed up by the military, the CIA, NSA, FBI and the DEA. Each group had cross-functional team members with the sole responsibility of sharing all information so that nothing would get misinterpreted or fall between the cracks. In less than five days, the DEA team, headed by Deputy Director Jim Carlone, came to the conclusion with precise certainty that twenty-one drug cartels, located in Mexico, Central and South America, were behind the attack.

Over the last three days, ending today at noon and with the help of eight foreign governments, we concluded Operation Clean Sweep. Thirty-three cartel locations, including drug manufacturing sites, were overrun by United States Special Forces from all branches of the military. At these thirty-three locations, we captured potential suspects and escorted all others onto buses provided by the local governments to either deliver them back to their homes or to some point of safety.

Within an hour of evacuation, the United States military conducted bombing raids on these facilities. At this time, over 350 captured suspects are being processed at various locations throughout the US, Puerto Rico and Mexico. All will be brought to trial in the US. I want to thank everyone involved in this effort, and trust the American people will support our decision to act.

To all foreign countries who wish to do us harm, I offer this warning: be careful. Think long and hard before you attack us, anywhere in the world. We will find you, and we will cause you much pain. And yes, that is a threat.

For everyone watching or listening, I ask that you talk to your friends and neighbors about what you heard tonight. This tragedy offers us a real chance to face and give up our dependence on illegal drugs. We have captured today's kingpins and leveled their manufacturing sites. There is not a doubt in my mind that they will rebuild, that others will take the place of those now spending their days and nights in American jails. When they rebuild, we will return and we will destroy. But – are we, like Sisyphus of old, doomed to roll a huge boulder up a hill, only to have it roll back down, for all of eternity? We will, if we don't curb our appetite for these drugs and change our ways. People are dying in these drug wars, and remember, there is such a thing as guilt by association. We have to eliminate the source, and that is us.

Thank you and God Bless America.

Epilogue

February 10, 2013
Holy Spirit Mission

SEEING THE YELLOW BUS coming down the dusty drive towards Holy Spirit Mission sets my heart racing. Sitting beside me, Clare feels my nervousness, squeezes my hand and blows sweetly in my ear. Fina charges down the driveway, barking wildly at the bus until it comes to a stop in front of the bench we're sitting on. The door swings open and Fina runs up the steps, jumping into Diego's lap as he turns off the ignition.

"You know something, Clare," Diego calls over to us, "I'm having trouble getting used to starting this thing with keys and not a screwdriver. Oh and by the way, I can't wait to paint it many colors."

Clare smiles as we stand up to meet our guests. My mother walks down the bus steps with a huge grin on her face, bringing a few stray tears to my eyes. As soon as her feet touch the ground, we hug for a while, which just doesn't seem long enough. Thanks to the research done by my mother and her team, the United States was able to break the backs of the drug cartels and gain new respect from the world community. When I finally let go of her, Clare takes my place hugging her, the two sharing secrets through whispers.

Feeling like I'm being watched, I turn back to the top of the bus's stairs and see Stella looking radiant in a red sundress, with a slightly forced smile on her face. When she gets to the bottom step, she cries out my name and jumps into my arms, then sees me wince. "Joey!" she cries. "Forgive me. I forgot. You're still recovering. Put me down!" I accept her apology, then, just to prove that I can, I carry her three times around a large tree before placing her gently on the bench.

But seeing two shadows coming down the aisle towards the door, I have to dig deep inside myself to be strong, knowing that at any minute I can break down completely. I look back at Clare for strength, then turn back around to find my best friend standing two feet from me.

"Oh, Mike, thank God you're okay," I say as he wraps his arms around me, giving me one of his famous hugs that also makes me wince, and leaves me breathless.

"Thanks for not forgetting about me, Joe." Mike says as he lets go of me.

"Never, Mike, never," I assure him. "I love you too much, buddy. I've missed you."

Behind him is his wife Joanne, looking well, but tired, coming down the stairs carrying Fina. I take the wonder dog from her, set her on the ground, then hold Joanne in my arms for a very special hug. She whispers "thank you" in my ear several times and continues to hold my hand as Uncle Diego emerges from the bus, luggage in both hands. He winks at me, then walks over to greet my mother, kissing her on the cheek.

"I would like to welcome everyone to Holy Spirit Mission!" shouts Clare. "I was informed yesterday by Jim Carlone and the Mexican Government that I am the new owner, so all of you can stay as long as you want! Do make yourselves at home and enjoy the Mexican way of life, which you may find as pleasant a change as I have. Please trust me when I say that the people of the local villages will welcome you with open arms. They are truly special and hold a great love for all. I learned that several years ago when I first arrived here as a total stranger."

My mind begins to wander as Clare talks about sleeping and eating arrangements. Looking at everyone around me, it's hard not to see how lucky I am. The Reserve approved my temporary retirement indefinitely, which means until I'm ready to go back or needed. My plan is to work with Clare at Holy Spirit and give back in some way. For the first time in my life, I feel like I'm free to do the right thing.

I strongly agree with our president that we all must do what's right for our country and stop being so selfish. We can no longer isolate ourselves from each other if we are to survive as a nation. I have fallen deeply in love with Clare, who holds so much goodness in her heart and is willing to share it with me. For that I am grateful.

Clare has just finished welcoming our close friends as I hear off in the distance children's voices getting louder. A few moments later, more than twenty children come scampering in our direction shouting "baseball, baseball." The children run up to Clare, Joanne, Stella and my mother, grabbing the hands of strangers and friends alike and pulling them out towards the middle of the field. Diego throws open the luggage locker on the side of the bus and starts pulling out boxes of new baseball equipment, including team shirts that have Holy Spirit Mission printed on the front and a picture of Fina on the back.

The kids quickly scramble into shirts, laughing as they model them for each other. Then the game is on, and we drop everything and join the children. Joanne is being lovingly mugged by the children, who make her giggle even without her knowing one word of Spanish. My mother and Stella are laughing so hard they both fall on the ground, an open invitation for some of the children to pile on top of them. Slowing down my senses, seeing Clare spin around in circles while holding on to several children, dust floating in the air around them, makes it all seem so unreal – and so real. My only hope at this moment is that one day I can make her this happy myself.

Mike assigns everyone to a team. The first pitch goes wild towards the end of the driveway. I run to shag the ball before Fina does so we don't have to stop the game and chase her around. At the end of the drive and near the road, I notice an all-too-familiar sight. Forgetting about the ball, I walk over to a large, brown-paper-wrapped box. My name is spelled out on the top, and of course there is no return address. This box differs from the others only in that it has a large brown envelope taped to the side. Glancing back at the field, I see most of the children laughing hysterically as they chase Fina through some tall grass, trying to get the baseball from her.

As I watch them, I tear open the side of the envelope and an item falls to the ground that I recognize right away. It's the mask that covered the right side of my father's burnt face. I think of him briefly and figure whatever's in the box can wait. Maybe I'll keep the tradition and open it on my birthday.

Walking back to the mission with the envelope in my hand, I hear Holy Spirit's bell start to ring. The *tres amigos* have done it. They've repaired the bell and put the tower back in working order, as they promised they would.

Standing in the field, I realize that no one's moving. Everyone is still, staring at the bell tower and listening to the beautiful sounds as they echo over the landscape. Mike turns to me, smiles and winks. Knowing what he's thinking, I begin to hum "Ring Them Bells." It's one of our favorite Bob Dylan songs, one that we sang together with JL Carlone, back on tours in the Middle East.

I glance back over at the box and think about what might be inside. Will the contents provide closure or more unanswered questions? Just then, my iPhone starts to vibrate in my pocket. I realize that I shouldn't get too comfortable with my new life here at Holy Spirit. While a few questions have been answered and the mission-accomplished banner can be waved, I feel the sudden urge to rip open the brown box and discover a new set of clues that will once again take me over the falls.